CITY OF LIES

A HARDBOILED MYSTERY

JANUARY BAIN

ROUGH
EDGES
PRESS

CITY OF LIES

For Don

CITY OF LIES

PROLOGUE

In the midst of chaos, there is also opportunity.
~Sun Tzu.

Hollywood, *March 1947*

"Is it true? You *must* tell me. I have to know. I can't bear to think about it. All those people dying in the camps. Oh my god!" She hid her face in her hands, her heavily pregnant body sagging against the plastered wall. Her thin shoulders shook with the intensity of her sobs.

All warfare is based on deception. Patience is the supreme virtue. He recited the lines in his mind, observing the excessive display with contempt. One more complication. Such a foolish woman. Did she not realize she was only necessary as long as she didn't create problems for him? He forced himself to speak the proper words. "Sweetheart, you mustn't upset yourself like this. It's not good for you or the baby."

1

He leaned down and picked up the small steel box from the floor. She had forced it open with a penknife, exposing the identify card, his Iron Cross Medal of Honor, and the creased photograph, the one of himself with his Fürer. He slipped them back inside, and closed the lid firmly.

"You're exaggerating all of this in your mind. I had nothing but a minor role. Insignificant in the scheme of things. I was helping those prisoners in the best way I could by being there." Having to belittle his role was repugnant, but defusing the situation was essential. "Does it matter now? The world has moved on. Turned their attention to the Soviets and the communist threat. Far bigger fish to fry."

"Does it *matter*?" She lifted her tear-stained face, her expression one of horror. "Of course, it matters. I'm about to have your baby. And it didn't look unimportant." She placed one hand over her stomach protectively. "I can't have my child's father be a—" She swallowed. "I just can't. Maybe you could turn yourself in. Get some kind of deal for doing that? Atone for things."

He sighed with exasperation. "I already have a deal and a new identity that guarantees me a future. I'm a legitimate refugee with a promised American citizenship in a few years. Now how would I have been able to get that if what you are suggesting is true?" The lies he'd crafted were brilliant, suggested he'd been forced into supporting the Nazi regime. He'd held the winning hand: letters of reference. And his honest hatred of all things communist made passing the lie detector tests simple. With his promise to aid in spying on his former homeland, he'd slipped right in with everyone wanting him.

Both the CIA and the FBI had been foaming at the mouth to recruit him.

He looked at the woman. He shouldn't have kept the incriminating evidence. Though some day, the pendulum would swing back again. People were doomed by their forgetfulness. Studying history was the only way to know the future.

He deliberately changed his expression to appear concerned. "How else am I to look after you and the baby? If they arrest me now for an old folly, you will have nothing. Is living on charity what you want? On the handouts from others thinking they're better than you are?"

In the light shed by the wrought iron lamppost outside the bedroom window, her skin looked gray and blotchy. He controlled a shudder of dislike. She had been so pretty nine months ago. Blonde, and slim, hungry for life. He'd been so patient, wanting a son to carry on his bloodline.

"What kind of deal lets a murderer go free? If the press ever hears about it, we'll be ostracized. The world never moves on from such horrors." She turned a defiant look upon him, her eyes flashing with more fire than he'd seen in weeks. Too bad it was about this.

"No need for them to ever become involved. What would be gained, a fatherless child? Perhaps the mother jailed for conspiracy? Hard to say you didn't know if they catch you red-handed with those items. And who would tell them anyway?"

She looked down and he knew. His heart hardened while his brain sharpened.

"Who have you told?"

She shook her head, biting her lower lip. "Addie's

promised not to say anything. I—I had to share it with someone. I just couldn't believe it or make sense of it. But she said if you don't voluntarily pay for your crimes, she'd *have* to do something. She was outraged by what she found out. It can't all be true. *Please*, say it isn't. You couldn't have done those vile things. Experimented on those prisoners. It just can't be. It makes me sick to my stomach even to think of it."

He ignored her pleas. "Does anyone else know? Think carefully. Was there anyone around when you and Addie conspired against me?"

"No, of course not. She promised to give us a couple of days to do the right thing. She wouldn't tell anyone at the paper, I'm certain. She's a good friend."

"That's good then." Just one more to kill to end this charade.

He slipped the icepick from his pocket and in one swift motion pulled her forward and drove it upward into her brain from the base of her neck. He held her through her death throes. "Shush, shush, sleep now, my pretty. You go to a far better place."

He laid her on her back on the grass. What to do about the child? It would help cover up the crime, make it so heinous that he would never be suspected. Something diabolical like the Black Dalia crime that had grabbed recent headlines. He held all the chips right now. The dossier he'd been secretly drafting on the agency gave him pull if they did not help him. No, on second thought, that wasn't the answer. It would be far better to hide this. More work, of course, but loose ends tied up never unraveled. But the seconds were ticking by, vital oxygen vanishing. He didn't want a brain-damaged child in the world. He set to work.

An hour later, he lay the female child, a huge disappointment, on the cold stone steps of the orphanage. Walked away without a single glance back to see if anyone answered the ringing of the bell. What did it matter? It wasn't the son he coveted.

CHAPTER 1
THE SOUNDS OF SILENCE

The streets were dark with something more than night.
—Raymond Chandler

HOLLYWOOD, APRIL 1968

"OF ALL THE dirty rotten maggoty things to do. That's *my* twist. You stole my ending," Claire Preston hissed at the movie screen.

The story about a woman going missing and the authorities arresting her abusive husband for murder had seemed familiar from the opening credits. His going to prison for life and swearing his innocence, with no one—not even his lawyer—believing him anything but guilty. Then the dramatic twist. Her showing up on screen *alive* at the end, twenty-five years later, in the visiting room at the prison and driving the knife home. The motive and name of the movie: *Retribution*. The woman had lost her unborn baby from the ongoing abuse and could never have another, more than enough motive to do the nasty. And all Claire's idea.

A plot she'd skimmed as a script reader from the seemingly endless slush pile over at New Pictures Studio. Someone had used her notes to save the lame script from the dustbin.

"Is there a problem here?" The usher shone a flashlight directly in her face, giving her a new target.

You bet your sweet ass there's a problem. "No problem. I was just leaving." It wasn't fair to take out her ire on the pimply-faced attendant in his ill-fitting burgundy jacket.

She fumed all the way down the red carpeted aisle to the street exit before shoving the cold metal door open with more force than strictly necessary, more upset with herself for letting it get to her, than by what she'd just witnessed.

The door clanked closed behind her, and the cool, moist air instantly enveloped her like a heavy embrace. An unusual turn of weather for LA in the fall, but welcomed. Maybe it would head off the usual rash of fires? She tugged the collar of her coat closed and yanked the belt tight around her waist. No credit for the idea, okay, she could live with that. But they could have at least said thank you or done something—taken her out for a drink or a decent meal or sent her flowers. Instead, they're pretending it never happened.

Not cool.

She got into her white Ford Fairlane in front of the Starlight Theatre at the headwaters of the Los Angeles River and headed west toward the Sunset Strip and her small apartment on Sycamore Avenue. Why had she bothered to stop and see the movie her friend Serena had insisted she'd like? Now she had to live with knowing what the studio was capable of. But then again, knowledge was power.

She pulled out a Salem cigarette, slipped it between her lips, then punched in the knob for the electric heater on the dash. When it was ready, she applied the red-hot wire to the tip while drawing the soothing heat deep into her lungs, feeling the head rush, before letting it escape into a series of satisfying smoke rings.

The sun was dying a slow death, making her squint in self-defense. The glare kept her from seeing what needed to be seen, a black dog streaking out in front of her car on the bridge. She braked hard, catching sight of it at the last second, slamming her left foot right down to the floorboards, the cigarette flying out of her mouth.

Her body slammed forward, the seat belt cutting painfully into her chest. The vehicle lurched sideways and into the path of another vehicle, eastbound. The blacktop vanished. Unable to comprehend the speed at which her world had imploded, Claire was helpless, the vehicle air born. Something wet dripped into her eyes, stinging, and making her blink rapidly in efforts to see clearly.

"Oh my god!" The words burst from numb lips, her hands clutching at the steering wheel in horror.

The car slammed into the water a few seconds later, a river swollen and angry from a torrential rainstorm earlier in the day. Terrified, she watched the water rising around her. She struggled to undo her seat belt, but her hands shook so badly it seemed an impossible challenge. Finally, as the precious seconds ticked away, the catch on the lock clicked and released. She was free. *Thank you.*

She focused on what she could see outside the side window. The danger was not over. The water was rising, rolling in waves and pushing against the glass. Right. *You were supposed to open it.* She reached for the mechanism on the door, fumbled with it, then began to twist it in a circle, rolling down the window on the driver's side. Water began spilling in immediately, making her mouth dry with fear. The water was cold, and pushed against her, soaking her instantly.

Shivering, she kicked off her shoes, then wormed her way through the narrow space. Coming nose-to-nose with a black shadow, she screamed, swallowing mouthfuls of the foul water. Then realized it was the dog. The black dog she'd nearly hit.

They swam together to the shore, his presence a small comfort. He pulled at her dress with his teeth, helping her onto the bank, as if he was trying to make up for her what had happened.

She managed to croak out a few words. "Hey, boy, looks like we're in this together."

He chuffed an answer and lay down at her side. Overhead she could see people standing on the bridge, some pointing fingers down at them. Hopefully someone would call the cops. Something dripped into her eyes again and she touched her forehead. She was bleeding from a deep cut on the side of her face. She lay against the dog, shivering from shock and cold. Then everything faded to black.

CHAPTER 2
STILL WATERS
RUN DEEP

I was neat, clean, shaved and sober, and I didn't care who knew it. I was everything the well-dressed private detective ought to be.

—Raymond Chandler, *The Big Sleep*

HOLLYWOOD, OCTOBER 1968

"NICE FAMILY." The young woman who had introduced herself as Claire Preston crossed her shapely legs and nodded at the prominently displayed photo on his desk.

"I like to think so," Jake Sterling said, his tone noncommittal. His new client was a looker while he was Mr. Average, average height, average looks, only things not average were his dogged search for the truth and his ability to take a hit, bullet or otherwise. But for once he wished he hadn't bothered to set out the picture of a smiling woman and her two-point-three kids.

"I hope you're better at being a private eye than you are at finding out that your wife cheats on you, with any man willing to shell out a dollar ninety-five at the five and dime." She raised a sardonic eyebrow before shifting her weight to her other hip. And very trim hips they were. But apparently her brain was even sharper. He had bought the photograph from Woolworths for exactly a buck ninety-five.

"The truth will set you free, John 8:32," Bishop squawked twice, adding a little sidestep on the wooden dowel for emphasis, preening with self-importance. His shimmery green feathers caught the shafts of light drifting through the venetian blinds, adding an unholy glow.

"Optimistic, isn't he?" His possible new client took out a pack of Salems and nudged one out from its snug location with long slender fingers, the tips varnished to a high-gloss red. It made him want to slip into a matching convertible, turn up the music on the rebel song, "I Fought the Law" by the Bobby Fuller Four, and hand the redhead a mickey of lemon gin.

He couldn't hold back the chuckle this time, though it escaped sounding more like a strangled snort. She had him dead to rights. He picked up his lighter, leaned forward in tandem with her, and lit the tip of her cigarette. She laid cool fingers against his hand to keep the light steady.

"Bishop has an uncanny way of pointing out my shortcoming. Just like my father intended, no doubt."

"Rather conflicts with the motto on your business card. *Nothing but the truth.*" She inhaled, filling admirable lungs, and blew out such a perfect concentric smoke ring he had to stop himself from applauding.

He picked up the offending item from the scarred top of the old mahogany desktop he was proud to be sitting behind. His father had spent thirty years slaving over it selling insurance, week in and week out. He slipped the eight by ten photo in the top drawer, face down. "Clients like a family man. Care for a drink, Miss Preston?"

She shrugged shapely pale shoulders but didn't turn him down. "Claire, please. It's five p.m. somewhere, if that matters. Who's the parrot named after?"

He reached into his bottom drawer and drew out the mickey of Jim Beam and two tumblers. Filled both with three fingers worth, half emptying the bottle, then handed one across the desk. Their fingers brushed again as she took it from him. "From a quote. *It was a blonde. A blonde to make a bishop kick a hole in a stained-glass window.*"

"Good thing I'm a redhead. Raymond Chandler, *Farewell, My Lovely.* You as big a fan as your father?"

"*It seemed like a nice neighborhood to have bad habits in.*"

She smiled that Mona Lisa smile again before efficiently tapping the end of her Salem twice against the huge glass ashtray still sparkling from a recent cleaning. When she sat back, her brown suede mini skirt rose another half inch, making him sweat in the air conditioning he'd cranked up to maximum setting before Mae Dixon, his bossy and essential secretary, had ushered in his last client of the day. The small rose tattoo peeking at him was the final coup de grâce. He yanked at his tie, releasing its stranglehold.

"You read a lot, Mr. Sterling?"

"Please, call me Jake. Guilty. You?"

"It's what I do daily to keep body and soul intact." She gave a grimace, quirking red-rouged lips downward at the corners like she'd just eaten something unagreeable. Picking up the glass of whiskey, she took a large gulp, the liquid working its way sensuously down her creamy white throat. His best guess, a real redhead. The conveniently located beauty mark near the edge of her mouth sealed the siren deal.

He looked into her arresting green eyes shining like an alley cat's in the streetlight before taking a good slug of his own Jim Beam. "Doesn't appear to be agreeing with you. And here I was betting on your being an actress. An even less agreeable occupation."

"Good place to learn the lying, stealing, mannerisms of Hollywood as anywhere—reading scripts. And I leave the acting profession to my friend, Serena Sands."

"You want to become a mystery writer exposing the underbelly of Hollywood? Come work for me. Nothing like the real world to give a writer excellent fodder. In fact, you'll need to work hard to make your book more plausible than what truly goes down in this city of lies."

She stubbed out the cigarette, then immediately lit another before he could lean forward to assist. He noted her fingers trembled ever so slightly. She blew another perfect smoke ring. Impressive. She was the kind of female he almost hoped would say she needed his help to kill someone, and to bury the body in the desert, so she'd be in his debt forever. Not that he would do it, of course, though he had never been properly tested. Until now.

"Maybe I will. Do you believe in fate, Jake?"

The rebel song still high jacking his brain slowed down a bit. "I like to think I have a hand in my own destiny, that if I don't care for the cards dealt, I can reshuffle the deck. Helps me sleep at night."

She gave him a slight nod, her glittering Veronica

Lake pageboy swinging forward against her shoulder, shadowing half her face. Too bad she was a decade younger and a ten. On a good day he might be a solid six —six and a half.

"Yeah, though I walk through the valley of the shadow of death, I will fear no evil. Psalms 23:4."

We both ignored Bishop this time. She finished her drink in one last dainty gulp, the slender column of her throat undulating as she swallowed. He poured them both another, not bothering to ask.

"I sense a story here." He took another slug of whiskey to brace himself and waited.

"I'm not certain where to begin." She sucked in her plump bottom lip and chewed on it thoughtfully.

"I got nothing but time." A complete lie. He was due at his weekly Thursday night porker game in exactly twenty-eight minutes. Something told him if he was smart he should have excused himself, but curiosity is a ferocious beast. Not happy until its offspring are well fed. And so far, curiosity hasn't killed this cat. Tried, just hadn't succeeded. "Start at the beginning."

And she did, beginning with the usual tale of woe. Children often swear their square parents couldn't possibly be related to them. He got it. But in this case, she was probably right. Discovered a paper that proved she was adopted as a newborn.

She pulled said paper out from her sleek handbag and handed it over. He scanned the document, an adoption record. Mother and father unknown. Name of the child: Mary Claire. No last name. The Los Angeles Orphans Home on North El Centro across from the Paramount Pictures lot was listed on the header. Except it was now called the Hollywood Home for Children.

"My mother died six months ago, and when I was cleaning out the house, I discovered it inside a locked box hidden in the back of a closet." She took another swallow of the liquor, her eyes unfocused. And not from the booze. "Along with an antique brooch and this old scrap of fabric. Maybe I was wrapped up in it, who knows?" She set the small length of cloth and the impressive three-inch brooch on his desk. The unusual design with the large black pearl in the center and six filigree leaf-like silver extensions spiraling outward gave the appearance of a large flower. He turned the piece over, noting that the clasp had been expertly repaired.

"I'm sorry for your loss." He glanced at the tiny rosebud pattern on the rectangular piece of material. Could be from a dress? Curtains?

She shrugged. "It was a long time coming. I was prepared. She was more than ready."

"Still. Losing a parent's rough."

Her green eyes filled with tears she angrily blinked away. "If anyone had asked, I would have said my parents were my real ones. I even look a bit like my mom, and she had an excuse for the red hair since hers was dark brown and my father's black. A great-aunt, deceased. Shared an old black-and-white photo that hid her hair color. But now I need to know the truth. About who I am, and where I came from."

"I can only imagine." Both his parents were alive and living in a retirement community in Florida. Happy as a pair of clams according to his mother's weekly one-sided phone call. "So, you want me to find your birth parents? Though I warn you, this isn't much to go on." He gave a nod to the skimpy items arrayed on the desk.

"I understand. But the home's a place to start, right?"

"Yes, I would start there." He sat up straighter. "But don't get your hopes up. Adoption records are kept sealed for a reason. And there's no last name listed. Unless someone worked there at the time knows something helpful that they're willing to share, it might be a dead end. And sometimes it's best not to know. You've had good parents, right?"

"Yes. But now that I'm essentially an orphan again, I'd like to find out if I have any living relatives." She hesitated and got that thousand-yard stare that usually heralded more secrets to spill. His gut tightened.

"A few months back, I had what you might call a near death experience. I was in a car that crashed into the Los Angeles River just after a heavy rainstorm—I had swerved to avoid a dog—and the doctor discovered I have a heart condition. Fortunately, the doctors were able to repair the small hole. But since then, I've been having these terrifying dreams. Like a movie running over and over in my head." She hesitated, like she was reluctant to share the content. *Good, only the facts, please.* "I wonder if somehow it's connected?"

"You might want to talk to someone about that." He leaned back in his chair, ran a hand over the stubble on his chin. He needed a shave. And a haircut wouldn't hurt. Looking like a hippie wouldn't bring in the clients. Then he had a better idea. "Maybe what you're remembering in your dreams is just the bad plot from a B movie? You've said yourself, you read a lot of stories."

She pressed her lips together, eyes narrowed with concentration. She stubbed out her red-tipped cigarette and sat up straighter. Sometimes the prettiest packages hide the deepest, darkest secrets. "The dog, Marlowe, survived intact from the accident, if you're wondering,

17

and lives with me. A sweet black lab. In a way he saved my life. I wouldn't have known about the heart condition otherwise." She grimaced, making even that expression look good. It took him a full second to recall *which* dog she was referring to. "I have money, an inheritance, so spend it and find out everything you can. That's all I ask."

"Great name for a dog. Marlowe."

He drilled his fingernails on the desk. Everyone hides something. Says one thing while believing another. A certain wariness around those amazing emerald eyes convinced him her truth was not unknown to her. She was an old soul in a young body type, if such a thing existed. "You were a newborn when the past happened, *if* anything untoward happened at all. You're most likely are the product of an unmarried woman who couldn't care for you the way she thought you deserved and decided to do the right thing. I might as well tell you, I'm a man of facts. Only believe what can be proved beyond reasonable doubt. I might not be the right one to take on your case."

"You are *exactly* the one to take on my case. I want the truth, as your slogan promises, fake family aside." She used one hand to wave the indiscretion away. He didn't have the grace to blush. "I can handle it, whatever you find out. Because I'm afraid. Afraid that I'll be labeled crazy if it turns out my nightmares are real. And even crazier if there're not."

He was a sucker for a pretty girl in distress. They both knew it.

"Fine. I'll be in touch soon."

"Is the job offer still on the table?" She swung that wealth of titian hair back from her Madonna-like face and gave him a direct look right in the solar plexus.

No. He'd said it in a moment of weakness. *But I never say anything I can't back up. Maybe that should be the new motto for my business card?* He took a second to consider while the decision hung between them like a pregnant walrus. On the plus side she was bright, educated, and would make most men spill their guts. Two guys coming through the door with guns would be less distracting. Problem, ditto for the negative side. She'd never suffer fools gladly.

"I think you might want to keep your day job until you see what the position entails. It's not all fun and glory. My business interests involve cheating spouses in divorce cases, background checks for perspective employers, helping lawyers get the facts for their clients, insurance fraud, sometimes even private security for celebrities." He ticked them off on one hand. "Tomorrow's Saturday. I will be checking out the home first thing in the morning."

"I've always admired Kate Warner of the Pinkertons. Believe I'd enjoy being a master of disguise in real life over the movies any day of the week."

"You might be too bright for this job."

"Why? You've chosen it." The glint of good humor was his undoing.

She held out her hand for a shake and he grasped at it, pumping it more than adequately. And just when he thought it couldn't get any worse. What had he been thinking, suggesting she come along with him? But he was a man of his word. What he said would happen, happened.

"Where should I send the thank-you card?" he asked.

Her lush mane swayed again as she cocked her head sideways, striking him in the kisser. "For what?"

"For pulling you out of the river."

A smug grin was her only response before she made a graceful pirouette that an exacting ballet teacher would admire, then headed out of his office. Though watching Claire leave wasn't quite as good as admiring her sashay into his office in her mini skirt, sleeveless top, and white go-go boots, it did beat poker hands down.

CHAPTER 3
LIFE IS TOO SHORT

I SHOULD HAVE LEFT OUT THE PART ABOUT HAVING *nightmares. Now he's going to think I'm certifiable.* At least she hadn't spilled the actual night terror that had plagued her for months. More thanks to him, really, than her.

Claire rubbed her aching neck as she drove west on Sunset Boulevard, trying to soothe the tension away before it crept up into her brain. It was that damn accident. A sickening vertigo overcame her, and she swallowed hard against it, blinking her eyes repeatedly until the sensation vanished and the street scene of Grauman's Chinese Theatre with its stylized bronze-green pagoda roof and the guardian lions came back into focus. But least there was some good news, Jack had suggested they look into her case together. Then she groaned, remembering the party she'd promised to attend tonight. Serena was not known for wanting to go home before the cock crowed and went back to bed.

She parked her brand-new white Volkswagen bug between the yellow lines in the numbered space behind the apartment complex and slid out of the driver's seat.

Catching a glimpse of Herman Blackwell striding purposely toward her, she groaned.

"Claire, I'm glad I caught you. Do you know anything about *that?*" Herman asked, pointing at a white circle drawn on the pavement a few yards away.

"No." The white chalk marks appeared to be drawn around something brown and lumpy and laying dead center. "Is that what I think it is?"

He bobbed his head, his greased hair unable to follow suit. "Disgusting behavior. If I knew who it was, *boy*, look out."

Right. "Well, only one person in this building has a dog other than me, far as I know, and you know Marlowe's not to blame. Why not ask the other owner? Make them pick it up?" *Maybe because he's a freakin' body builder?*

"Don't worry, I will. But I can't be certain who did it without seeing it *actually* happen. False accusations and all. Could have been anyone out walking their dog from another location."

"Well, good luck with that."

She moved to walk around him, but he held up a sweaty looking palm the color of the belly of a dead fish.

"You should know that it's been decided by the owner's that *all* tenants *must* keep the noise level down after ten-thirty, not eleven o'clock as was posted earlier, no exceptions. We have children in this block now."

"One child that visits once a week in the afternoons." Not that she cared, but the guy was just too annoying. And he needed help keeping his facts straight.

His lips thinned against his too-white teeth as he struggled to keep the smile in place. "That's bound to change now."

"Well, since Serena and I prefer to party *away* from

the apartment," she shrugged with indifference, "it's none of my concern."

His expression shifted. "I noticed that. Always like a good party myself if it's attended by a pretty girl who needs an escort. This city's not safe for young girls like you." He lowered his voice, his eyes smoldering. "I've heard all about those casting couch sessions. Tsk-tsk. I'd hate to think of you *ever* being placed in that dangerous situation."

"Don't worry, Herman, I can take care of myself. I've never wanted to be an actress and fly that close to the sun. Making and then tearing down careers is too much a blood sport in this town to interest me."

"Say, I'm pretty much done writing my screenplay. Think you could give it a looksee? Might need a word or two changed here and there, though I have been over it with a fine-toothed comb." His smugness wasn't convincing, though she knew it probably masked insecurity. Weren't most people insecure and trying to act like they weren't these days?

She counted to three, trying to come up with a plausible excuse. "I'm a bit busy at the moment, even thinking of changing jobs. I'm probably not the right person to ask."

Disappointment clouded his face. "But I value your opinion. What kind of job? I would kill for the one you already have."

She didn't want to jinx her chances by talking about it. The private investigation field had always intrigued her and working with Jake Sterling just might be her ticket to an interesting future. "Trust me, you don't want to hand in your script to a studio without copywriting it in some way first. Like turning it into a novel or getting a legitimate agent. It's a cutthroat industry and ideas are stolen at a whim and a stroke of the pen."

"See, that's why I need your help. You've got the inside scoop. Maybe I could buy you dinner in trade?" His face shone with such hope. He wouldn't be a bad-looking guy if he'd wash the oil out of his hair and remove the stick up his butt.

"No." She let out a deep breath. "I'll do it. No need to thank me. But maybe you could go easier on everyone? It *is* nineteen sixty-eight."

"Thanks! I'll drop it off later if you're going to be home? Explain a few things you'll need to know to understand my intentions. Like on page eleven, the heroine's backstory includes betrayal by her husband and that's why she decides—"

Her headache that she'd been keeping at bay, pounced in a blast of fury. "No, sorry, I have to go out. Just slide it under the door and leave your notes pinned to the top. I can't get to it for a few days anyway."

"Well, sure, that's okay, I guess. I truly appreciate your input. Maybe I'll even dedicate it to you? You probably don't realize this, but you've kind of been my muse of late."

"O-kay. Sorry, but I have to split. Serena's expecting me."

"Yes, of course, I didn't mean to hold you up. But could you explain to your roommate the new rules? She never seems to take my going to all the trouble of telling her what she needs to know, seriously enough." His mouth pinched in the telling.

"Leave it with me." She made a quick getaway, her stomach churning. She flew up the stairs and dropped her keys trying to unlock the door in time. Ten seconds later she emptied the contents of her stomach into the toilet of the empty apartment, holding her hair back from her face in clenched fists, her dog Marlowe milling about and looking concerned. Wiping her mouth with a trembling hand, she surveyed herself in the mirror. Pale, but better.

"I'm okay, boy, just a headache," she reassured the black lab. His nails clicked on the tile as he exited the bathroom.

She opened the medicine cabinet, then took out a small bottle and shook a couple of white tablets into the palm of her hand. She tossed them into her mouth and crunched them down, the flavor making her grimace. She filled a glass with water and washed away the bitterness.

Suddenly Serena's face appeared in the mirror beside her own, making her startle. She hadn't heard her come in over the roaring in her ears. The gorgeous blonde's tan face with the high cheekbones, short straight nose, little-girl dimples, and sky-blue eyes was reflected back, her expression one of sympathy. Didn't hurt that her innocent face was atop the body of a goddess who exuded sexuality. No male of the species seemed to be able to see her when Serena was around.

"Another headache, hon?"

"Yeah, but it's fading fast," she fibbed, then realized it actually was easing.

"Are we still on for tonight? I really want to go. It's kind of a big deal. I'm up for a part in that new film, *Hollywood Nights.* You know Elle, she's insisting I be there. And I need my good luck charm by my side."

Elle was Serena's pushy talent agent. Effective strategy. Only the squeaky wheel got the part for a client in Hollywood. Or a wannabee starlet willing to cross the line. She'd long given up on warning her of the dark side

25

of Hollywood, and Serena insisted she understood the fame game. Claire wasn't so certain. Her friend had stars in her eyes, believing she was just one director, one producer, one perfect moment away from being discovered. Well, maybe she was. She was pretty enough, smart enough, and photogenic enough judging by her still photographs, but could she handle the twenty-four hour a day pressure being famous brought? Could anyone?

Claire had decided early on she never wanted fame bad enough to pay any price. She wanted her freedom, her anonymity, and the ability to just be herself. She'd spent her childhood devouring books. Writers were left alone. Irony then, since the accident, she was becoming less and less certain of who she was when she got a few precious moments to herself to write. Made writing so much harder. Strange cracks in her psyche let in unexpected thoughts and emotions. Then this new development of discovering she'd been adopted and the ground had shifted right out from under her, making the earth feel as unstable beneath her feet as the San Andreas fault lines that ran under Los Angeles. Was that why everyone partied so hard here? Being reminded constantly of their mortality?

"Where's this important party being held anyway?"

"Get this, on exclusive Cielo Drive, in Beverly Hills, baby!"

"Huh."

"So, let's get you fixed up. I'm thinking that cherry-red dress with all the fancy beadwork."

"And I'm thinking a little black number. You're the one who's supposed to shine, girlfriend, not me. I just want to watch the crowd, maybe overhear an interesting conversation or two. I need to get a real ear for the way people talk. Dialogue spices up novels and screenplays."

"Nobody in real life talks or acts like they do in the movies." Serena put one hand on a slim hip, imitating a dizzy actress type. "Oh, I think there's an intruder in the basement. I think I'll go down there in the dark holding a flashlight because the power's been cut, check it out in my see-through nightie."

Claire laughed. "Then trip on the last step and land on the floor conveniently losing hold of said flashlight. Scramble fetchingly around in the light now focused on my half-nude body where the nightie has ripped exposing my full breasts and taunt belly, surprise written all over my face. Yeah, right." She scoffed. "I want to write something that *matters*. Expose the world behind the façade."

"You will. But in the meantime, we gotta run." Serena checked her makeup in the mirror and fluffed her lion's mane.

"Word of warning. I don't want to be late tonight. I have an early call."

"But tomorrow's *Saturday*. I was depending on you to be there for me." She whirled around from the mirror and gave her a beseeching look.

"I met with that private investigator today. The one recommended by Elle."

Serena's eyes narrowed thoughtfully as she picked up a tube from the vanity selection and applied a fresh layer of shiny red lip gloss. "Yeah, what did he have to say?"

"That I'm welcomed to go with him tomorrow to check things out. Learn how a real investigator operates."

She gave a disgusted grunt. "Isn't that what you're paying him for?"

"I want to go along. Being a private eye's always been of interest to me. Besides, it will help with my writing."

Claire shrugged. "He even mentioned he might have a job for me."

"And not work for the studio? They pay pretty good and all you have to do is read all day long. You want to give that up for a stab at being a private dick? Snooping around and getting into other people's personal business." She wrinkled her nose before turning to the mirror and applying a dusting of face powder. "Strange occupation, if you ask me."

"Well, someone has to dig for the truth."

"This is Hollywood. No one wants the truth shoved in their faces, trust me."

Her words stunned. "Well, I do. I want to know where I came from. Why my mother gave me up." Tears prickled behind her eyelids.

"Oh, I'm sorry." She stopped her primping for a moment and bestowed a quick hug, her sweet floral perfume making Claire's nose twitch. "I didn't mean it. Now, let's get you glammed up. You're pale as a ghost."

"Okay, but I'm going home at midnight whether you're ready or not. We're taking separate vehicles otherwise."

"Midnight! The party will just be getting into full swing. Nobody that's anybody shows up before eleven. And I need you to drive so I can have a few. You know how nervous I get. Please, Claire, give me a break here. I'd do it for you."

"No later than one o'clock then. And that's final. Besides, I can't leave Marlowe alone until all hours. What if he starts barking, what then?"

A mutinous stare before a loud knocking on the apartment door interrupted. "I'll get that. You finish getting ready." Serena hurried away.

"But I need to explain a few things." Herman's voice

echoed into Claire's brain. She quietly closed the bathroom door. Maybe it was time to move on? She could afford a place of her own now even though she'd give every red cent she'd inherited for one more day with her mother.

She took a few minutes to fix her makeup, then combed her hair smooth, adding a sparkly barrette on one section tucked behind her ear for glamour while letting the other side swoop forward in a lush wave. A good a place to hide as any. And her mother had loved Veronica Lake movies. In some strange way she felt she was honoring her when she emulated the star.

With the conversation heating up in the other room, she tiptoed out of the bathroom and down the short hallway to her bedroom. Marlowe jumped off the end of the bed and strode over to give her legs some serious loving. She bent down and gave him a hug.

"You're getting fat, big guy." After a proper reunion, he jumped back onto the bed, his golden-brown eyes continuing to watch her every movement.

Pulling the short black cocktail dress from her closet, she tugged it on and struggled with the back zip. With a loud sigh, she stepped into her patent leather matching stiletto heels. No doubt she'd regret it in an hour. But the best way to blend in was to look the part, and there was never any doubt everyone at a Beverly Hills party would be dressed to kill. And looking good was power. The coin of the realm. Visible currency. And all too fleeting. Hmm, maybe her book would be about stars and aging? No, *Valley of the Dolls* had already landed that story hands down.

Now Jake Sterling was an interesting man. She could see basing a character in a story on him. Her pulse quickened. An opportunity to apprentice with a real private investigator didn't come around often. She intended to make the most of it.

"Are you ready yet? I got rid of that Nazi wannabee for you. What a piece of work." Serena's voice echoed down the hallway.

"Be right there."

One final check in the dresser mirror that she was fit for company, and she joined her friend who was perched on the arm of the sofa.

"You owe me one. Herman's screenplay is on the table." Serena lit a cigarette and gave her a glance filled with meaning. She blew out the smoke, then smiled. "You look gorgeous by the way."

"Thanks, so do you."

"Why, this old rag? Only paid three hundred dollars for it."

"What? For one dress, Serena!"

"Don't worry. I kept the tags attached, tucked inside. I'll take it back tomorrow."

Claire shook her head. That was more than their combined rent on their apartment. "What if something gets spilled on it?"

"Don't jinx me. I'll be careful. Not like I can afford the clothes I need on my pittance of a salary. And if I don't look like a success, how will I ever *become* a success?"

"Okay. Just let me feed Marlowe, and we're good to go."

She opened a tin of dog food with the can opener and the lab was instantly at her side, his tail waving with delight. She placed the offering in his dish and refreshed his water. "I'll be back later to take you for a walk, I promise."

Claire picked up her keys from the kitchen counter.

"I'll drive, but if you're staying outrageously late, you'll have to catch a ride with someone else."

Serena pouted. "You've been no fun since that damn accident."

She chose to ignore the dig. Much as she liked her witty, cool friend, it was becoming mostly all about what was best for her career. She went through boyfriends like a head cold goes through tissue. Sure, it was the sixties. But freedom should mean more than just hopping from bed to bed.

"You need to get laid. That's what the pill was invented for."

"When I find the right guy. Coming?" Claire opened the door to the apartment.

"Oh, *please*! This day and age, he'll expect you to be an expert lay. Guys are not into those virginal types anymore. They're usually a cold fish in bed."

She didn't let her friend know her words had struck home. It was true she'd never felt such an overwhelming desire to have a guy that she threw caution to the wind and ignored the fact VD and STDs existed. Did that make her frigid?

"And guys don't want the town pump either." Soon as she said the words, she wished she could claw them back. The hardest part of having had the head injury, was the blurting out of what she was thinking if she wasn't paying enough attention or was overly emotional. "Oh, I'm sorry, Serena, I didn't mean that." She rubbed her forehead. "I'm just a bit off today."

Serena gave her a reproachful look that cut her as surely as if a hot knife had drawn a sharp line through exposed flesh. "Just for that, you'd better be prepared to wait for me even if it takes all damn night."

"Fine."

Serena stomped down the stairs ahead of her, her squared shoulders an act of defiance.

In the parking lot, they both carefully avoided the white circle, giving it a wide berth. Claire sighed, if only it was as easy to avoid stepping in it in relationships.

"That Herman's such a dud. Everyone knows who's responsible," Serena muttered before lighting up a cigarette.

"Sam outweighs him by a good forty pounds—all solid muscle. He's right to be cautious."

"Well, I don't intend to be cautious tonight. I heard today that the director's wife has just thrown him out for fooling around with the maid. And since I'm such an easy lay, might as well use it to my advantage. Might win me the part. I got a lot more to offer than the help."

"I'm sorry. I shouldn't have said that. I apologize. Can we just forget about it and move on?"

Serena shrugged, knocking off the ashes from her cigarette into the metal ashtray. "Sure, why not?"

Though her tone was brittle, Claire chose to accept it at face value. But come Monday, she was looking for a new apartment. Sans roommate.

CHAPTER 4
WHAT'S YOUR BAG?

CLAIRE PARKED HALFWAY DOWN THE HILL. THE SOUNDS from the Hi-Fi system muffled, but recognizable. "Help" by The Beatles.

"Help, I need someone," Serena sang along, her goodwill restored it seemed by the music. She had a good voice too, well-trained. Along with dance lessons, the former Miss Ohio was poised to make a showing. She didn't need to sleep around to win a part. Somehow, she must convince her. A good friend would do that much at least.

Walking up the hill together, dancing along to the driving beat, her heart lightened with each step. Yeah, this was the ticket. She just needed to get over herself.

Claire pulled open one of the double doors to the three-story colonial with a full-length front portico and Corinthian columns, letting out the coolness of the air conditioning and exposing the glittering palace within with its array of burnished chrome and butter-soft leather. People milled about, their bright frocks and psychedelic suits as mesmerizing as Antoinette's Versailles. The guests all wore masks, hiding faces and minds brilliant at appearing to be someone else, *anyone* other than themselves. She even doubted many of them had any idea who they were without a role to play.

"Serena Sands! Come in, come in. And who's your gorgeous plus one?"

Their hostess, big-boned with even bigger hair, was dressed in a wildly patterned caftan, zigzagged diagonals of rainbow colors that would elicit another attack of vertigo if Claire stared too long. The woman had on a tri-colored mask with bright feathers attached at the sides that swayed around her face.

"Claire Preston. Anita Wilson."

"Nice to meet you."

"Likewise. The bar's over there along with the masks. Grab whatever you like." Anita pointed a finger with an inch-long nail encrusted with multi-diamond chips at the sideboard where another guest was busy prepping a drink. "Oh Albert, nice that you could make it!" Anita already had her focus shifted to the next guest.

Claire followed Serena's lead and headed for the bar.

"What would you like?"

"A white wine spritzer, heavy on the spritzer."

While Serena prepared their drinks, Claire choose a simple mask of midnight blue with silver filigree around the edges. She surveyed the crowd as she pulled it on. Easy to tell who the director of the promised movie was. He was surrounded by a bevy of starlets all vying with cleavage and gestures for his attention. Fascinating when you want to be a writer. She would miss the parties once she moved out. Or more like miss observing. No matter how she tried, she never felt a part of things. Maybe she'd always known she was adopted on some unconscious level? An outsider.

"Here you go." Serena handed over the drink. "I've got to find Elle. Will you be okay alone?"

"Sure. Go do what you need to. Oh, don't forget to take a mask."

"Right-o." Serena surveyed the choices lined up on the sideboard to the right of the impressive display of alcohol, then picked up one that looked like a tigress. On her it flashed exotic, her sapphire eyes shining through the holes like jewels.

"Nice choice."

She watched her friend strut her way through the pack using those admirable rolling hips, garnering admiring glances from all quarters. Men and women. Serena had once, in a drunken state, told an acquaintance she was bi, and it hadn't hurt her cache one bit by the revelation which made the gossip rounds. Times really were a-changin'.

"So, abandoned again, I see, Claire." Deanna St. James joined her, unmistakable even in the lioness mask, same as she apparently was with her flame-red hair. A middle-aged writer for a tell-all rag, she often made an appearance at the same parties Claire attended, no doubt looking for fodder for the insatiable gossip mill. She was looking solid tonight. A simple, black, very expensive dress with a gorgeous brooch pinned to the front. It brought to mind the piece of jewelry she'd left with Jake today. Would he be able to find her mother? Was she alive, and maybe wanting to be reunited? She'd had many daydreams since the discovery of being adopted out as an infant. And they didn't all end happily.

"Serena's here to network. I'm just here to make sure she's okay."

"Elle should see to that. She will be taking a big enough percentage for the rest of her life."

"She'll earn it, no doubt. And I'm driving. Not much for drinking, so I don't mind." She'd never give Deanna anything if she could help it. It would be used against Serena in a heartbeat.

"Bet you don't know the scoop on Elle?" The coyness was clogging, but to be for-armed beat being in the dark any day.

"No, I don't." She took a sip of the refreshing wine spritzer, enjoying the bubbles that tickled her nose. Would she want to get the goods on others if she ended up working for Jake? No, it was different. She wasn't out to gossip, just to help solve puzzles.

"She had it out with hubby last night. Sent him packing. Caught him playing the field with a starlet, up and comer, who fled the scene—naked. Already changed the locks, had his ass fired from the agency, and contacted her lawyer. Serena better look out for her, she's a barracuda when it comes to money."

"Well, isn't that what actresses need? Someone to look out for them? Make sure they're compensated fairly?"

"Yeah, but Elle carries it too far at times. The things she's asked her clients to do when trying to get a job." Deanna shook her head, her eyes darkened by some emotion. "Well, I just hope Serena knows what she's doing."

"Even a director or producer can only go so far, right? And the girl always has the choice. Serena would never do something she didn't want to."

"Hon, you're naive if you think that. I've yet to see limits on what people will do to achieve fame. And what they'll do to keep it." She shook her head. "You have no idea what goes on in this shanty town. The glitter's fool's gold. And it covers up a system that chews up newcomers and spits them out regular as a Swiss timepiece."

The conversation was making her stomach hurt. Surely the *Valley of the Dolls* was only a work of fiction? The milling crowd suddenly morphed into tawdry marionettes in a stage play, their every action suspect.

Deanna lowered her voice, and her eyes, outlined by the edges of her mask, took on a more sinister appearance. "There are things I've discovered over the years, things so vile I can't even report on. Sickening, disgusting things." She took a swallow of her scotch. "I'm glad you're not one of them, Claire. Smart girl to keep away from that lot because money and power always wins over youth. And beauty—it's so damn fleeting." She waved a hand at the milling crowd. "And if you think it's bad now, some of the worst crimes happened back in the forties after the war when we opened our doors to the world." She took another gulp of the alcohol and finished the glass. "Sorry, I seem to be in a maudlin mood tonight. Maybe it's time I left this business for good." She set her glass down and straightened her mask. "I'll make myself scarce. Take care now."

Claire watched the woman walk away, her black dress the color of mourning. She glanced down at her own somber choice. Next time she was wearing the red number. But Deanna's warning had struck home. She wanted to get some fresh air but felt duty-bound to keep an eye out for Serena.

The minutes dragged by, the song changed to "These Boots Are Made For Walkin'," its upbeat tempo perking up her mood. Her bladder began squawking and she left her station to locate a bathroom. Hiking down a side hallway that a guest pointed out led to a powder room, she nearly knocked into a couple straightening their clothing as they lurched from an open doorway. Behind them the fixtures of a bathroom were visible.

"Oops, sorry, sweetheart," the older man said, a wolfish grin he probably thought of as charming well cemented in place. A thin skim of hair was plastered to his mottled scalp and his Lone Ranger mask was askew. The odor of alcohol and weed saturated his breath and clothing, making Claire take a step backward from the noxious cloud.

A young blonde woman stared at her, her eyes narrowed, checking to see if she was going to be foolish enough to be competition. *Don't worry, I have no interest in second-hand goods.* Her hair could use a good combing too, and it appeared she'd lost both her mask and her bra somewhere, evidenced by her clearly visible nipples through the thin silk of her white dress.

"If you'll excuse me," Claire said, giving them a wide berth.

"You look like you could use a drink or a pick-me-up." The man reached into the breast pocket of his Madras jacket and pulled out a micky and a small bottle of pills. "Here you go. Have your pick. You know, you remind me of someone. Yeah, that's it, Veronica Lake. Except you're even rarer. A redhead. My favorite color."

"No, I'm good." Claire held up a cease-and-desist hand, but she didn't back away any further. *When an animal spots new prey in the wild, a possible target mustn't let any visible signs of fear escape.* Advice from a nature program came to mind and made her stand her ground.

"She don't need nothing. Leave her alone, why don't you? Let me take care of you. I can get it up, just give me another chance, you'll see." The blonde tugged on his jacket, trying to pull him along.

Excellent grammar. Another plus for using drugs.

"Don't give me that." He swatted the blonde's hand away, his ruddy skin flushing redder. No doubt due to the implied slur by Miss Grammar 1968 on his manhood. "Do you know who I am? What I can do for you?"

"Thanks, but I'm not a starlet. I read scripts for a living."

He swayed backward, then lurched forward to correct his balance. "What! A gal who looks like you? Say, aren't you a little young for the job? Come on. You must provide your boss with some little extras. Just talk to me, baby. I got the pull too."

Claire relaxed a bit. She could outrun this guy in a New York minute. He was toast. She'd not often run into such a disgusting persona, but then, she hadn't been to that many Beverly Hills parties. Maybe they thought they could get away with it? Isolate a victim and pounce? Those nature programs were turning out to be a good dress rehearsal for the human world after all. Except animals were more honest in their way of going about things. "If you can rock my world the way you rock that combover, you must really be something."

"That smart mouth's going to get you in trouble." He punctuated his remarks with a fetching scowl.

"Hey, I need a drink. She's said she's not interested. Let's go."

"*Everyone's* interested, baby. Just this one thinks she smarter and better than the rest of us, playing it coy." His charming expression vanished, replaced by a meanness that promised retribution.

Time to go. Claire made a two-step dash for the bathroom door, slammed it shut, and clicked the lock.

A loud pounding on the door made her back away. Was he strong enough to bust through? Maybe she'd underestimated his inebriated state and he was only playing at being drunk? She glanced around the room, noting the large window that overlooked the inner courtyard. In a pinch, she could get out. And the gold Academy Award statue for best actress perched on the shelf above the toilet would make a perfect weapon. Apparently, their hostess had a quirky sense of humor or knew more people would have time to study it in here.

The pounding died away after a few rather long seconds of her standing near the pried open window, statue in one raised hand. Good. She took a deep breath, put the gold man back in his place of honor, and made use of the facilities. Checking her appearance in the full-length mirror, she smoothed down a wayward strand of bright hair. *Enough is enough.* No more Hollywood parties, no matter how much Serena begged, borrowed, or bribed.

Exiting the bathroom with caution, she peered around the half-closed door, alert to any letches lurking in the hallway. Empty. Perfect. She strode quickly back into the ballroom, preferring to be surrounded by chattering magpies over being separated from the herd.

She couldn't spot Serena from the edge of the crowd. She began to circulate, trying to catch a glimpse of her friend. As the seconds ticked by, her recent rash with disaster loomed ever more important in her mind. *Please, let her be okay.*

But after a thorough check through the crowd, she came up empty. Finally spotting Elle near the swimming pool, she rushed up to her, interrupting a conversation between her and a tall man with shiny black hair and equally dark eyes that reminded her of a hawk with his sharp features. Elle was perfectly put together as always, her brunette bob hugging her cheekbones.

"Have you seen Serena?" she asked, unable to stop the words from spilling out.

Elle frowned. The man gave her an appraising look.

"Not lately." She looked put out. "If you find her, tell her I'd like a word."

"Elle, introduce us, please." The tone was commanding and rubbed Claire the wrong way after her earlier experience.

"Claire Preston, I'd like you to meet Dr. Richard Vogel. He's just taken a position as the new physician for New Pictures. Claire reads scripts for them."

The doctor held out his hand like a man used to commanding the play. "Pleased to meet you, Miss Claire Preston."

"Nice to meet you. You must be taking over for Dr. Jacobs? I heard he was retiring."

"Yes." His voice was clipped and precise, his hand colder. "And I'm pleased to say that you and I will have time for a nice chat very soon."

"What are you talking about?" Though she was needing to find Serena, his words took her off-guard.

"For your physical, of course. I'm making it my first order of business to check out *all* employees. And see if any require victim shots to improve their existing health or pep up their energy. I have concocted my own special brand, approved by the studio. What's best for the employee, is best for the company." His tone struck her as a tad arrogant. But then, didn't most doctors have a god complex? Or at least their nurses seemed to think so. Even kindly old Doc Jacobs had been high-handed at times, driving his nurse Betty to distraction during immunizations.

"I don't think I need vitamins to sit in the back office and read scripts. Plus, I have my own physician. Why waste the studio's money?"

"I'm afraid it's mandatory. And aren't you a bit young to be a full-time script reader?"

She gave a noncommittal shrug, ignoring the hackles rising on her neck. "The powers that be wanted someone who understands the new generation and what they want to see up on the big screen. Older people often aren't in the groove. Excuse me, I need to find someone."

"Describe your friend." That annoying tone again. Deanna came up while they were talking, stood quietly nearby drinking a bottle of water.

"You probably don't know her."

"Serena Sands is slightly taller than our Claire here, blonde and beyond gorgeous, and up for a sweet part in a big picture scheduled to begin shooting next month," Elle said, her lips quirking upward at the corners, no doubt thinking of her commission. "And I think I can speak with authority in that she will definitely need your special brand of vitamins to keep up with the filming schedule. The studio wants filming completed in time for post-production in late fall, and then have the film released before Christmas to be in contention for this year's Oscars. Going to be a tight squeeze."

"I shall be pleased to make sure our starlet's in peak physical form."

Oops. Before I forget. "Thanks, Elle, for the recommendation of that PI. He's exactly the guy I needed to help me."

"Good. I hope it bears fruit for you. Everyone should know where they came from."

"What private investigator?" Dr. Vogel asked.

She shook her head discretely at Elle. Last thing she wanted was the doctor knowing any more of her private business.

Claire left the pair self-congratulating each other and

made another swing of the room, beyond desperate to catch a glimpse of Serena. Maybe she'd gone back to the car? Seemed an odd choice, but she was at a loss now. She took off her mask, tossed it away and rushed outside, taking the front steps as quickly as her high heels would allow. She made her way back down the sloping driveway, keeping a sharp lookout. The click of her stilettos on pavement and the steady hum of cicadas and other insects echoed the drumbeat marching in her head.

Halfway down the driveway she heard a mewing sound a short distance way. Was some creature in distress? She stopped walking and listened. It seemed to be coming from the bushes. She left the sidewalk, her heels sinking into the grass and loamy soil, making it difficult to keep her shoes on. She tugged them off and held them in her hands.

"He—lp." The fearful, muffled word spoken barely above a whisper struck with force.

"Who's there?" Claire swept the area, her eyes alert for any tiny movement.

No answer.

She rounded a hedge. Serena lay prone on the ground, her dress in disarray, a gag tied around her mouth. Her mask was gone. Claire dropped her shoes and sprang into action. She fell to her knees and tore off the gag which gave off a peculiar sweet, clogging odor. "Good heavens, Serena, what's happened? Did you fall?" It was obvious something far more sinister than a simple fall had occurred, but she couldn't bring herself to say the words.

"Claire."

"Do you need a doctor?" She was afraid to move her. What if something was broken? "Are you able to sit up?"

Claire used a shaking hand to push back Serena's hair from her face. Her eyes were unfocused, but her face was untouched by any bruising.

"Help me up."

Claire grabbed her shoulders and aided her into a sitting position. "What happened? Are you all right?"

"I'm okay. Someone attacked me. Pushed me up against a tree, stuffed that gag in my mouth and tried to rape me. When he couldn't, he got so angry. He pushed me to the ground and took off. Something on that rag made me woozy and I went unconscious for a while. Or at least I think so." Serena rubbed at her forehead.

"Did you see them?"

"No, they were behind me the whole time. But I think I was able to scratch his face."

"I'll get the doctor. You need to be seen to. And we need to contact the police too."

"No! I don't want anyone to know about any of this."

"But he attacked you!" Claire looked around, adrenaline flooding her system and making her jittery. "What if he's still here? Watching?"

"He's long gone. Couldn't even get it up." Serena's expression shifted. Her mouth downturned with disgust.

"We have to call someone. We can't let him get away with it. Maybe next time he'll be able to—" She couldn't bring herself to say the hated word.

"No. Absolutely not. It's my call, and I say no. I won't have this standing in my way of getting the part."

"What has one thing to do with the other?" Claire stroked her friend's back.

"I'd be seen as soiled goods." Serena shook her head. "No, leave it alone."

"But we can't just walk away. We need someone to look into this. Make sure this guy doesn't strike again."

Jake Sterling's face came to mind. His expertise could be useful. "Can I at least call the private eye I contacted today and have him look into it?"

She ignored the question. "Help me to my feet. The wooziness has passed."

She pulled Serena to a standing position, kept an arm around her just in case. "Would you let me do that at least? Call Jake Sterling? We can't let this happen to anyone else."

"Fine. But not here. I don't want anyone knowing at the party. We'll call him from home. Oh no, look at my dress! It's stained. I'll never get my money back now."

"Don't worry about the dress. I'll pay for it. I have money now."

"You'd do that for me? You're a good friend, Claire. I don't say that often enough. Don't ever leave me, you're the only friend I can count on." Serena's voice wobbled a bit.

She swallowed, tears prickling the back of her eyes. So much for moving out. "Of course, I'm not going anywhere. I wasn't such a good friend earlier when I made that stupid comment about the town pump."

"All forgotten. I shouldn't have called you frigid."

"Well, you might be right. I seem to find it rather easy to turn guys down flat."

"Nah, you're just picky. You can tell when a guy just wants into your pants and has zipola to offer otherwise. Not a bad thing." They held onto each other and slowly made their way down the hill.

Claire helped her friend into the car, then looked back at the mansion perched on the hill. In a thousand years none of this would matter. Shaking her head, she decided the strange turns tonight had affected her more than she realized. She got into the driver's seat, noting the downturn to Serena's mouth. At least this was a moment she could do something about.

"Did you hear about Elle chasing a naked woman away from her husband last night?"

"Yeah? I'd like to have seen that." Serena gave her a wobbly smile.

"I always wondered how a hearing man married Elle."

It took a moment for it to sink in, before peels of laughter erupted from her friend. "I shouldn't laugh, Elle works hard to find me opportunities." Serena wiped her eyes with the back of her fingers.

"You are careful, right? You won't let her talk you into anything you don't want to do for a part?"

"What are you implying?"

"It was just something Deanna said tonight."

"Deanna's always stirring things up. It's her job. I'm fine. I know my own mind. Leave it alone."

"Just want you to know, I'm here for you."

"I know. Me too."

Claire pulled out two cigarettes from the pack laying on the dash and pushed in the electric lighter. She waited a few seconds and lit the tips before handing one off to Serena.

"Thanks."

They smoked in silence; Claire worried her words had fallen on deaf ears.

CHAPTER 5
THE GOOD, THE BAD, AND THE UGLY

"Morning," Jake said as Claire slipped into his classic Highland green Ford Mustang, elevating it to superstar status in an instant. She was wearing a simple black knee-length dress. Looked good with the lustrous strand of pearls and matching low-heeled pumps, though he missed yesterday's mini skirt. The female scent she graced the front seat with reminded him of flowers blooming in a summer breeze. He took a deep breath that did nothing to steady his pulse.

"Cool ride. Expecting an eleven-minute race today?" she quipped, giving him a knowing smile.

"Well, if it's good enough for Steve McQueen. Of course, I owned it first." He shrugged, pretending a modest indifference. She was looking too fine today, same as yesterday. No doubt, same tomorrow. What was he thinking, asking her to come along?

"Screened *Bullitt* last week. Huge box office bonanza for Warner Brothers and Steve's own Solar Productions. Jacqueline Bisset looked fabulous too." She slanted her emerald-green doe-eyes his way, that fabulous side-wave of red hair falling forward to frame what was the most

47

gorgeous face that had ever graced his car. Yup, too much temptation for this former LAPD detective and lapsed Catholic. Maybe it was past time to sit his butt back down in a pew?

"Hmm." No point in disagreeing about the gorgeous Jacqueline Bisset. He liked a woman who was unafraid to compliment another.

"There's something I need you to look into, but it's kind of sensitive."

"A development in the case?" He turned to give her a look. She appeared pensive; her lush lips highlighted by a soft-pink lip gloss quirked to one side.

"No, nothing like that. It's my actress friend, Serena Sands, she had a bad experience at a party last night." She went on to fill him in on what had occurred.

"And you're just telling me all this *now*?" A surge of emotion railroaded his best intentions. "Darn it, Claire, you should have called me. I would have come running." What if the guy had attacked Claire? His blood boiled. "No more going to parties unescorted. Call me first."

"It's never happened before. And I can't be calling you every time I have to go to a party. Besides, the guy couldn't ah—follow through on his intentions, if you know what I mean."

"Yeah, I got the picture." He grimaced. "Any ideas who could have done it?" He observed her with a laser sharp focus, trying to see inside the youthful idealism she probably thought protected her. Memo: nothing protects a person from the evils of a certain segment of the population but due diligence, being prepared, and raw courage. And even then, all you've done is hardened the target. Some creep will always be trying to find a chink in the best defense. Why make it easy for him?

"Maybe. A guy who banged on the door to the bathroom."

"While you were in it?"

"Yeah. But I stalled him. And I had an open window and a heavy Oscar in my hands to even the score. I'm a big girl, Jake. I know how to handle creeps."

"That's not the point. You shouldn't have to handle an asshole like that. You should be protected from such things." She had courage and smarts, with some training he could make her a whole lot safer, starting with his patented self-defense course.

"No one gets off scot-free. Like I said, I can take care of myself." The apprehensive flash that came and went on her pretty face in a nanosecond belied her words.

"I can help train you with a variety of ways to protect yourself." He pressed on. "Why do you think it was him? Other than his deplorable actions toward you."

"The girl he was with made allusions to being able to, quote, 'Let me take care of you. I can get it up, just give me another chance, you'll see.'" She grimaced with distaste. "Seems logical the two events could definitely be connected."

"Do you have a name for this guy?"

"No. And I didn't see his face either. Everyone was wearing masks."

"Convenient."

"But I did see the woman's face. I'd recognize her again. And the guy did have a bad combover, and Serena thinks she scratched his face. I don't think he liked it much when I referenced said combover. So, you can add 'quick to anger' to the plus side of his resume."

The gleam in her eyes told a good tale. Claire intrigued him, and he recognized in her a select fellowship of not taking life too seriously. Refreshing in someone so young. Even as it worried him.

"Good. While that's something anyway. Soon as we've interviewed the administrator at the home, I'll be checking it out. Personally."

She nodded. "Are they expecting us at the home?"

"I prefer a good ambush. Catches them unprepared. Vulnerable people make mistakes."

"You're a bad boy, Jake." The way she purred the words gave the opposite meaning.

Just give me one night to show you how bad. Damn it. Why couldn't she have been born ten years earlier? She was too young for him. And if they were going to work together, that shut the door on any possible romantic intentions, no matter how attractive he found her. "Stick with me, and I'll have you earning your private eye badge in no time."

"What does that take?"

"Well, you have no former police training, I'm guessing?"

"No, just an English major from UCLA with some screenwriting credits. Oh, and a minor in psychology I particularly enjoyed." She drew a cigarette pack from her bag and offered him one. He pulled out his lighter and lit them both. She took a deep breath of hers before exhaling a few smoke rings and adding, "I take it you have. What went wrong?"

"No point in rehashing old news. Suffice to say my partner was into certain misdealings I personally found offensive. I prefer to call my own shots, even if it means a drop in pay and no pension." He took a deep drag on his cig, driving with one hand on the wheel.

"There's a story there I'd like to hear sometime. But I

understand. Not enough money in this world to buy my soul either."

"I think our writer friend Chandler had something wise to say about it. 'Down these mean streets a man must go who is not himself mean, who is neither tarnished nor afraid.' Same goes for a woman. But to answer your question, yes, California has requirements for becoming a private investigator. We've just recently amalgamated into one group as of September. The fee's thirty bucks a year. But it takes three years to be fully qualified plus an examination. Nothing you can't handle if you're serious about it. Oh, and you'll need to attend some CALI district meetings for credit. There's also a yearly convention which is useful for gaining contacts. Best part, most are big on ethics."

"Sounds like a plan."

He gave her a look as they arrived at their destination, the Hollywood orphanage, which was overshadowed by the water tower of Paramount Studios. He parked in front of the two-story red-brick institution with numerous cottages for children set to the back of the acreage. "Thank you for dressing the part today. Just let me do the talking. You all right with that?"

"Sure. I'll take notes." She slanted a glance at him, taking no prisoners.

He disembarked and went around and opened the passenger door for her. She stubbed out her cigarette in the ashtray, then got out and moved to join him, the scent of her perfume giving him a head rush.

"Your momma certainly taught you right," she quipped before turning serious. "Last thing I want is to be a distraction today."

"Lady, that's not possible—today or any day. But good try. You ready?"

She gave him a wan smile and took a deep breath. "Ready as I'm going to be."

He took her arm and walked her down the cement sidewalk to the wide entranceway and up the three steps to the door. On the top step he observed her downward study of the landing and he knew she had to be wondering if that was where she'd been left as a newborn.

He pressed the bell and listened to it echoing deep inside what was probably the most haunted building on the street. Had to be, considering what had transpired over the decades. Though maybe the back lots of the studios would win the dubious title.

The door swung open slowly. There stood a very old, birdlike woman, her skin loose and parched for lack of moisture, networked by deep lines and fractures. She was an exotic variety of human these days what with the tidal wave of humanity having been born since the end of the war. Her eyes defied her years though, intelligent and deep-set. She gave them a glare.

"You here from the city? I told them I don't need any more of their bull malarkey. Regulation *this*, regulation *that*. Never leave a body alone, the shysters."

"No, ma'am. We're not with the city or any government agency."

"That's something then. Come in, come in! Don't stand there like a pair of ninnies."

Jake kept a straight face with difficulty. He didn't dare look at Claire.

"Aw, nice picture of Marilyn Monroe," he said, noting the lineup of former residents on proud display, led by their most famous one.

"Bah, that one, always complaining about cleaning

toilets." The woman made a sound of disgust, her face soured.

"I would imagine, being an actress, she had a way of fudging the truth to craft a history better suited to her needs. The American public eats up a bad luck story. I'm certain you did everything in your power to make her and all the children into fine young citizens."

She took a moment as if to gauge whether or not he was being facetious. Apparently found his expression sincere enough to answer. "Yes, exactly. Why, I've told everyone who would listen, we treat all the youngsters *exactly* the same. Make sure all their needs are met and they can go out into the world proper like."

"You've worked here a long time. Seen a lot, I would imagine, over the years. Lots of orphans dropped off on your doorstep?" he asked casually.

"Of course." She bobbed her head in full agreement. "All kinds of children have made their way through these halls, bunked down in the cottages out back. And lots of them went on to make something of themselves. Best you can do, make a child face up to things. When life hands you lemons, add sugar and make a pitcher of lemonade, I always say."

"Good advice. Were you working here in nineteen forty-seven? Just after the Black Dahlia murder?"

"Oh, terrible thing. Every self-respecting woman was afraid to go out after dark. Of course, the victim didn't associate with the best of people, if you know what I mean, being a chippy. Call a spade a spade, I always say." She shook her head, and her mouth tightened with disapproval creating even more well-deserved canyons across her upper lip.

He kept watch on Claire as she made her way down the row of photos, her expression closed.

"Was there a baby left on the doorstep a couple of months later, after the murder? Sometime in mid-March?"

"You'd need to look at the records to check on it." The woman's birdlike glance peered at him before moving over to rest on Claire with renewed interest.

"We were hoping to see the administrator, Mrs. Holmes?" He handed her a business card. She took it without bothering to read it.

"No appointment, eh. *Harrumph.* Young people these days. Can't be bothered doing it the correct way." Hands on bony hips, she pursed her lips.

"I see you're starting another food drive." Jake nodded at the poster. "Fill the Larder is an admirable charity. Please, accept this as my donation to the worthy cause." He reached in his pocket, then handed over a pair of Jacksons.

"I'll see it gets to the right committee." She slipped the forty dollars in the bodice of her dress. "Wait here. I'll be right back." She tottered off down the hall like a glacier, though that's not giving the glacier enough credit.

"Nice to see a few of their residents went on to fame and fortune," Claire said, rejoining him.

"You've grown up just fine, have a degree from UCLA, work in Hollywood in the movie business without selling your soul for a job, and are doing quite well for yourself by all appearances. Though I have to wonder about your choice of friends?"

"My friends? You mean Serena? It's not her fault about last night." Claire's face colored with outrage.

He held up his hands in surrender. "Take it easy. I meant no offense. It's the industry that's ripe with corruption. The casting couch exists, whether we like it or not."

She raised a hand to push the wave of hair back from her face. The sunlight shone brighter through a spotless window right onto her person. That's when he saw it. A thin pink scar running along the side of her face from her forehead to her earlobe, kept hidden by her hairstyle. Had to be her recent accident. No wonder she was prone to nightmares. Well, he had his own scars. Some visible, some not.

As the minutes ticked by with their congenial hostess still MIA, he fingered the items hidden in the depths of his suit jacket pocket, antsy to get on with things. The wait was taking a toll on his companion as well. A small frown had appeared between her arched eyebrows that were an exact match for her hair color.

"I wish I had a cigarette," she said, her tone wistful.

"And a fifth of bourbon wouldn't go amiss. Only two things harder than waiting. A screaming baby and people who use *your* instead of *you're*."

He earned a satisfying snort. She began to tick them off on her fingers. "Too many exclamation marks, failure to use a hyphen to connect two words for compound adjectives, misusing apostrophes, oh, and speaking of things requiring an exclamation mark—" She nodded at their attentive hostess now barreling down the hallway at a clip a sloth would admire. "There she is now."

He hid his grin and made himself wait for the woman to rejoin them. Then he felt a twinge of guilt when he realized she was out of breath. By the blush now staining Claire's cheeks, she was experiencing a similar setback.

"Against my better judgment, Mrs. Holmes will see you now. Follow me. Keep in mind she's a *very* busy woman. Don't wear out your welcome."

That helped ease the guilt sufficiently. "Please, just

point the way. We've taken up too much of your time already."

Those birdlike eyes pinned him in place. "Last door at the end of the hall. Use your manners. See you knock before you enter."

"Thank you, ma'am."

Side by side, they traversed the length of the hallway in a burst of pent-up energy.

He knocked briskly on the wooden door, admiring the nameplate of Mrs. F. Holmes, administrator. He glanced at Claire. "You okay?"

She nodded, her frown deepening. "I need to know. No matter what we learn, I can't live the rest of my life not knowing where I came from."

CHAPTER 6
TURN ME LOOSE

THE ADMINISTRATOR SAT BEHIND A GARGANTUAN DESK, though her broad smile made up for the barrier. Her pleasant face was surrounded by a flattering layered hair style. She was thirty-two, according to her dossier, meaning she'd not been around when Claire had been dropped off. The F stood for Fiona. Known for her charity work. If she could help, she probably would, was his preliminary assessment.

"Good morning, please, have a seat."

Jake waited for Claire to sit before he reached across the desk and offered his hand to the woman, allowing his suit jacket to fall open to make sure she observed the badge pinned to his belt. She returned a firm handshake, her eyes flitting over his person. He made introductions, then sat down.

"Louisa was saying you wanted to speak with me?"

Good. A woman who gets right to the point. He pulled out his wallet and flashed his Private Investigators license. "Yes, I do have a few questions for you. Does the home keep records on every child that comes through here?"

"We do." She pointed at the three-drawer filing cabinet behind her desk. "Each child in our care has a case file."

"Right back to the eighteen-eighties when the home was founded?"

"Yes. Though most of those are housed in the basement. What can I do for you? Are you wanting a record of a specific child? We don't just let anyone look through our records. Privacy for both child and birth parents is critical. You'll need to fill out a form before we can consider your request."

"This young woman you see before you recently learned her adoption had been hidden from her since birth. Her adopted parents have died, and she's an orphan all over again. She wants to know where she came from. Maybe find a living relative to connect with? Surely, we can help her with now that circumstances have changed so drastically? Offer her a helping hand without all the red tape?"

"I am sorry for your loss." The woman's dark expressive eyes flitted to Claire. "But it's not only your feelings at stake here. What if your birth parents are unable to handle the stress of you showing up after all these years or, worse yet, don't want to see you? There could be tragic consequences. On both sides."

"You have my word I won't contact them unless they want to see me." Claire paused. Her expression turned pensive. "Perhaps you could check with whomever is listed in the file? See if they want to see me? I desperately need to know where I came from. What if I have inherited some health condition—I've already had a small hole in my heart repaired—and what if my mother needs my help now that she's older? I should be there for her."

The administrator looked thoughtful, a fingernail

clicking against her front teeth. "You make some valid points. Yes, I could act as the liaison between the parties." Then she grimaced. "But the records you want are among hundreds, if not thousands, in the basement. And I simply do not have the time right now to check them all. It could be weeks until I can get around to it. We're right in the middle of raising funds to keep this place going. That has to take priority, you understand."

"Of course. But what if I gave you my word to bring the file directly to you? I'm bonded," Jake said, giving his most sincere expression. "I do have these things that were left for Claire by her adopted mother." He reached into his suit pocket and pulled out the folder paper, brooch, and the piece of material. He laid them down on the desk.

"These may prove useful." She picked up the official document issued by their office and studied it. "Louisa was here back in the day. Let me call her and have her take a look at the brooch and material. See if they will twig any memory for her?"

"We'd appreciate any help you can give us." He reached into his pants pocket and brought out a couple more Jacksons, tucked them in the jar sitting prominently on her desk. "A little something for the children."

"The children thank you. This doesn't change anything about what I can or can't do for you, you understand, Mr. Sterling? I'll be back shortly." The woman got up and left the room.

"Do you think she'll let us comb through the records?"

"I don't see why not. Saves her the time. Plus, we're not asking for anything unreasonable here. You could fill out a form and have the county do the work for you, but it takes longer. She'd still have to hand over the information eventually."

Claire nodded. "Right. Let's hope Louisa remembers something useful."

"I wouldn't get my hopes up. She doesn't seem the kind to be any more helpful than necessary."

The second hand on the mantel clock on the bookshelf behind the woman's desk ticked off the seconds. The timepiece was surrounded by manuals and cheap knickknacks. A few drawings by children hung on the light-colored walls. A tall narrow window looked out onto the street. A view of Paramount's water tower was visible, looming over the landscape on tri-pod legs, its blue and white logo of a cresting mountain iconic, if not a reality. Hollywood and the movies. Nothing more than a state of mind, a sleight of hand, an illusion only projected in celluloid. He shook his head, feeling the weight, living in a city of crushed hopes and dreams.

"What if we don't find anything helpful in my file? What's the next step?"

"Checking out newspaper accounts around the time."

She frowned. "But wouldn't a crime have to have occurred to have any mention of a baby dropped off at an orphanage? It's such an unimportant event otherwise."

She was too clever by half. "Perhaps. But also, in context of what was going on at the time. It's a long shot."

"What about hospitals?" She looked less stressed now that she was making a mental list. Good. Action was his drug of choice.

"We'll check on it. Could have been a home birth. Unattended. Or maybe there's a midwife that knows something? I warn you; this could take a great deal of time and money if we don't find a good lead here today. Best pray for that."

"We could break up the job. I mean, I can make time to help. Whatever you need done, I'm more than willing to do. Earn my own pair of gumshoes." Her enthusiasm warmed the cockles of his heart.

"Then there's the brooch. I'd make the rounds of the jewelers and pawn shops, see if I can dig up any intel. You can assist with that chore if you want. But I warn you, it might take weeks of tramping around Hollywood with no guarantee of success."

The door opened and in swept the administrator. A longish moment later Louisa followed suit. "Sorry to keep you waiting. But Louisa was right in the middle of something. So, take a look, would you please, see if you recognize anything?"

Louisa tottered over to the desk; her expression bored as any self-respecting teenager. She glanced at the items, then her expression shifted dramatically. Her thin gray eyebrows soared upward and her mouth dropped open.

"You're her." She swung around and pointed an accusatory boney finger right at Claire.

Claire sat up straighter. "What do you mean? What do you know about me?"

"Terrible thing. You poor tyke. Dropped off in nothing but your birth caul and a piece of bloody fabric. And a ridiculous brooch pinned to it all. *Tsk tsk*. Well, looks like you did okay for yourself. Grown up fine. Be glad you were left here. At least we were able to find you a decent home. Newborns are easier to place, you see. It's the older ones who suffer most." The old woman shook her head. "You want my advice, leave this alone, dearie. You got your good life. Let the past lie where it belongs, I always say, no good comes of digging and messing about."

"Is there anything else you can tell us? Was there an investigation at all? Were the authorities contacted?" he asked.

"You'd have to check the files. No need to, was my personal opinion, she was fine here. Didn't take but a couple of weeks before a nice, young couple came along and took her away with them." The woman's expression had shifted. Turned sly. She gave the impression she might know more than she was prepared to say. Would a couple more Jacksons open the vault?

"Did you see her records? Anything in them that could help identify her birth mother?"

"Can't say, but I doubt it. Most females who did things like that don't want to be identified." She sniffed her disapproval. "Women today use the pill to avoid pregnancy. No better morals, in my opinion. Just 'cause you don't get caught, don't mean you're not a chippy. All this free love bull malarkey. Makes me sick to my stomach."

"Thank you, Louisa. We won't keep you any longer." Mrs. F. Holmes's face flushed a far rosier color.

Louisa harrumphed again for good measure, then she shambled out of the office, not bothering to close the door.

The administrator busied herself with opening and closing a desk drawer, drawing out a page of paper in the process. "Here's the form you need to fill out. However, it's only a formality. I'll let you get on with things. You have my permission to search the records in the base-ment." She handed it to him.

"Thank you." He folded it in three and tucked it in the

breast pocket of his suit jacket. Then picked up the other items and stashed them.

Claire added her thanks and they all stood up.

"If you'll follow me."

The three of them trooped down the hallway, overtaking Louisa. She waved them on with a frown. They rounded a hallway and made their way past a second series of doors.

"It's through here." Mrs. Holmes stopped in front of a door and unlocked it, using one of a series of keys hanging from her belt. Then switched on a light switch. A musty smell emulated up the steep staircase, making his nose twitch. "The boxes are all clearly marked as to month, and year. The case files are all laid out by number and are moved into permanent storage when the child turns eighteen. Like I say, there's quite a pile of them, I'm afraid. No one wants to spend much more time down there than necessary." She gave a short nervous laugh. "Some employees have complained about visits from our resident ghost. They tend to set a box down and make a hasty retreat."

"Thank you. We'll bring the file by when we have recovered it," he restated his promise.

"I'd appreciate it."

The woman strode off, her heels making an officious tattoo on the tile floor.

"You ready?" he asked.

Claire nodded, her expression pensive. "Not overly fond of ghosts."

"Don't worry. They usually take a dislike to me and stay clear." He thought for a second, then asked, "Who do you think killed the chauffeur in *The Big Sleep*?"

She chuckled. "Finally, the sixty-four-thousand-dollar question. Even Chandler didn't know and he wrote the book. Might as well ask me when Harry Houdini's going to contact the world again?"

"We've got to sit down together sometime and discuss murder plots."

"Anytime, detective."

Mission accomplished, he walked through the open doorway and began to descend the staircase.

She followed him down the narrow steps. At the bottom, he glanced around and groaned. Boxes were piled everywhere in the dimly lit chasm. The floor was made of hardpacked dirt and only added to the dismal smells emanating around them. Had something curled up and died down here? "Lot of files."

"No kidding." They stood side by side, surveying the huge, low-ceiling room with its series of cement pillars holding up the three-story structure. "Phttt. Sure stinks. Looks like the spiders have had a heyday," she added.

"Now the fun begins. You know, I could drive you home first? You're not exactly dressed for this kind of activity."

"No, I'm staying. The quicker we get through this mess, the better. Plus, I need to learn everything the job entails. You can't hog all the fun stuff for yourself."

"Okay, if you're certain?"

She nodded. "I am. What's the game plan?"

"You start on that row—" he pointed a short distance away. "And I'll start over there."

Other than the sounds of boxes being shoved about, silence descended. It was dusty, dirty work, and he felt bad he'd pulled her into it. Not kicking and screaming, but still.

The upper floor creaked and resettled with a series of loud pops every few minutes, making him look up. Dust descended from the ceiling in waves, obscuring the view from the few bare light bulbs still working. He sneezed often, his eyes watering. Spooky place all right. Just the spot to film a horror movie. Perhaps *Night of the Dead* or—

"Over here, I've found the box!" Claire half-shouted, her excitement obvious.

He hurried to join her, noting the month and year were correct: January to June 1947. Each year had been broken up into two separate boxes.

"Nice work. You're my new lucky charm." He gave her a grin and an appreciative pat on the back.

"We aim to please, sir."

She was a mess, covered in dirt and cobwebs and God knows what else, but with that lovely smile, she looked like an angel caught in a snow globe.

"Okay, let's see what we have." He pulled out her paperwork to check the file number, then made his way through the brown manilla folders, ticking off each one in turn. When he came to the spot where hers should be, he found nothing. He went past to be certain, then went back again in case they were slightly out of order. "Doesn't seem to be here."

"But it has to be! It's the right box."

"Yes, it's the right box. But your record's still missing."

CHAPTER 7
DON'T LET THEM SEE YOU SWEAT

"Now what? Mrs. Holmes is going to think we absconded with it." Claire was filled with dismay. She'd gone from pure exhilaration to sinking into the quagmire of despair in a matter of minutes. *Why my records?*

"Let's check a couple of other boxes, see if other files are missing as well. Could be a coincidence."

Claire grimly set to work, hoping Jake's reasoning would prove correct.

"They're all here in the half-dozen boxes I've checked. *Every last one*. Mine's the only one missing."

"Same here." He stopped searching, then picked up the offending box from 1947. "We'll need to hide this one so no one else knows about the missing file until we find out what's going on. We'll say we couldn't find it. Hand in the paperwork like we want them to sleuth it out."

"Good idea. Buy us some time." She took a look around. "Where?"

"We'll bury it way at the back under a pile. You heard Mrs. Holmes, no one's likely to look that hard. In fact, I'd expect her to be right unhappy we didn't find the file for them in the first place."

They set about the task. Finally satisfied their slight-of-hand would hold, they ascended the staircase back to the land of the living.

"Do you play pool?" Jake asked, holding the door open for her. The question took her by surprise, though not as much as their appearance in the brighter daylight.

She reached out and began to brush some of the spider webs and dirt off his suit jacket. "You're a mess, Mr. Sterling."

He shrugged, reaching for something in her hair, then showing her a string of spider webs on his fingers. "Beats bodily fluids."

"Right. Your job as a cop. Did you ever get shot at?" The question spilled out before she thought better of it. Blame it on a very discombobulating morning. She finished brushing the obvious debris from his jacket and stepped back to brush off the front of her dress.

"Yeah. I have had a couple of holes plugged in me." *If you're not in trouble, you're not doing your job.* "Bad enough when it's a criminal shooting it, but when my own part-ner's gun misfires, well, let's just say it's time to rethink your career choice."

"Is that why you left the force?"

"It was time to go anyway. Much prefer running my own business, calling my own shots, if you'll pardon the lame pun."

"To answer your question, yes, I've played pool and table tennis. There's an exercise setup at the studio, in the lounge. Why do you ask?"

"Best place to gain intel I know of, other than a bar. My advice, practice lots. Catches the punters off-guard.

Okay, I'm going to drop you off and begin looking into who attacked your friend."

"I can help there as well."

"Absolutely not." Jake's expression turned grim. "I'll need to be free to make my feelings clear about conduct unbecoming a human being."

The steeliness of his tone more than convinced her.

"I have some vacation time owed me."

"Save it. When the investigation heats up, then we'll see."

"What about the form? I could fill it out and send it in."

Jake drew it from his breast pocket and gave it a quick perusal. "Not much to it. I'll drop it off later."

"What are you two doing to my nice clean floor?" Louisa was tottering up to them, her face a mask of outraged anger.

"Sorry about that. The basement was pretty dirty," she said.

"You should have been more careful. Don't know why it was so important to you, knowing the dismal facts of your beginning, that you'd get into such a state?" The old woman shook her head, her lips pursed with displeasure.

"Are you sure you don't know anything more about my case? It would mean a lot to me to find my birth mother. I recently lost my adopted mother to cancer and my father died of a heart attack years ago." She swallowed the pain.

"Terrible thing, the cancer." The woman's expression shifted, her tone becoming less angry.

Jake reached into his wallet, drew out the last of his Jacksons and handed them to the woman who immediately tucked them away. "Anything you can remember would be appreciated."

"Well, there's one thing. Not sure if it helps, but the day after you were abandoned—"

Claire winced at the word.

Louisa lowered her voice, her beady eyes bright with the memory. "A bigshot came a-calling. Some federal agency"—she made a sound of disgust, her face souring —"and he was all up in the administrator's face. Thomas Crane ran the place in those days. Weak as water he was. No backbone. Capitulated to whatever the boss man wanted. The man came and talked to me as well, demanded I hand over anything I had connected to you. I said I had nothing. Why should I hand over anyway to the likes of him?"

"You kept the items?"

"I did. Hid them away, and when you were adopted, handed them over to your parents in secrecy. They rightfully belonged to you. The brooch looked to be expensive. It had an antique look about it."

"Thank you, it was kind of you."

The woman blustered, obviously not used to being thanked. "Wasn't anything any self-respecting person wouldn't do. The government has no right to be all up in our faces. What's it to them, the possessions of an abandoned baby?"

"We appreciate your telling us, Louisa. Very helpful." Jake held out his hand for a shake.

The pair shook hands. Impulsively, Claire gave the woman a quick hug of thanks.

Was that a tear she dashed away with the big service hanky she pulled out of a pocket?

"Did the pair of you find the file you were looking

for?" Louisa blew her nose noisily and tucked the hand-kerchief in her apron pocket.

"No, we're going to have leave it to the county. Let them locate it," Jake said.

"*Phttt.* No point. That man likely took it with him."

"You said he was federal. Any idea of his connections? FBI, CIA?" Jake pressed.

"None. Thought himself so *la-ti-dah* important. I have to go. The children will be wanting their lunch."

They parted ways. On the front sidewalk, Claire looked back at the top step she'd been placed on so long ago. A strange yearning struck a lonesome chord deep in her chest, making her feel less a part of humanity and a more a piece of rubbish someone would throw away.

"If it's any comfort, I'm a strong believer it's within us to heal ourselves. But—" He stopped talking to pull another string of cobweb from his suit jacket and continued, "After that experience, I'll need to pull a Chandler, rub two nickels together and hope they're not too shy to mate this month."

"I'll reimburse you."

"That's not what I was suggesting. The money was well spent. We know a heck of a lot more now than we arrived."

"Why would my case be of any interest to a federal agency?" She turned from staring at the top step to look at Jake. He appeared pleased.

"A sixty-four-thousand-dollar question. Okay, I'll drop you off."

He pulled up at her apartment complex. "Remember. Don't forget to call me if you receive another party invite."

"I won't, Daddy."

His chagrined expression was worth it.

She hurried into the building, intending to take Marlowe for a walk before settling down to read a couple of scripts she'd promised her supervisor she'd make an assessment on this weekend. She made a face thinking of her weaselly boss. She'd learned to keep from making recommendations for what the author could have done to make the script better or more commercial, to saying it wasn't up to studio standards. That way, she wasn't so pissed when they used her ideas to make a movie. She intended to save all her notes in a file for her *own* use one day. She was paid to suggest viable scripts, not paid to write them. Now, that would be sweet money. Maybe one day.

"So, what did you think of my script?" She was in the process of unlocking the door to her suite when Herman accosted her, sidling up before she could escape.

"Sorry, I've been out. There's been no time yet to read it yet. But I will get to it. Then I'll let you know."

She ignored his disappointed expression and continued on inside, closing the door with relief. Everyone wanted something. Usually for free.

"Hey buddy, time for walkies?" Marlowe dashed up to her, his toenails clicking on the black-and-white tile. His short bark of greeting suggested it was about time. She stroked his thick black fur and patted his head before pulling his leash off the hook near the door and latching it to his collar. She'd shower and change later. Picking up a baggie and her keys, she opened the door. "Let's go, bud."

They took off at a sprint, making their way down the carpeted hallway and out the side door to the street in a flash of fur and dusty clothing. The metal door clicked shut behind them, and she followed the excited dog onto the sidewalk leading to the park for their daily exercise, only one block away. It was one of the best parts of living in the apartment block, the close proximity to a green space.

The park was nearly deserted allowing her to give the inquisitive Marlowe free rein to check out every tree and shrub for evidence of other doggie competition. He promptly set to work, using his highly developed scent of smell to sleuth in every nook and crevice. She followed along behind, enjoying the fresh air and sunshine after the morning spent in the dismal basement. It would be nice to get the smell of dirt and mildew out of her nostrils.

Near a section of the path that led to a thick strand of trees her sixth sense went on high alert when Marlowe growled deep in his throat, making her skin crawl.

"What is it, boy? Someone out there?" They both stopped in their tracks. She held on more tightly to his leash.

A twig snapped. He growled again, a sharp warning that decided her. "Let's head back. We both need to eat, and I need a shower."

She wasn't sure he was going to cooperate, but after a final growl, he turned and obediently set a path back to the apartment. Minutes later they were safely inside. She opened a can of food for him. The way he chuffed down the food he'd obviously already forgotten the incident.

But the experience left her unnerved. It was the first time Marlowe had given her warning of something suspicious going on anywhere. Maybe it had just been another dog he hadn't liked? She hoped so. They both liked the park. Or maybe it was time to start carrying pepper spray or a weapon? She'd always felt safe with the large dog at her side, but she didn't want anything to happen to them if it could be avoided. Yes, time to shore up defenses. Maybe she'd ask Jake for his recommendations. He packed heat. She'd witnessed the bulge under his jacket.

Mind made up, she headed for a shower and a night of reading. She'd call Jake tomorrow.

CHAPTER 8
THE EVIL MEN DO LIVES ON

HE KNEW BEST. NEVER DRAW ATTENTION TO YOURSELF. Never take risks. He lived for the hunt. For the planning. For proving he alone could lower the chance of exposure to near zero, by considering each and every contingency. For choosing due diligence and precision. And all his exquisite planning had paid off each and every time. Perfectly. *The supreme art of war is to subdue the enemy without fighting.*

He had hit his stride these past years. Not a whiff of anyone ever having suspected his experiments had continued unbated since the war. And he'd done it all by having discovered the perfect disposal site, making him the ultimate revenant. The one who preyed on primal fears, who lies waiting in the darkest corners of the human mind and survived by calculating the energy of the living as they died. It amazed him how much the human body could endure.

Other than the crime that still made him wince with the memory of such unseemly passion, all the others had been carried out with such supreme care it was a shame they would not go down in the annals of history. The crimes to beat. All so well hidden no one in the coming centuries would ever find the bodies.

He sniffed the air now as she ventured closer. *Aww.* The delicious smell of fear wafted in on the slight breeze as he crouched camouflaged by the close-growing bushes. Soon would be the seminal moment when she realized he had her in his sights. Chosen. One to be sacrificed in the name of science. Then the dance could begin. Ah, the moment of clarity when she knew that there would be no escape. The wide-eyed stare as the last breath left the body after it gave forth all its secrets. He licked his lips, keeping his eyes focused on the woman. Soon the time would be upon them. But not before he was ready.

Until then, a wise revenant stood and watched and gained important intel, even though every muscle in his body twitched for relief. Victory only honored the prepared and the brave. He took out his little black book and made careful notes in his precise handwriting.

CHAPTER 9

PREPARATION IS KEY

JAKE DROVE DOWN THE STREET, CHECKING FOR THE
address of the man he suspected of attacking Serena
Sands. The MO fit after a couple of phone calls to the
right parties. And his housekeeper had admitted the man
had scratches on his cheek, courtesy of last night's
masquerade. The place appeared deserted, but he could
see the man's black Porsche parked haphazardly in the
curved driveway. He'd obviously driven home under the
influence. Jake's lips thinned, and he squinted his eyes at
the sight. Nothing he detested more than a man, or a
woman for that matter, who endangered others with
their feckless behavior.

He exited the Mustang, checked his weapon was
secured, and began the hundred-yard-stalk down the
recently repaired asphalt to the low-slung ranch-style
house set back on five hobby acres of prime land.

The fragrance of blooming hydrangea tickled his
senses, and he sneezed three times in succession. Darn
allergies. He reached into his pocket and withdrew a foil
wrapped sample from his favorite pharmacist. Popped

one. He didn't want watery eyes to impair Operation Limp Willie.

At the front doors, he pressed the doorbell, keeping an eye out for any movement. The housekeeper answered his ring, her expression sullen. She perked up a bit when he gave his name, like she suspected what was coming.

"Detective Jake," she said, her smile slowly widening to Cheshire Cat size.

"Is Mr. Costanza around?" It was just too satisfying that the guy's first name was William.

"Yeah, he's out back by the aquarium, feeding that disgusting fish of his. He has a big shark, thinks it's a nice thing to brag about. Some people are too rich, in my opinion."

"A shark. Interesting. Guess Willie best be careful it doesn't bite him in a tender spot or two."

She erupted with a peel of laughter that far outweighed his comment, then wiped the tears from her eyes with the corner of her apron. He had to assume humor was a stingy commodity in the household. "From your lips to God's ears. Come with me, I'll lead you right to him."

"Is he alone?"

"He is at the moment. Better hurry."

He followed the comely, rather twitchy young maid through the spacious house, the air conditioning cooling him down admirably by the time they'd reached the patio doors. The window view led to the expansive backyard where the main feature stuck out like a gardener's sore thumb. The thousands-of-gallons water structure shrieked of money. The maid was right. Too much dough cannot guarantee taste.

The maid departed with a final unearned chortle on

his part, and he walked back out into the heat, perspiration once again breaking out under his armpits. The guy couldn't have gone for, say, an inside hobby collecting stamps or building model planes?

He strode down the cobbled pathway to the far side of the structure, where he could hear a man speaking, or was it crooning, To someone named Big Tiger.

Big Tiger turned out to be the pet shark of the man he was looking for, said fish being proximately nine to nine-and-a-half feet long. The cold-eyed creature was swimming relentlessly in the now-visible water of the tank, this end being all glass. That made it far too easy to see some of the world's sharpest teeth. It would take a dentist of some fortitude to scale those pearly whites to a proper shine. At the moment his choppers were unseemly, filled as they were with the raw bits of blood and gore from the diet Limp Willie was in the process of feeding him.

The biting end of the serrated edge of the knife the guy was using to cut up the chunks of fish for the even bigger fish in the tank winked in the bright sunshine, drawing his full attention. It took no imagination to see it hooking into his own guts and cutting clean through, making his day shorter than intended.

Jake decided to keep the warning part of this impromptu meeting quiet until the knife was safely stowed.

Limp Willie looked up and caught sight of him, frowning with concentration. He dropped the hunk of smelly fish he was holding back into the bucket, but he held onto the knife.

Might be a shorter meeting than intended. Keeping a close watch on the weapon, he advanced closer and managed a smile, even with his lips feeling like they were stuck to his front teeth. "Mr. William Costanza?"

"I am."

"Jake Sterling, of Sterling Private Investigators. I was hoping to ask you a few questions? Would you have a moment? Or is this a bad time?"

The guy had a worse combover than expected, even after Claire's description.

"What do you want to know?" The guy's paunch suggested he wasn't in the best of physical conditioning, though his beefy arms, visible in the muscle shirt, suggested otherwise.

"Last night a girl was attacked at a party you attended in Beverly Hills. She's named you as the attacker." It wasn't entirely correct, but a good offense is the best defense. Ask any lineman.

Limp Willie squinted, his lips turning downward in disgust. "You mean that ditsy blonde who's trying to trick me into paying her palimony?"

"No, I don't believe you've got the right female. The one with the complaint is certainly not suing you at the moment for anything. She's the one you forced yourself on near a tree in the yard, using a rag soaked in chloroform."

The man's face turned a dull red as he jerked up the knife to chest level, pointing it in Jake's direction. "She said that? What a lying bitch. She wanted it. I don't need to attack anyone."

"She did not want it and neither did she actually get it, right, Willie?"

Apparently, he'd gone too far, for Willie charged at him, giving a series of quick backhanded slashes in a row, dancing around like a fencing master who desperately needed to show off his rusty prowess.

Jake ducked and dived away from the slashes, then slipped inside Willie's reach, so for the next backhanded slash he was too close in for him to get any muscle behind it. Quick as lightning, he switched into a more advantageous position. With his chest to Constanza's back, he snaked his arm inside his elbow like he wanted to square-dance, then grabbed a handful of the wife-beater shirt between his shoulder blades. With his other hand, he snatched at his free arm. The improvised armlock neutralized the knife, but the rat shark began trying to chew on his arm with impressively sharp teeth of his own.

His grip was slipping, and he used all his strength to heave the man one way, twisted his hip the other, and put him on the ground with an ankle sweep. The knife clattered out of Willie's fat sausage fingers, landing on the paving stones. Jake picked it up and tossed it into the bushes.

The scrap was over in mere seconds. Jake took the opportunity to give the warning he'd come to offer, crouching over the guy. He was winded, though his sparing mate looked even worse for the encounter, his muscle shirt ripped to shreds exposing his ample center of gravity.

"Okay, Willie, now that I have your full attention, here's the deal. You will cease and desist—"

The sounds of running footsteps slapping on cement alerted him to incoming.

"Ha, now you're in for it. My bodyguards finally getting their asses into gear," the guy wheezed.

Jake hauled Willie to his feet, by what was left of his sleeveless tee, the strip around his neck. Too bad it half-chocked him in the process. "Tell them to lay off. Or I'll need to step this up a notch and call my friends at the LAPD."

"You don't scare me. Do you realize who my friends are? Bigger bullies than the LAPD can ever hope to have."

"You okay, Mr. Constanza?" the taller of the two newly arrived bodyguards asked with deference, his eyeballs pinballing back and forth.

"No, I'm far from okay. Where have you been? This guy attacked me on your watch. See him out and don't make it a soft landing."

"Sorry, we were called away on a false alarm. You heard him, buddy. March."

Jake held up his hands. "I was going anyway. Just wanted to give your boss fair warning. Don't attack innocent women."

"Innocent, my ass! You've not heard the end of this, *Mr.* Sterling." Reference to the fact he was no longer officially with the LAPD.

Jake shrugged. "Don't imagine I have. You want to finish this like a man, let me know." He straightened his jacket, then followed the two bozos through the house and out the front door, knowing what was coming next. Every muscle in his body was tense and on high alert by the time they arrived on the front steps. Both men looked like they could handle themselves physically, if not mentally.

He never got used to waltzing into what any sane person had to assume was danger, whether it be a home of the guy who had pulled the trigger or held the knife or swung the pipe. Twelve years on the force had taught him that. A knot of anxiety started to unravel somewhere behind his belly button and spread throughout his body. And the waiting is the worse time. Action relieved anxiety.

"Time to send a clear message, buddy. Nothing personal, you understand, just doing our job."

Tall clown acted first, sucker punching a fast one to his midsection after the shorter clown grabbed hold of him from behind. Jake grunted in pain, then struck out with one well-aimed kick to the taller man's loins. It connected. When the guy bent over to cradle the offended appendages, he swung around and tried grabbing the other one by the neck, fully intending to punch him. The guy ducked his move and made a neat sideways step.

"Get him!" tall clown screamed his displeasure, still holding his nuts.

"I got you now, asshole!" The short guy charged, knocking both of them to the ground. The smell of freshly cut grass assailed him as the clown landed on top and Jake jerked his body hard in efforts to dislodge him. The taller guy was coming round enough to reenlist. Unfortunate development. He grabbed Jake around the neck with one beefy arm. Squeezed hard. Jake sneezed loudly three times and the guy loosened his hold, then jerked him to his feet. It wasn't looking good. Turns out he was a decent fortune teller.

The bigger man caught him with a haymaker across the cheekbone. Things began to go dim, and black spots danced in his vision. The guy hit him a couple more times for good measure, but his face had gone numb, making it wasted effort.

When the guy finally let go, he slumped to the ground. The shorter clown decided it was the ideal opportunity to kick him in the ribs. Opportunists galore in Hollywood.

"Okay, enough."

Jake had to agree. More than enough. No matter what, no good deed ever goes unpunished.

He took the cue, staggered to his feet, and began to limp away as the front door slammed shut. He'd gotten off lucky, even though blood was dripping from his nose and his right side was on fire. In his experience, guys with dick problems leaned toward escalating retaliations to make up for their obvious short comings. And no doubt, Limp Willie, with his disturbing need for a shark tank, wouldn't be taking any of this on consignment. Maybe it was time to call his last friend who might listen to his tale of woe.

CHAPTER 10
A HARD DAY'S NIGHT

UGH. MONDAY MORNING. IT WAS NOT CLAIRE'S FAVORITE time of day. Staff meeting followed by pep talk followed by commissaries among participants. Someone's feelings *always* got hurt. Seemed to depend on the whims of an egomaniac. Keeping her head down and steady the course was Monday's usual modus operando. She cradled a large thermos of strong black coffee in her hands sitting at her desk, staring at the poster of *Casablanca* while waiting for the weekly migration of all the minions to the conference room.

"You got anything decent to pitch? I don't know why I ask, of course you do. You got the best track record around for sniffing out a winning script." Tess Evans, from one cubicle over, came in and leaned against the partition, carrying a steaming cup of coffee and nibbling on a honey-glazed donut. Five nine, thin, with long fair hair parted exactly in the center, she'd been voted most likely to be a model in high school. She looked as sullen as a Monday morning hangover; her mouth adorned by shiny red lipstick downturned at the corners. The fragrance of sweet sugar, vanilla, and cream made

Claire's mouth water. But the question of the day took her mind off the need for empty calories.

"I do as it happens." She smiled in memory of the competent script she'd skimmed through last night. An unexpected surprise. She hoped she could report back a positive outcome to the writer. One of the best parts of her job was making an unknown writer's day. She hoped he knew what he was in for, negotiations with the resident shark.

"Must be good judging by that smug smile. Lucky you. I got nothing, nada, even though I read a ton of stinking scripts last week." Tess took another sip of her coffee while rolling her eyes.

Claire winced. "Most are. Luck of the draw what we get to read."

The ding of the call to the staff meeting resounded throughout the office.

"It's showtime," Tess said. She scarfed down the last of her donut, then blotted her lips with a tissue she nabbed off of Claire's desk, dropping the red-smeared item in the wastebasket before making an elegant turn on sky-high heels. Yup, she could have been a model, probably to be voted most loved by her fellow posers for her inability to gain an ounce no matter what she consumed.

Claire picked up the promising script and joined her colleague. She was as ready as she could be for the fishbowl.

"Morning, people. I hope everyone's prepared to blow me away today." The chair of the meeting, Cuthbert Murdock, sat in the place of honor at the head of the humongous wooden table hand polished bi-weekly with beeswax by his adoring secretary, Wendy, who sat at his side, pencil poised over her stenographers' pad. Her pleasant, vacant expression told her full story. Cuthbert, on the other hand, was a fussy man with deliberate movements and dark, beady eyes. He favored a fedora that would have looked better in nineteen sixty-two and had a face that would have been more at home in Barrows, Alaska, during long periods of no sunlight, but it didn't stop him from wearing alligator boots made in Florida. Oh, and a bolo tie that would look better on the dance floor in a Texas honky tonk.

Nods ensued all around the conference table from the script staff of seven, though most avoided eye contact. No one wanted to be first.

"Okay, why don't you begin, David? Tell us what you've got for us today?"

David Miller cleared his throat. "Okay, it's a coming-of-age story. Three childhood friends—"

"Okay, I'll stop you right there. A coming-of-age story is not going to happen right now. We want action, people, *action*."

"Okay, next up..." Cuthbert looked about to do an *eeny, meeny, miny, moe* pantomime before he nodded at the young man sitting slumped back in his chair beside Tess, looking like he was trying do a disappearing act. "Tommy Jones."

Tommy's forehead was creased with lines of concentration. He rubbed at his chin, his face still breaking out with latent teenage acne, and then sniffed loudly making our boss wince. Tommy had asthma, and most Monday mornings he had to use his inhaler. At the moment it was clutched in his right hand as picked up the script he was going to recommend.

"*Murder in the Maples*. A story about passion, betrayal, and the murder of a well-off family involved with a new-age cult that demands unquestioning sacrifice from all its members, rich or poor. The story juxtapositions the haves against the have-nots as it thunders to its murderous conclusion." Tommy's Adam's apple twitched with nervousness. We all pretended the ceiling was far more interesting as Cuthbert pursed his lips, considering his pronouncement from on high.

"Hmm, maybe if we make them a family of vampires. The cult aspect/devil worship angle always sells. *Thank you, Roman Polanski.* Mark that one as a possibility, Wendy."

Nice. Tommy wouldn't need to use his inhaler. Cuthbert then went on to turn down the next three scripts in fast order.

He snapped his fingers. "Okay Miss Preston, you're our last big hope here. Spill."

She glanced at the studio mural of Mount Everest painted on the far wall. It offered encouragement every time she sat at this table, imagining herself scaling the highest peak. Taking a deep breath while trying not to think of the fact that the future hopes for a good screenwriter hung in the balance, she began her pitch.

"*Hell on Heels.* The revenge story of a single mother against a motorcycle gang that kidnapped her daughter, plied her with drugs, abandoning her body eight months later on the side of the road. She goes on a rampage, infiltrates the club as a biker's old lady, intending to take them all down, one by one."

"I like it. But let's change it to *Hell on Wheels* and the protagonist to male. More plausible that way."

Hell no. "I believe the world's ready for this, it's timely. Television now has a kickass female in Batgirl. Why not take the lead in movies?" Claire's heart rate increased; the sound echoed in her ears. She understood a woman's need for revenge. In similar circumstances as the heroine in the script, she could see herself hitting the road and demanding her own vigilante justice for a beloved daughter. The female lead was the main reason she'd enjoyed Herman's script, after becoming invested in the mother's journey from trailer trash to redemption row.

"Batgirl's a one-off. Women don't want to follow a real woman acting in such a dastardly thing. A cartoon character is the only one to get away with it. Trust me. A male protagonist works best."

Steam *had* to be rising out of the top of her head. "I think the story works so well is because it *is* a female taking a stand for justice."

A startled hiss of collective breath though no verbal response in aid of her radical idea. She was on her own, but she wasn't going to let it stop her. Not this time.

"Miss Preston, I'm a few years older and a whole lot more experienced than yourself on the interests of the fairer sex. Perhaps we can agree that my take on what women *do* or *do not* want has more veracity." The condescending pompousness to his tone did not endear him to the females in the room. And maybe not the males, judging by Tommy's grimace and steely-eyed furtive glance at the man in charge.

She shook her head. "You might have a few more years experience, but I think I know my generation. And it's not the same as my mother's. I'm willing to go out on a limb here and say that women are changing their collective psyche. We want action as well. We're no longer content to sit back and let the male of the species take charge. Not when it comes to doing the right thing."

"And you think the right thing is doing unspeakable things to males who have harmed your daughter?"

Claire gave him a direct look. "No more than those

animals deserved. Why can't a female mete out justice as well as a male? We have female police officers, female judges, female lawyers. Heck, one day we'll probably even have female serial killers."

"Ever hear of Belle Gunness, Lizzie Borden, Clementine Barnabet or Martha Beck? Their exploits alone would make your hair curl," Tess asked with deliberate nonchalance, staring off into the middle distance and not meeting anyone's eyes.

"We're not talking about the criminally insane here." Cuthbert's expression had frozen into an unflattering scowl, his displeasure obvious. He pinched the sagging skin on his throat between his thumb and forefinger. His dark eyes flashed his displeasure.

"You don't think some scumbags treating your daughter like a piece of garbage isn't cause to exhibit a little psychotic behavior?" Claire asked. The thin ice beneath her feet may have started cracking but she was holding her ground.

"The public's simply not ready to accept it. So, it's not going to happen. Not at my studio. Not ever." Cuthbert stood up, signaling the end of the meeting. "We'll contact the writer and let him know we'll be optioning his screenplay, with necessary changes, of course. Make sure you give Wendy his address."

Cuthbert and his assistant marched double-time from the room without a backward glance. She'd gotten off lightly, though that didn't mean she wouldn't be fired by the end of the day, even though she had the best track record for spotting a winning script on the team. She had a little money in the bank not earmarked for finding her birth mother, the possibility of a new job, and her soul unsold, which should keep her from jumping off the

Hollywood sign anytime soon. Unfortunately, there was precedent to that action as well.

"Cheez, girlfriend, what got into you?" Tess asked. They joined the flock of prison escapees scurrying into the hallway. "Cuthbert didn't even bother with his awesome pep talk today."

"Don't you ever get sick of the misogyny that exists in Hollywood's back lots and boardrooms?"

"I haven't got the luxury of worrying if a female or a male takes the lead in any given film. I meant to tell you this—" She shrugged. "But I've taken in my sister's kids for the time being. She's going through another tough time."

Tough time was a euphemism for going through hell. Tess's older sister Meri had a huge drug problem causing most of her tough times. And the entire family's as well.

"I'm sorry. And yet you supported me in there with your female serial killer list. Thank you." She felt guilty now, not wanting her ideas to cost Tess. "If there's anything I can do, please, just say. If you need money or anything, I'm here for you." She laid a comforting hand on Tess's shoulder, never sure of what she should say or do.

"I appreciate it. But it is what it is. But this time I might sue for custody. It's bad for the kids, you know, being carted back and forth between households like yo-yos. So, I need this job. It pays well and will keep a roof over baby Seth and Jennifer's heads."

"If you need me to babysit, I'm there for you."

"Mom's looking after them during the day. I don't know what I'd do without her help. But its kind of unfair to her. She's raised us and now she's being called upon to help raise her grandkids."

"My guess, she loves it. She's still young and she adores them."

"I might take you up on the babysitting offer. You know, you aren't the femme fatale that everyone thinks you are with that cool, beyond gorgeous, exterior. You got a soft heart, girlfriend. Make sure it doesn't get you into trouble."

She ignored the sideways compliment. Truth be told, she preferred the label of being a hard case. Kept her protected. "Just let me know the date and time. I gotta go and make the call to the author of the winning script. I wish I had better news about how they want to gut his story."

"He won't care. He's getting recognition."

"You don't know my neighbor." Claire winced. "He's a stickler about the tiniest thing. You'll never guess what he did this weekend?" She gave Tess the bare facts about the highly charged doggie doodoo incident as they headed for their cubicles.

Tess laughed so hard tears ran down her cheeks, running through the pancake makeup she'd applied. She grabbed another tissue off Claire's desk and blotted her face. "Cool. They should put that in a script. Wouldn't Cuthbert be perfect for the role? The way he's always turning his nose up what we offer him. Well, not you, but the rest of us. I thought Tommy was going to have another attack this morning."

Claire shook her head. "Not like we don't want what's best for the studio too. Why hire us if you won't listen to our suggestions?" Then she remembered they were not above "borrowing" suggestions, if warranted. Dog eat dog world, all right. Maybe she needed to adopt even more of that femme fatale vibe.

"Call up your writer guy. I wanna hear his reaction."

"Yeah, me too." She sat down and flicked through her Rolodex until she came to the card with the correct name, address, and phone number. She'd entered the data this morning with high hopes for this moment.

She grabbed the desk phone and punched in the numbers on one of the fancy new touchtone telephones the company had recently installed that President Kennedy had made famous at Christmas.

"Herman Blackwell here. How may I help you?"

"Herman, this is Claire. I have news. Good and bad. Which do you want first?"

"Is it about my screenplay?" His high squeaky voice suggested he'd just joined a harem, and not as a player.

She held the phone a few inches away from her ear. "Yes, they liked it, but wanted the protagonist to be male, rather than female. Are you okay with that?"

"Who cares! I get paid, right?"

"Yes, you'll be paid. I have no part in those negotiations. I'm only the messenger."

"Thank you, thank you, thank you! I can't thank you enough!"

"Aww, but you can. Anyway, expect a call from Cuthbert Murdock's secretary Wendy. She'll set up the meeting."

"But you'll be there, right, to have my back?" The eagerness in his voice only added to her misgivings.

"Sorry, it doesn't work that way. My job is finished once I've recommended a script. You should think about getting a lawyer who knows the industry to represent you. They can best advise you."

"But I want you."

She sighed. Could she do that? Would they even let her into the meeting? "I can't promise anything, but I can ask." Last thing she wanted to do. She was not an experienced barracuda, regardless of how she appeared to the world.

"Thank you. Thank—"

She interrupted. "I'll let you go to tell your family and friends the good news."

"Yes, right. I'll see you later. I can hardly wait."

Oh boy. "Not sure when I'll be home. So please, don't wait up."

Tess popped her head in again as she lay the phone back into its cradle. "Wendy was just by and left the schedule for the doctor's appointments. You're up to bat after lunch."

She groaned. "They could have least gone in alphabetical order."

"So, was I right? Did he sell his soul for the opportunity?"

"Yup. Selling your soul to the devil is a full-time occupation in Hollywood."

CHAPTER 11
A ROCK AND A HARD PLACE

WARNING DELIVERED, JAKE GRUNTED AND FORCED HIS battered body into the Mustang. A quick trip back to the office to make himself presentable, then he was calling on his old pal Mann at the agency. The intel from the children's home courtesy of the old housekeeper about the important visitor right after Claire was born was a huge red flag. Someone knew about her birth, someone who didn't want her origins to come to light. And he wanted to talk to that someone.

He entered through the back door of his office and slipped into the bathroom, wanting to avoid an explanation with his nosy but essential secretary. Mae was too qualified for the job or the salary, but she kept his business interests running like a top.

The view of his mug in the overhead mirror suggested she might be better at the job of secretary than he was at being an interrogator. He filled the small sink with tepid water and dashed a few handfuls onto his face, wincing at the sting to his battered nose. After drying his face with a brown paper towel, he threw it in the trash. He pulled up his shirt tails and inspected his

ribs. A large bruise was glowing darkish purple. He carefully pressed against the area and let out a low growl. His
verdict of a couple of cracked ribs seemed about right.
He grabbed some ace bandages from the cupboard under
the sink and took off his jacket and shirt. Winding the
cloth around his upper body with a firm hand, he tied
them off and redressed. It would have to do. Good thing
he had recently stocked up on Jim Bean.

"*It is mine to revenge; I will repay*. Deuteronomy,"
Bishop proudly announced, hopping back and forth on
his perch as Jake crept inch by inch into his office.
Grimacing, he lowered his body into the chair.

"I gotta teach you some new schtick, Bishop. That
one's wearing thin."

"There you are! What the heck happened to you?"
Mae swept into the room, her ample bosom doing a fine
impression of the front end of an ocean liner sheathed in
solid paisley brocade. She carried a handful of messages
clutched in her right hand. She gave him the once over
and stood directly in front of him, waiting for an answer.
Her dark hair was perfectly groomed, tucked into those
sausage curls she favored. Her arched eyebrows were
pencil thin, her cheeks pinked, and her lipstick deep red
as per usual. A very trustworthy sort who had more than
once earned his admiration. Though she was under the
mistaken impression he needed a second mother.

"Let's just say a land shark and I had a disagreement
over the proper protocols for dating and leave it at that."

She arched one thin brow. "Well, you got a busy day
lined up." She held up the sheath of messages.

"Put off what you can and set any can't-get-out-of-it
meetings for late in the day or early tomorrow morning.
I've got to see a man about a file."

"Breaking out of prison, are we?"

He chuckled, then winced as the action annoyed his ribs. "No, but before this is over, who knows. I may need you to bake me a cake."

"Are we discussing the adoption case or something else?"

"The adoption one, but there's a connection. It was her friend that was on the receiving end of the unwanted courtship rituals."

"Friend, eh. This new case has got you going in circles already. My, but Claire Preston is some looker."

"Yeah, well, she's easy enough on the eyes. But the case intrigues me anyway." He stared at his small library of books housed in the shabby bookcase. Mostly Raymond Chandler mysteries and a couple of manuals on the private eye business. He should lend those to Claire. Help her bone up for her future exam. Huh, he was getting a bit ahead of himself.

"She's a little out of your league, boss. Be careful."

"Now when am I *not* careful?"

She raised her eyebrows, her glance lingering over his obvious injuries. "Right. If you need me, call. I'll be out front, guarding the realm."

"I'll be leaving shortly. I probably don't say this enough, but thank you, Mae."

"You certainly do not say it enough." And with that the door closed firmly behind her ample assets.

He reached down to open the bottom drawer of his desk, wincing. This was going to get old fast. He dragged out the full bottle of whiskey and broke the seal on the neck. The satisfying glug, glug that followed his tipping it up to his mouth soothed his inner beast. He had a good couple of swallows, then tucked it away. He needed to keep his wits about him.

He picked up the phone and dialed the number from

memory, his forefinger enjoying each satisfying swoop of the seven-digit number. The new touchtone phones didn't have half the satisfaction of a good old rotary in a proper solemn color. Black.

"Agent Mann." His contact barked from the other end of the line.

"It's Jake."

"What do you need?" A legitimate response. The guy was rough, but honest. And knew he owed him big time. Jake had once saved his butt on a case of mistaken identity that could have spelled sudden death to his career and future pension.

"I'm involved in a case that's taken an odd twist and I need to know why. A file's gone missing from the children's orphanage right here in Hollywood. Maybe be a one-off, but it was observed that the feds were very interested in the outcome back in the day. I need to know why? Can we meet today?"

"Hmm. FBI or CIA?"

"Could be either. The eyewitness couldn't say." He went on to share the name, date, and the small bit of intel he had.

"Okay. Let me look into. Can you give me a day or two? Got my hands full right now with a cold case. The Black Dalia's reared its ugly head again. Get this—the suspect with a string of alias has been speaking in the third person, says he's speaking for the killer as an informant. Personally, I think it's more likely the bastard's unwilling to hang himself for it. Classic decoy defense. Unfortunately, Short fell into the low-life's orbit."

Jake gave a low whistle. "Ya got my sympathy. Be careful—the real story for that case resides on the dark side of the moon. The victim was so horribly overkilled. Call me when you know anything, all right?"

"Yeah. Soon, I promise."

He hung up and realized he now had the afternoon free. Time to make some house calls.

He picked up the phone and buzzed Mae. "I'm on my way out. Should be back before you leave for the day."

"I managed to push everything aside until tomorrow, except an Edward Smith who said it was rather urgent. He's scheduled for seven o'clock."

"Fine. Thanks, Mae."

"Twice in one day. I should buy a lottery ticket."

He heard the smile in her tone. "Get one for me. My luck's bound to improve."

"You don't believe in luck. You're always spouting on about how luck is the potential enemy, calling luck the temptress, a seductive whisper taking you away from data and facts." She quoted him word for word.

"Maybe I've changed. Maybe I'd rather be lucky than smart."

"You'll never change, boss. Everything's black and white, logical with you."

"Are you suggesting I'm sadly lacking in passion?"

"No, just have a good moral compass. My advice, hold on to it, this city has a way of bending the needle away from true north before you realize it."

"Mae, you're one of a kind."

"Get on with you. But while I got your ear, I'd advise you to quit handing out so many twenty-dollar bills. Our emergency kitty will go the way of the dodo bird if we're not careful. And don't forget your appointment."

"Now when have I ever done that?"

He stopped the communique right there, tucked the wrapped brooch in his suit pocket, and got up from his desk before he could think better of it. His ribs squawked louder than his chair, but he managed to shamble out the back door to his Mustang and pour himself into the driver's seat. He drove down the alley and onto the Strip, the one point seven mile stretch of nightclubs, shops, and restaurants that had been dubbed the epicenter of counterculture in America. If music, sex, and drugs turned your crank, it was epitomized by the Whiskey-a-Go-Go, a hot spot he avoided like the plague. He parked a half-block down from Sunset Pawn and killed the motor.

Pushing open the front door of the business, the odor of sadness and neglect filled his nostrils while the overhead doorbell rankled his eardrums, making him stifle an urge to sneeze.

"Hey, Jake, how's it hanging, buddy?" Bill Salander, the proprietor of the largest pawn shop on the Strip, came out from behind the long counter that ran along one side of the shotgun style building to greet him. His Howdy-Doody looks belied a sharp intelligence. The guy could squeeze a nickel and make change for a dollar.

"Hanging same as yesterday."

Bill gave him a closer perusal. "Then yesterday must have been a doozy."

Jake shrugged. "Had a disagreement with a guy over how to treat women. Set him back a day or two."

"You ever think of hanging up that white hat and join with the rest of us, you might make it past forty. So, what can I do you for?"

"I have an item I need to know the provenance of. It's been hidden away for two decades, but I'm hoping to find out anything possible. If it was ever pawned, and if you have paperwork on it?" He took the brooch from his pocket, carefully unwrapped it, and handed it over.

Bill gave a low whistle as he inspected it. "Nice piece, worth a pretty penny." He shook his large head that was a size too large for his body. "Two decades is a long time. I've been here twelve and a half years myself. Gunny's your best bet. He's been here since the twenties."

Jake followed him down the hallway of the narrow building, a path wore down by thousands of shod and unshod feet toward the curtained-off storeroom.

"Hey, Gunny. You decent?" Bill called out before yanking back the curtain and exposing the old man perched on a stool and reading a newspaper. The walls were a series of shelves holding items that appeared to have given up the ghost of owner's past.

"*Phttt*, never," Gunny said, yanking his mouth into a grimace of a smile. "No mileage in it." He laid the news-paper down on the large bench covered with a pile of things appearing to need fixing, bits and pieces strewn haphazardly about. He got up from his perch, stiff and awkward in his movements. "I know now why old pros-titutes are so darn good at hand jobs. What can I do for you?" His white hair was more disturbed than usual, floating around his pronounced ornery expression with all the consistency of spider webs. They both ignored the intel on ladies of the evening.

"Jakes needs intel on this brooch. Ever seen it before?"

Gunny took the jewelry from his outstretched hand. "Hmm, nice piece." He turned it over and inspected the back before placing it right side up. He scratched his balding head, and a white wave of dandruff floated lazily to the shoulders of his faded blue work shirt. The denim cloth was so old the name on the patch over his pocket was barely recognizable. "Hard to forget such a fancy piece. Been a long time though. Twenty years at least. Where did you find it?"

"Hidden away by a woman who adopted a baby

twenty-one years ago. Just came to light and the girl's all grown up and looking for her birth mother. Anything you can remember would be helpful."

"How helpful?"

Jake pulled out a pair of Jacksons and tucked them into Gunny's shirt pocket. "Very helpful."

Gunny patted his pocket, buttoning down the flap for good measure. "Seems I do remember a young woman, a starlet judging by her pretty blonde looks, needing to raise a few bucks to keep body and soul together. She pawned it a few times, but always came back and retrieved it. Said it was a family heirloom. I kept hoping she'd leave it one day, kind of wanted it for Martha. Such a pretty piece and if you knew anything about Martha, she loved her jewelry. Collected it by the bucketful. Kept me broke, but she was worth it. Fancy piece who cooked and took out the garbage. Impossible to come by these days." He shook his head sadly.

"Remember anything else about the girl? Was she expecting a child any of the times you saw her?" Jake leaned against the bench on his good side, enjoying the head rush of getting intel right off the hop. Or maybe that was just a slight concussion from earlier.

"Can't rightly say. Maybe? She sometimes wore this loose wool coat with a fur collar. It kept you from seeing her figure. She did come in with a guy that one time." The grooves round his mouth deepened and he rubbed at the back of his neck.

"What did he look like?"

The look in Gunny's faded blue eyes sharpened to chisel points. "He was a piece of work I pegged for trouble soon as I spotted him. Nazi bastard. Thought he was so clever, hiding behind America's tit. But I saw right through the disguise to his stinking black heart."

"What made you think he was a former Nazi?" Jake didn't bother to hide his surprise.

"You doubt me? I fought in WW1, young man, and I tell you, he didn't fight for our side. Accent was off, body language all wrong. He was no American solder. He fought for the enemy. Some fool let those villains in after the war. I wouldn't have served him if it came to that. I don't need blood money. But he made a point of standing around waiting for the girl to retrieve her goods."

"Ever see him again?"

"Nah. And that was the last I seen of her too. Always wondered about it. If she was okay, you know?"

"You had your doubts? Why?"

"He was a former Nazi, for Christ's sake!" he hissed in a loud voice. "No telling the harm they could do. I get that we needed intel on the Russkies during that damn Cold War, but that wasn't the way to go about it." The elderly man shook his head, his thin cheeks turning splotchy red from his burst of anger.

"You see any more of his ilk after that?" Jake kept his breaths shallow, avoiding the pain of his ribs rubbing against raw flesh.

"Once or twice. I didn't encourage them to darken our doorway again. Some business isn't worth it." The octogenarian shook his head.

"Would you recognize the guy again?"

"Been two decades, but hard to forget those eyes. Cold and black like a shark. And twice as evil."

"Good. That's helpful, Gunny."

The old man smiled, exposing yellowed teeth. "How helpful?"

"Now, I think Jake's been more than generous, Gunny," Bill said, his voice tinged by caution.

"How about I buy you a drink next time I come by? I might need you to identify the guy."

"Sure, glad to." Gunny licked his lips. "I'm a man who enjoys a drink. I hope you nail the bastard. That piece of shit was up to something. No way a monster like that could keep his nose clean all these years. And if you find out his past crimes, all the better."

Before Jake followed Bill from the room, he tucked another Jackson in Gunny's pocket, slipping it under the flap. "First drink's on me."

Rewarded with a toothy grin, Jake made his way back to the front of the store, not comfortable with what the new intel might mean to Claire.

"You looked like you swallowed a lemon."

"Much as you want to help a client discover the truth, you always hope the information you dig up doesn't disturb the world view they have of themselves."

"You thinking the guy might be her father?"

"Maybe. But I'm hoping he's a red herring. Your records don't happen to go that far back? Maybe we catch a break?"

Bill shook his head. "I doubt the pawn slips are still around. There was a water pipe that burst not long after I started working here and a whole lot of records got destroyed. But I'll take a look. Maybe we get lucky."

"Thanks. I'd appreciate it."

"How much?" Bill's question took him by surprise, but the man quickly slapped him on the back. "Just kidding, Jake. I owe you a few favors as it."

"Thanks, call me if you find out anything."

"Will do. And try not to get into any more altercations this week."

"I make no promises I can't keep."

"Aw, shit, not them again! I told them to clear off last week, and here they are back. Bad for business."

Jake followed Bill's self-righteous anger. It was obviously directed at a group of young hippies standing outside his shop, singing and dancing and chanting with nary a care using a couple of tambourines. All long-haired females under twenty, the group of a dozen or so were barefooted, one held a baby, and there was a hat strategically positioned on the sidewalk near mother and child with a sign that read: *Death of the self is the greatest form of love.*

The sight was not uncommon, but the words of the message chilled him to the marrow.

"I miss the fifties. Everyone was working hard to get ahead."

"Not a fan of Flower Power and hippie love-ins?"

"They don't get it. Nobody wants them hanging around bothering customers. Go get a real job. Stop this begging and have some respect for yourself. Look, they've even dragged a baby into it. I mean, how low can you go!"

"Not the baby's fault." Jake checked his pockets for another Jackson and found a couple strays.

Bill shook his head. "You shouldn't be encouraging them. I'll never get rid of them."

"Don't worry, I gotta plan."

Jake hit the sidewalk, the heat of the late afternoon sun baking dusty mirages along the length of congested Sunset. He sighed. Another twenty-four-rush hour going nowhere.

He walked up to the woman with the baby who stood a bit away from the main group. She was clean at least and the baby looked well enough attended, its chubby legs busy bike peddling the air while it sucked away on a tiny fist, drool running down its chin. She swiped the drool away with the shirttail of her off-white embroidered peasant blouse.

"I got an offer you shouldn't refuse."

"What's that, mister?" She switched the baby to the other arm.

"You take this show a few blocks away and I'll give you some cash. You stay, and I'll keep it for myself."

She licked her lips. She gave him a sideways glance from under thick eyelashes suggesting she knew her way around a proposition.

"Not that kind of thing, lady, forty bucks to mosey along."

"Forty dollars? For real? My name's Sunshine, not lady."

He showed her the bills. "But only when you move along, Sunshine."

She narrowed her doe-shaped eyes. "Charlie calls this our lucky corner. We always do well here, so he's not going to like us moving. And how do I know you're not going to renege on the deal?"

"Who's Charlie?"

"He's just the greatest man who ever lived!" An instant change came over the woman. Her expression beatified, making her almost beautiful. "He knows *everything*. He knows what's coming, what needs to be changed, what we have to do, like Jesus. You need to meet Charlie. Change your life, mister, for the better."

"I'll pass." Seemed there was a new Messiah or guru popping up on every street corner these days. And the young were so needful of someone to follow, someone to make sense of their teenage angst that every generation experienced to some extent, they'd give credence to all kinds of crazy ideas. Of course, it didn't help that the latest generational spit had never been deeper. Mistrust on both sides was growing. He felt the cracks growing wider and deeper with each passing day, a whirlwind in the making. "But I give you my word I'll hand over the money."

"Give me a sec." She went over to the main group and spent a short time talking to them. A couple of the women gave him a hard look.

"Okay. But pay me first." She held out a hand, palm up.

He shrugged and handed it to her. Stood with his arms over his chest. Waited.

She began to walk away, and the others soon followed. He turned to observe Bill who was still standing in the window, watching the proceedings. His old friend smiled and nodded, adding a thumbs up for good measure.

Okay. A bite to eat then back to the office to work on some long overdue reports before his appointment. Good as Mae was, some things he had to do himself. He couldn't expect her to invent the facts for billing on a case, tempting as it was.

CHAPTER 12
ROOM WITHOUT A VIEW

CLAIRE KEPT HER HEAD DOWN FOR THE REST OF THE morning, trying to keep her mind on the business at hand, going through the Monday morning slush pile of scripts. But the dream from the night before kept pushing itself to the forefront of her feverish brain. The usual nightmare that had kept her up for hours last night because it had changed, it had become more real with details that still gnawed at her. She could smell the musty, rundown old house, the air sharp with mold. Hear the sharp screech of a barn owl as it flew overhead. The dark wood furniture was dulled by dust and she felt she could stretch out a finger and draw in it.

Then she stood in front of a photograph as she always did. Black and white, it was of a young woman, slim and pretty and smiling for the camera from where it sat on a mantle. The woman wore the brooch she'd recently found, and her dress was adorned with the tiny rosebuds of the scrap of fabric. When the blonde woman stepped out of the photograph, it was electrifying. Something brand new. And it felt too real. Like it was happening right now.

For the first time, the woman spoke. Turned and looked right at her. Claire remembered the eyes staring right into her soul. She spoke two impossible words. "Find me."

She wanted to step forward to hug the woman, but she was frozen to the spot. Paralyzed. Unable to move even one tiny muscle.

Then a menacing presence appeared just beyond the darkness. It made her want to scream at the woman to run away. When she finally was able to move, it was too late. The woman had moved back into the photo. Now only a cardboard cutout remained. Was she her mother? What did it all mean?

"Earth to Claire."

Tess was trying to get her attention, waving a hand in front of her face. She blinked her eyes, the strange vision fading, but the odd sensation lingered. "Yeah, what is it?"

"It's past one o'clock. Have you forgotten?"

"What? Oh, right, the doctor's appointment. I had a lot of things to take care of first. I'll go now."

She pushed back her office chair and got to her feet, moving past her friend. Last thing she felt like doing, seeing *that* guy. Well, maybe he could recommend a therapist. Not like she didn't need someone who might make sense of her crazy dreams and thoughts. She checked her wristwatch and realized it was ten past one. She quickly made her way out of the building and onto the back lot where the medical office was located. Behind the building, Quonset huts filled with movie memorabilia stretched as far as the eye could see. When she had the time, she loved to stroll down those endless isles, filled as they were with old, dusty, long-forgotten props no one could bear to part with. Besides, who knew what would be useful again?

Her steps lagged as she reached her favorite prop ever designed by the studio for a movie. A gleaming Excalibur, set in stone, was given the place of honor in the middle of the grass field, surrounded by a circle of white rose bushes. With a glance filled with reverence for the icon, she wished as always it was her destiny to be able to draw the sword from the stone. Inherit its legacy. Use it to cut a righteous swath through the world. But then again, it hadn't ended that well the last time it had been drawn. One final look, and she sprinted the last few yards to the medical building.

Opening the door, she stepped inside the low bunkerlike cement building, thankful for the coolness after the hot sweaty jog across the open field, the dry grass tickling and annoying her bare shins.

She walked the dozen steps to the reception desk and was greeted by a new, white-coated male nurse with dark dress pants and shiny black shoes. The guy even had a tie visible at the top of his lab coat for heaven's sake.

"Claire Preston?" he asked, a frown tugging at the skin of his face. The young man, only few years older than herself, was standing with a clipboard in one hand and a pencil in the other.

"Present," she quipped.

"We expected you eighteen minutes ago." His dark eyes condemned her behavior as much as if she'd committed a capital offense. She instantly missed old doc, Jacobs, and his sweet nurse, Betty.

"Excuse my tardiness." She quirked her lips into a tight smile.

"The doctor's time is valuable. Have a seat." He dismissed her, then punctuated his remarks by making a dramatic checkmark by what she had to assume was her name on the officious clipboard.

She sat, choosing the chair furthest away from Annoying Man. There were a dozen plastic and chrome chairs lined up against the front wall of the building and down the two sides forming a U-shape. The walls were painted an uninspiring beige and the wall-to-wall rug matched, though it did appear to be freshly shampooed from the medicinal odor of disinfectant wafting in the air around her.

The clock overhead ticked off the seconds with a rather harsh thud of its second hand. She looked around the recently redecorated office, finding its sterile nature made a harsh first impression. There were no magazines on the rack that normally held them. No glass container with all-day lollipops. And no smiling Nurse Betty.

She waited ten very long minutes, pretending the man at the desk didn't exist and wishing she'd thought to bring along a paperback to read. Finally, the sounds of a door opening and muffled voices drew her attention. The male nurse perked up as well and waited expectantly for whomever was advancing down the hallway.

Dr. Vogel appeared first. Then right behind him a slender young girl who looked no older than eighteen, her face wreathed in smiles, her long, center-parted light hair hugging her cheeks. She wore striped bellbottoms and a white blouse with lace cuffs frilling out over her wrists. Claire instantly recognized her from the music industry. What was she doing there? Were they going to make a movie for the studio?

She watched the good doctor kiss the back of the singer's hand and bid her a gracious goodbye. Interesting.

Then her full name was called by the nurse, like there

was a bevy of studio employees champing at the bit. She made the point of looking around the waiting room before getting to her feet. *Who me?*

Dr. Vogel's dark eyes turned her way as she approached the desk and her stomach clenched. She wished she was anywhere else. Her recent experiences with the health system were unavoidable after the accident, and were fine for the most part, but she still didn't feel comfortable back in that situation. Too much time when things spun out of her control. Only one good thing came out of it. Her sweet and courageous dog, Marlowe. Right then she wished the pair of them were together, laying on the sofa, and watching a rerun of Perry Mason.

"Aw, Miss Preston. We meet again."

"Doctor." She acknowledged him with a polite head nod.

His nurse pursed his lips and busied himself restacking a pile of files.

"I'm so glad I didn't keep you waiting," she said with a nod. Doctors were notorious for keeping their patients waiting. And obviously no one cooled their heels today except her. Ten minutes she'd never get back.

"My apologies for keeping you waiting."

Did his nurse just roll his eyes? Not cool.

"I was running a bit late myself, so no apologies necessary."

"Well, come on back then. We'll take a look at you."

The collective "we" was jarring. When he held open the door to the smaller cubicle that housed the tools of his trade, she almost expected to see another body. But it was only the two of them. Intimate and intimidating.

"Okay, Miss Preston, please have a seat. If you would be so kind as to answer a few questions for me first?"

"Call me Claire. And sure, ask away, doctor." She didn't want to flunk cooperation as well as punctuality. She sat kitty-corner to him at the small desk that made close interactions possible. The room, about ten by eight, was a bit claustrophobic, with the black exam table with the ubiquitous white paper covering taking up most of it. Ask her anything but to spend time on that torture table.

"Fine, Claire it is. How would you rate your health out of ten? Ten being the best."

"Physical health? Ten most days, I guess."

"You differentiate?"

"Excuse me?"

"Between physical health and mental health?"

"No, I don't." She rubbed at her forehead. The line of the scar had begun to ache. Meant a headache would likely follow.

"Explain, please."

"If your mind is happy about things in your life, then it follows, your body will feel better—healthier."

"Your life is happy? On a scale of one to ten, where would you place it?"

"I don't know. About an eight, I guess. Higher some days." Not this day though.

"So, you do differentiate?" His dark eyes bore into hers.

The headache bloomed and she swallowed. "I guess, a bit."

He made a couple of notes and she wished she could read upside down writing. Would be useful in the investigative field, she imagined. Suddenly she wished she were asking the questions, instead of Dr. Vogel.

"Are you sexually active?"

She startled, uncomfortable with the question. What was the best answer to keep him off her back? "No."

"You hesitated for a moment there."

She shrugged, staring at a poster of a woman's reproductive system on the wall which did nothing for her nerves. "Rather uncomfortable with the question."

"I thought women of your generation were all about offering free love?" He softened his inappropriate remark with a self-depreciating smile. She liked him a bit better.

"I'm a firm believer that stereotypes misinform more than they help."

"Touché, Claire. All right, have you had any health crisis in the past year?"

"Does an accident count?"

He nodded sagely. "Of course."

She briefly explained what had happened.

"You obviously have been able to move on quite well. You appear to be in complete control of your faculties. Any headaches or other problems since the accident?"

"Headaches, but it was to be expected after the thump on the head." She'd rather not be reminded of that or the strange thoughts that sometimes entered her mind unbidden. She pressed her lips together and willed away the most recent nightmare with its hard to phantom twist. She could still see the eyes of the woman, imploring her to help. *Where are you? Are you still alive?*

"Have you talked to anyone about what happened?"

She shrugged. "My roommate Serena has helped. And my dog Marlowe is a good listener."

"Marlowe?"

"For the famous detective. Raymond Chandler wrote the books."

"I shall check them out. You enjoy mysteries?"

"I do. You?"

113

"We're talking about you. Okay, next question. Do you ever have trouble sleeping?"

"I have dreams. They wake me up."

"Night terrors?"

She nodded.

"I can help with that. Pills will help you sleep through the night. Also, you might want to spend time talking to someone. Having an accident that frightening at such a young age can leave lasting problems if you don't deal with them."

The idea of having lasting problems made her sit up and take notice. "Yes, I would like to talk to a therapist, if you think it would help?"

"I do. Okay, enough questions. I'll need to take your vitals and then you can be on your way."

She took a deep breath. Thank God. No talk of an internal exam. Her nerves eased. She was going to refuse anyway, but this made it easier. He remained silent while he listened to her heart and lungs, then took her blood pressure.

Five minutes later he pronounced her healthy and fit. He went to a cupboard, unlocked it, then pulled out two prescription bottles. He stuffed them into a small paper sack and handed it to her. "One will help you sleep, the other's for morning drowsiness. Okay, I'll see you back here on Friday, same time."

"What for?"

"To begin your therapy, of course. You did say you wanted to speak with someone about the recurring nightmares?"

"Yes, but—"

"I'm a trained therapist, Claire. I'm your best bet to get to the source of your anxieties. I insist, I won't even charge the studio for my valuable time. I find your case intrigues me. I also believe there's a lot you're not telling me or remembering that I can help you navigate. And, if I can be so modest, I might be able to use your experiences for a future book. Without any reference to your name, of course. And the studio will not hear a word of anything you tell me. You have my word." The firmness of his tone and the generosity of his offer made it impossible to say no.

Her earlier elation deflated. Last thing she wanted was to spill her guts to this guy. A therapist connected to the studio who might have access to her chart filled her with dismay, no matter what he promised. The studio heads were notorious for poking their noses into every-one's business. She had envisioned a female to talk to, not a middle-aged square. Plus, she'd taken the trouble to share so little, how could her case possibly interest him? The thought of all she would have to hide from him made her head hurt worse. She swallowed the bile that rose in the back of her throat, wishing she had a breath mint.

"I'll see you on Friday. One p.m. Sharp. If I can make the drive from my ranch to the city on time, you can certainly make it across the lot, right?"

"You live on a ranch?" The idea held such appeal for her that for a moment she forgot where she was and who she was talking to. "It's a dream of mine, to own prop-erty one day."

"Yes." He pursed his lips with disapproval. "Unfortu-nately, a bit too close to a group of hippies. You'd think Spahn would know better. Take my advice, watch where you buy your acreage. I've owned it for decades and now in the past year the worst kind of neighbors have moved in. Always running late too, I would imagine." He gave her a pointed glance, jarring her right out of her moment of interest.

She got up feeling like an errant school child, holding the brown paper bag in one hand, and unsure of how to get out of detention. Short of quitting her job, she was stuck. She went to say something, but when she glanced at him, he was already immersed in writing something down in her file. Nothing to do but leave and dread coming back on Friday.

At the reception desk she strode past the male nurse without a backward glance. She'd had quite enough of him.

CHAPTER 13
A MAN WITH A PROBLEM

THE SOUND OF THE DOOR BUZZER IN THE OUTER ROOM alerted him to someone incoming. Jake looked over at the mantle clock resting on the top of the bookcase. Mr. Smith was punctual. Good start. The sounds were followed by footsteps of a hurried uneven gait, then the expected knock on his inner door. Brisk. Client on a mission.

"Come in." Jake remained seated, his body not up to the usual social conventions.

His first impression as the guy closed the door behind and turned to look at Jake was that he was a tall man. Stooped and nervous. Not as powerful as expected from his knock and with a bad foot encased in mismatched shoes, one larger than the other. He wore a houndstooth sports jacket with patches on the sleeves, carried an old leather satchel, and wore tinted, black-framed eyeglasses. His hair was dark with streaks of harsh gray on both sides.

"Jake Sterling, I presume?" he asked. His voice was even toned, without any inflection. He'd guess a university professor or an accountant. The guy's eyebrows rose slightly as he caught the battered state of his face.

"Yes, and you must be Mr. Smith. Please, have a seat. I'd get up, but I've had quite a day."

"Yes, that is obvious. I hope you're okay with this meeting? I did push your secretary for the earliest possible time. Perhaps I should reschedule?" Definitely a university professor with his need to enunciate such complete sentences. He could only pray he wasn't overly wordy.

"I am, if we can get right to it?"

"Of course. I only ask in good conscious. But I do have a rather pressing case." The man took a moment to sit down, setting the briefcase fuzzily on the floor to the right of the chair leg, lined it up perpendicular.

"Go on."

"It's complicated, but I seemed to have found myself in the crosshairs of someone who wishes me harm. I have no idea who it is, a former student upset over his grade or someone that didn't like my interaction with them or a colleague looking to push me out the door. I don't know, but I've been getting threatening notes for weeks now. I've been to the police, of course, but they say they can't do anything until he strikes. By then it would be too late, in my personal opinion, Mr. Sterling, shared by a few of the men in blue. In fact, it was a suggestion from one of LAPD's finest I hire a private investigator."

"The name's Jake. And you are quite right, it would be too late. Who recommended my services, Mr. Smith?"

"What do you mean? And please, call me Edward."

"The officer who suggested you hire a PI?"

"I didn't get his name. You understand, this has all been rather upsetting to me. I'm just a man with a love of history and imparting knowledge to students. To think someone wants to see me dead—" He shrugged. "I find it rather hard to fathom."

"I see. Do you have those notes with you?"

"I've brought them all with me. The police have already checked for fingerprints but came up empty. They've mostly been left on my car under a wind shield wiper in the staff parking lot or slid under my office door at the university." Edward reached down to retrieve his briefcase, taking a moment to unbuckle the front section.

"None at your place of residency? Are you married?"

"No to both your questions. Divorced. And a man should feel safe in his own home."

"He should. What brought all this to a head now? You said it's been going on for months?"

"It's been escalating. A note every day this past week. Not random like before." The professor handed him a sheath of notes all individually bound in plastic protectors, all numbered and dated. His sleeve slipped up a couple of inches in the process, revealing an ugly scar on his wrist. Poor bastard. Jake took the offering and began to leaf through them. Each piece of paper appeared to be from a similar white notepad. Newspaper letters, individually hand cut, were used to make the threats, the words appearing more chilling with their autonomy. The statements were short and to the point, along the lines of "kill yourself or I'll do it for you." Professor Smith had certainly pissed someone off.

"Are you teaching classes right now?" He looked up at the man, finding the tinted glasses, though not as dark as sunglasses, off-putting. He liked to look a man straight in the eyes. Get a proper reading. Maybe the guy had sensitive eyes? Or maybe he didn't want to be seen too well? *Just because I'm paranoid, doesn't mean I don't have a reason to be.*

"No, this semester I'm overseeing a select group of students writing their thesis over at UCLA, so I'm not exposed to a large number of students at any given time."

"Good." Jake finished looking at the damning evidence and sat back. "I think you need someone with more time than I can presently spare. I generally take on only one case at a time and I'm right in the thick of things at the moment. And looking at this, you need someone working full-time. A team can provide security round the clock. I don't like the way it's going—obviously escalating. You are most likely in harm's way, professor. But that's something you already know."

"I would be able to pay you well. And offer a bonus when you find the person responsible."

"It's not about the money."

"How about I hire a security detail? Would that free you up to concentrate on finding the perpetrator?"

"Maybe. Cameras need to be installed ASAP. Over the door to your office, where you park your car at work, and even around your home in case he changes his MO and decides to take his message there." He paused and took out a pack of cigarettes, offering the man one. He declined and pulled out a pipe instead. "You have no idea who could be behind this? No short list of possible suspects?"

The professor made a ritual of taking a pinch of fragrant tobacco from the pouch he pulled from his inner breast pocket, tamping it down in the old-fashioned, curved-stemmed cherrywood pipe with a calabash bowl. A lot of people referenced the distinctive pipe a Sherlock Holmes, but he could tell this was of a more recent make. American, made by the Pioneer company, with its ivory rim, Vulcanite joiner, and fancy stem. A bit much even for a professor of history. And Philip Marlowe would definitely not approve. Or his creator for that matter.

They smoked in silence for a couple of minutes. Then the professor pulled out a slip of paper from his jacket pocket, handing it over with a grimace and a slight tremor to his hand. "I did make a list, as it happens. The guy may or may not be on it. I added short descriptions of each person in case that helps. I only know a couple of the addresses, and who knows if they're current? Students move around all the time."

Jake glanced down at the half-dozen names. "Good. And if you think of any others, call it in."

"Does that mean you'll take the case?"

He rubbed his chin thoughtfully. His gut roiled, uncertain. He'd like to have gotten a better reading on the man first. But he sensed the guy needed his help, under all that pompousness, which worked for him.

"You need those dark lenses?"

"I have sensitive pupils to light. My ophthalmologist prescribed them. They do help."

"You wear them all the time? Even at night?"

"Especially at night. The glare of headlights is excruciating otherwise." The man finished his pipe, knocking out the spent coals into the ashtray on the desk.

"Okay, professor. I'll look into it. I can recommend a security detail if you like?"

"No, thank you, I have someone in mind. An acquaintance in the business."

That surprised Jake. Not many people showed that kind of initiative. "Okay, then. Well, I'll check in with you once a day. What time is best?" He stubbed out his cigarette.

"How about I call you? I'm in and out so much, it's easier if I take care of it." Not an unknown request, but not common either.

"We're in the same boat there. But I'm usually available first thing in the morning, or last thing a night. You can call me at home." Jake handed over his business card with his home phone number scribbled on the back.

The professor lumbered to his feet, leaned over the desk, and offered his hand. "Thank you, Jake. I appreciate your help. And your discretion. I wouldn't want word of this to leak out at the university among my peers. Doesn't look good, you know, a professor disliked this much."

The man's hand was dry, but he had a firm handshake. Jake immediately liked him better. "Lots of psychopaths in the world. Not your fault you ran into one."

"Too true."

He watched the man leave the room, dragging his right foot. His gut roiled again. Had he just made a mistake taking on two cases at once? Sure, the guy needed his help, handicapped as he was, but he needed a PI with more time on his hands than Jake. Well, sleep was overrated anyway.

CHAPTER 14
HISTORY REPEATS

HE WOULD HAVE PREFERRED THE NIGHT. BUT THE DARING
of such an event had pleased him beyond measure. And
he had perfected the disguise. One that would draw little
attention and yet facilitate the proper course of actions.
Securing the next human for the experiment was vital to
his ongoing work. Otherwise his treatise would come to
a standstill. And he was so close to understanding the
far-ranging effects of pain on the body and the psyche.
Finding the fine line between life and death, the sweet
spot that balanced the equation on a knife's edge, was
what riveted the scientist in him. Allowed him to record
brilliant data that would live on well after him. That he
had to keep it secret until his death was no deterrent.
Most important people were not famous until death. His
work would live on, like Leonardo da Vinci, he was a
master of his own domain.

He licked his lips, watching the young woman leave
the restaurant with the bag of takeout food. She was so
beautiful, so full of life. She had the potential to surpass
all the others and increase his data tenfold. And if the

prescribed experiments also brought him profound pleasure, so be it. Nothing is gained without passion. Without commitment. And without knowing what the essentials are for victory. *He will win who, prepares himself, waits to take the enemy unprepared.*

CHAPTER 15
THE HORROR OF WAR

CLAIRE DRILLED HER FINGERNAILS ON THE SOFA ARM, waiting for Jake to pick up. She glanced at the clock. Not quite seven o'clock in the morning. Jake had shared he worked all kinds of hours when on a case. Marlowe watched her from his favorite spot on the living room rug, nose buried under paws, but his ears twitchy and alert, ready to pick up on the slightest sound. Mr. Bat Ears. Of course, if the noise was from opening a can or rustling a packet of dry dog food, he'd rouse from a dead sleep in a nanosecond.

"Jake Sterling, private investigations."

The sound of his low timber voice filled her with reassurance even as her anxiety threatened to spill over.

"Jake, its Claire."

"What's up?" She closed her eyes.

"It's Serena. She didn't come home last night. She never does that, not unless she calls me first." Had her recent altercation at the party been more upsetting than she'd let on?

"Do you know where she was headed last night?"

"That's the thing. She was supposed to pick up some

takeout for dinner. We'd planned an evening in, watching TV and doing girl things."

"Is she expected anywhere this morning?"

"She has a meeting with her agent scheduled for nine on the calendar. I can't see her missing it."

"Okay, wait until then, call the agent, and see if she's there. In the meantime, does she have other friends she might stay with?"

Claire chewed on a fingernail, trying to come up with some close enough friends of her roommate that she would just ditch her for them. "I can't think of anyone offhand. She does keep a small address book in her nightstand." She didn't like the idea of invading Serena's privacy; they were good about staying out of each other's bedrooms but worry gnawed heavily enough to consider it.

"Well, if she doesn't make her appointment, it would be time to start calling around. Can you do that?"

"Yes, I'll call in and take the day off. There's something else, maybe it's important, I'm not sure?"

"What?"

"The other day, when I was out walking Marlowe at the park, I heard something in a wooded area. Spooked me. I mean, it may be nothing. But whatever it was made my dog growl."

"You're mentioning it, so it's something. Hmm. You say Serena's never done anything like this before? Shown up late the next morning?" The intensity of his voice drilled the words into her head.

"A time or two, but not when we've had specific plans. Do you think that's all this is?" She glanced at Marlowe, who was sitting up now and watching her intently.

"Can't say. But I'll call you after nine and see if she's shown up at her appointment. We'll go from there."

"Okay." She made herself stand down. Nothing more could be done at the moment. "How's the investigation going?"

"I've got intel. I'll tell you when we hook up. Call me if she shows?"

"I will. Jake, do you think she's all right?" She swallowed her fear and her reluctance to show her feelings, wanting in the worst way to be reassured her friend was going to be fine.

"Chances are good she'll show up this morning. When did you last see her?"

"Yesterday at breakfast. We decided on the Chinese food then." She rubbed her forehead, wishing she hadn't taken the sleeping pill the studio doctor had prescribed. It was making her feel like she was wrapped in cotton batten. She looked at the counter where she'd left the other pill bottle. Maybe one of the pick-me-ups chock full of vitamins and energy boosters was in order?

She ended the call and gave her dog an inquiring glance. "You want to go for walkies, Marlow?"

An instant chuff from the dog, and she got up from the sofa and went to get his leash, ignoring the pill bottle. She'd call in her absence for the day when they got back. She needed to clear her head in the worse way.

She clipped on Marlowe's lead to his collar and they made their way to the front lobby. She looked out onto the street, dismayed to see the Santa Ana winds had picked up overnight. The hard times had hit. Again. The hot hell wind was the bane of every LA resident's existence. Worse than tremors in the ground, was the searing winds that dried out every blade of grass and anything that moved. Whatever social unrest was blooming this week was bound to get worse when tempers flared from this uncontrollable wind. She sighed. Nineteen sixty-eight was proving to be the worse year for rioting since it all began in February in South Carolina. Only a matter of time until LA joined in. The world was becoming increasingly chaotic, and now, with Serena missing, the world was shifting like quicksand under her very feet. She pulled herself together with difficulty. It was not the time for allowing the city to suck her down into the quagmire. It was the time to gird her loins and be strong. Pep talk over, she addressed Marlowe who waited patiently by her side.

"Ready to go, boy? I can't do anything about the damn wind, I'm sorry."

He wagged his tail, and she pushed open the front door of the apartment block, holding on tight to his leash.

It is what it is.

"Claire, good to see you!"

She blinked her eyes, the fine grit carried by the wind annoying the sensitive retinas. Herman stood there; a grin so wide she worried he'd be spitting sand all day long.

"Morning. I guess I don't have to ask how you're doing?"

"Beyond ecstatic. I can't thank you enough."

"I think twelve times will do it."

He laughed, looking happier than she'd ever seen him. It helped buoy her mood a little. "Yeah, guess I've been overdoing it. Say, why are you not at work?"

"I took off today. It's Serena. Have you seen her at all? I'm worried about her; she didn't show last night."

He scratched his head and pursed his lips. "You know, I did. About six o'clock last night."

His words made her heart want to leap out of her chest. "Where? What was she doing?"

"She was out back in the parking lot. She was helping this guy load something into the back of his van. He had a broken wrist or something. I spotted a white cast. He had a box and was having trouble with it. I was going to help, but Mrs. Ferguson from 5A stopped to talk about the next block meeting, and I got waylaid talking about particulars. When I looked again, the van was gone as was the bag of food she was carrying. I assumed she went inside. You're saying she didn't make it?"

"No, she didn't. And that's why I'm worried. What did this van look like? Was it one you recognized?"

"No, not one of ours, a large white van with no windows. The guy was tall, I remember. I do know the license plate. I always memorize them." He pulled out a small pad of paper and carefully jotted down the numbers, handing it to her.

"Great. That's a real help, Herman."

He beamed before turning dead serious. "Let me know if you find out anything about Serena."

"Of course. Thanks for this." She waved the bit of paper in one hand before tucking it into her jean pocket. Her dog was pulling hard on his leash. "I've got to walk Marlowe now."

CHAPTER 16
AN EVIL WIND BLOWS

AH, SUCH A PRETTY LITTLE CAPTIVE.

He pushed back the tangle of fair hair that had fallen into her face, enjoying the quivers of fear that continually tremored throughout her body, trussed up as she was. She was his gift. He'd earned this moment. This time of release. When the high winds outside screamed their fury, he would find his pinnacle.

He was prepared. Checked there was still plenty of room in the deep well in the back of his property and that the grate was still holding the remains down below the water level and out of sight. He had chosen a victim he could only hope would live up to his high standards. Not the one who still roamed the streets of LA that he wanted to play cat-and-mouse with a while longer, but one who should live long enough to demonstrate the effects of deprivation and pain on the human body; offering up their body to science.

A favorite bit of the aria that played on the Hi-Fi in the other room and was sent through the four speakers in the corners of the room announced itself. He stopped dealing with the woman and played to the orchestra instead, making the controlled, magnificent hand gestures of a virtuoso as the melody played out in his mind along with the record. When the classic piece ended, he took a deep breath. Time to begin.

CHAPTER 17
RACING THE
WHIRLWIND

Jake pulled up in front of Claire's apartment and kept the motor running when he spotted her and Marlowe already in the foyer through the glass windows. She escorted her dog through the doorway and hurried over to help the animal into the back seat of his Mustang. She looked good, if slightly windblown, when she slid onto the front passenger seat. She smoothed down the ponytail she'd gathered the rest of her hair into at the crown of her head. The side swept wave was still in place, tucked behind one ear. Probably self-conscious about the hairline scar. She shouldn't be. Battle scars are hard won and dearly paid for.

"Thanks for picking us up," she said, clicking her seat belt into place and giving him with a tight smile before catching sight of his countenance. "My god, what happened to you?" She reached out and with cool fingers lightly touched the dark bruise on the side of his mouth. His nose was still swollen, but it was easier to breath today, though he sported a spectacular black eye. His ribs were bruised, not broken. Being a fast healer had helped from time to time in the past when cases heated up. He prayed this time would be no different.

"It's nothing. Just a slight disagreement with a loud-mouth. Okay, has anything happened since you got the information from the caretaker?" She'd called him to let him know that Serena hadn't shown up in her agent's office, and that no one had seen her last night except Herman in the parking lot. At least the guy had had the sense to get a license number on the van. Unfortunately, when he checked with LAPD, it had been reported as stolen a day earlier. Problem was, he couldn't even be certain the incident was connected. No fast-food bag was found on the ground, lost in a struggle. No screams heard. But his gut instinct agreed it was.

"No, nothing's changed since I reported it and gave them a photo of Serena."

"Okay, good."

"Do you think this has anything to do with the guy who attacked her at the party?"

"Maybe." He shrugged and punched in the electric lighter on the dash. "I intend to find out."

He lit two cigarettes, handing her one.

"Thanks."

"Where are we off to?" she asked, lowering the side window.

"The guy at the pawn shop came through. I've got an address, a bit faded from water damage, but still legible. And it's not far. I thought we'd check it out." While his guy at LAPD paid a visit to the shark guy with the bad combover who needed a wake-up call. Ted Bachman was just the man to administer it.

"An address? Whose address?" She swung her head around and gave him a steady shot from those luminous jade eyes, her bright ponytail dancing on her shoulders.

"The owner of your fancy pin."

Her hand fluttered to her throat. "My mother?"

"Maybe. The phone number wasn't listed, so I couldn't call ahead." He reached over and squeezed her hand. She took another long draw on the cigarette and let it drift out.

"Wow, that is something. My mother."

Her voice sounded tight and breathless. "I'll go in first. Find out what the deal is, okay? Otherwise, I'll leave the visit until another day. We clear?"

She nodded, but her mouth firmed into a straight line. She wasn't entirely happy with the admonishment. At least the trip would keep her mind off her missing friend.

They smoked in silence as he drove, taking the 101 into East LA, then the 60 toward Pomona. Traffic was heavy, and it took longer than he'd expected to reach the community of Wellington Heights. He pulled up in front of the rundown address and grimaced. Humble beginnings. The yard was overgrown, the curtains drawn. Someone had made a valiant attempt to plant a few flowers along the sidewalk. They had wilted from the drying wind, nearly overrun by weeds.

"We're here."

Claire stubbed out her third cigarette and tuned to look at a house she may or may not have a connection to.

She startled. Then turned wide eyes his way, her skin so pale she appeared translucent. "I know this house. I've seen it in my dreams."

"You've been here before? When?"

"I don't know. But I recognize it." She rubbed at the scar on the side of her face. "This house haunts me; a woman inside wants me to find her."

"You dreamed all this?" He knew she was hiding

secrets, but not such disturbing ones. You never know what a bump on the head can cause.

"I know it sounds crazy. But after the accident I began having these dreams. Well, more like nightmares. Bad enough that I think I may need help."

"Like a therapist's help?"

"Yeah. Friday I'm supposed to see the studio doctor and spill my guts." She grimaced and reached for another Salem.

He punched in the lighter, lit the cigarette for her, then watched her draw on it. Her fingers trembled slightly and he hesitated considering what was best for her. Take her home and come back?

"I'm okay. Maybe this will help me more than anything, you know? Finding out what the deal is."

"True. Okay, you promise to wait here until I come for you?"

"I do. Just don't take too long."

"We don't even know if anyone's home, so I might be right back." He got out and closed the driver's door. He made his way down the cracked sidewalk to the front stoop that was threatening to fall off.

He banged loudly on the front door. It was impossible to tell what color it had been originally. The wood was scuffed up and the small glass insert was cracked and dusty.

When no one answered, he tried again. Banged louder.

Slowly the door swung open. In the doorway stood a wizened old woman. She appeared older even than Gunny at the pawn shop, her hair beyond white, and her thin skin a network of lines and furrows.

"Hello, I'm Jake Sterling, of Sterling Private Investigations. I wondered if I might have a few minutes of your time?"

"Do I know you?" Her voice was as fragile as a baby bird's. She stood in the doorway, not moving aside to let him in. A very tiny protector of the realm.

He handed her his business card. She took it with hands that shook with obvious tremors.

"No, but I might know someone who knows you. Someone who might be related. Would you know anything about a baby girl left on the steps of a children's home in Hollywood twenty-one years ago? Given up for adoption? Perhaps a granddaughter of yours?" He pulled the brooch out of his pocket and showed it to her.

She stared at the jewelry, then at him like he was a ghost, her rheumy eyes behind her thick spectacles trying desperately to focus. Then down at the white card. He watched her read it, her thin lips sounding it out as she read the few lines it contained. Her well under five-foot person was covered by a loose-fitting blue housedress and her childlike feet were encased in worn slippers. She gave off the scent of lilacs and talcum powder.

"Maybe you'd better come in." She slowly shuffled aside and he followed her down the short hallway to a small living room that contained an overstuffed horsehair sofa and rocking chair. He caught a glimpse of the bathroom at the end of the hall, its door partially open. A bedroom was situated across from the living room, and he presumed a kitchen made up the last room on the main floor. She sat down in the rocking chair and gestured at the couch.

He sat. The room also had a small electric fireplace with a series of photographs of people placed on the wall above it. Mostly in black and white, some quite faded.

The room was dark and smelled moldy, of old possessions, too long neglected.

"I have a client who's looking for her mother. My investigations have led me to this address."

"Slow down, please." She waved a hand at him. "I know why you're here. It's been a long time coming."

He stifled his impatience.

"On that wall you will find a photograph of a young blonde girl wearing that brooch you have in your possession. A family heirloom by the way. Bring the picture to me."

He got up and went to inspect the more than fifty photographs dotting the wall. When he spotted the correct one, his stomach tensed. The woman was wearing a dress made of the same fabric he had the small sample of in his pocket. The exact same brooch graced her shoulder. He plucked it off the wall and studied it. The girl was so carefree, grinning at the camera, her pose with one hand on her hip rather capricious. She looked like a teenager of the forties, her hair rolled into sections on the sides of her head, the back down in a fluffed pageboy to her shoulders. She had a noticeable resemblance to Claire, her face as delicately put together, her eyes as large and beautiful, gleaming with a natural intelligence.

"Is this your granddaughter?"

She nodded. "Fiona was such a pretty girl. So full of life, she ran before she could walk. Wanted to be in moving pictures. She certainly had the looks for it."

He dutifully handed it to the woman. She traced a finger over the image, her face expressing a certain sadness that tugged at his heartstrings.

"Where's Fiona now?" He'd gotten the name off the

pawn slip as well. Fiona. No last name, but the all-important address.

"I don't know. We never heard from her again after she was home that last time. She was pregnant, and her mother was ashamed. The girl was unmarried." The old woman shook her head sorrowfully. "Terrible thing. Disowning your own."

"Did Fiona have any sisters or brothers?"

"No, she was an only child. Odd back in the day, but my daughter was abandoned by her useless husband, and Ruthie never remarried."

"Is Ruthie still alive?"

"No, she passed a few years back. The cancer took her."

"Do you have any other living relatives?"

"A younger brother who lives in San Francisco. But I haven't seen him in years. He's in a home now. Near the end. So, I have a great granddaughter, and she's looking for me?"

He nodded. At least Claire would get to meet her. Her almost to last living relative. "She's outside waiting to see if this is the right place. Shall I bring her in?"

The old woman put a hand to her hair. "I wish I'd known I was having company. I would have spruced up a bit."

Her vanity struck a chord in him. Such a human response. It made him smile even as bittersweet thoughts filled him of how little such things mattered. It was the time that was too short. He had a sudden urge to call him mom. Let her talk his ear off. "No matter how you look, Claire will be happy to meet you."

"Claire? That's her name?"

"Yes. And what may I say is yours?"

"I'm Alma. Alma Mary Clarin. Her great-grandmother." The happiness the woman was experiencing had taken ten years off her appearance. She beamed with anticipation. Aww. Good. It would be a nice reconciliation for Claire.

"I'll go and get her."

CHAPTER 18
A FAMILY LEGACY

CLAIRE WATCHED JAKE STRIDE DOWN THE SIDEWALK toward her, his short dark hair being yanked at by the merciless devil wind. She dropped her cigarette and ground it beneath the toe of her shoe. The moment was at hand and all she felt was numb. Confused. Worried she'd been on a wild goose chase that would not end well.

When he stood before her, he gave her a quick look before speaking. "I have good news and bad. The woman who lives in this house is your great-grandmother, Alma Mary Clarin. She lives alone. Your only other known living relative, her brother, lives in San Francisco. She hasn't seen your mother, Fiona, since she heard she was pregnant with you. Fiona's mother's name is Ruth. Apparently, Ruth didn't take well to having a pregnant, unmarried daughter. And I'm sorry, but Ruth died a few years back."

She held up a hand. "Stop, please. I need a moment." She took a few deep breaths and blinked away the sudden rush of hot tears that threatened to engulf her.

"I'm sorry about what happened to your mother, Claire."

"Me too. I can't imagine how alone she must have felt, her own mother not being willing to help out when she most needed it."

"We can still continue the search for her. She's got to be somewhere. She might have married, changed her name." The search had just become far more difficult if her own family was a dead end.

"If she hasn't come home in over two decades, I don't know." She shook her head. "I may have to face the fact she might be gone. For good."

"You don't know that. She might have felt that she was being driven away, and never forgave her family. It happens. Family splits are the hardest to heal. We often expect too much of the familial connection."

"Maybe." She took a ragged breath. "Okay. I got this."

"Good. I'll wait here."

"Thank you."

Claire made herself walk forward until she reached the front door. She was about to knock when it swung wide open. A tiny birdlike woman who looked to be ninety if she was a day peered up at her. Her wrinkled face was wreathed in smiles. "Claire, is it? I'm Alma. Your great-grandmother. Come in, dear."

Breathing easier, she stepped inside. The tiny woman immediately moved forward and hugged her tightly about the waist, her hands patting her as lightly as butterfly wings. She carefully hugged the woman back. The fragrance of lilacs and baby powder that entered her nostrils with each breath taken filled her with nostalgia for an earlier time.

She followed her great-grandmother into the living room and took a seat on the sofa, its stiff brown horsehide cover odd and unsettling beneath her. The woman took a seat in the rocking chair and began to rock slowly back and forth. Her hands lay quiet in her lap, worn and twisted with care.

"Now, my dear, I want to know all about you. What brought you here today?"

Claire took a deep breath and it all spilled out of her like a cleansing rain. The woman bent her head sideways like Jake's parrot, Bishop, taking in all the information. She nodded occasionally but didn't interrupt. Finally, the dam that had broken reduced to a trickle and she ran out of words.

"That's quite a tale, dear. But all I can say is how very glad I am it's brought you to my doorstep today. Now, before it's too late. I don't have as long as I'd like to get to know you." Her grandmother blotted her eyes with a tissue she pulled from a box near at hand, its top and sides hidden by a decorative croquet cover of bright yellow daisies.

Her stomach roiled. Time was the enemy in this situation.

"I wish I had known about you long ago."

"It is what it is, dear. Now, grab me that photo album in the cupboard over there. Top drawer."

She pointed at the sideboard pushed against the wall.

Claire got to her feet and went and opened the drawer, drawing out the old gray album with the faded script "Family" on the front.

She brought it to her grandmother and set it in her lap. She hovered by her side as the old woman opened it up. The woman rustled through the pages until she came to one. She pointed at it, her fingers trembling.

"This is a photo of Fiona with her young man. He

might be your father. The time is right. November 1946. A few months before you were born. She was already pregnant in this photo, it hardly shows, but I knew. It was after this that Ruthie, my daughter, said she wasn't to come home again unless she was married or had given the baby to a good family. I didn't cotton to it. Family's family, in my opinion. But my Ruthie, she had a religious streak a mile wide. Not sure how it happened, she sure didn't get it from me. You can have this. It might help you in your search. I do hope you find her, one way or the other. Maybe before I die." She struggled with the photo, tugging it away from the glued spots in the corners holding it in place.

"Don't talk about dying, Grandma. I just found you." Claire's throat tightened hearing the words as she took the photograph held out to her. The name *Grandma* slipped out, natural as could be. She looked at the photo and her heart faltered. The woman from her dreams stared back at her.

A knock on the front door startled her. Claire had to keep herself from leaping to her feet.

"That will be Eileen coming to check on me. She'll let herself in. She helps me out most days. Makes me a meal and tidies up. Lovely woman, if a little too religious for my liking." She winked mischievously at Claire. It warmed her heart even while she sat stunned by developments. The old woman made her feel part of something again.

She cleared her throat. "Thanks for the photograph. I'll bring it back when I've found things out."

"No need. You keep it. In fact, now that I know I have a granddaughter, you'll be inheriting all I have. It's not much, but a lifetime of memories."

She needed to get out of there, gain some perspective.

"Okay, but don't feel you have to. Well, I'll be going then. I will call you soon."

"That would be good. Oh, Eileen, I want you to meet someone."

The middle-aged woman stood in the doorway, her heavy bulk at odds with the narrow area. She carried a bag of groceries and she stopped dead when she caught sight of Claire, her expression suspicious.

"You have company?"

"Yes, my great granddaughter has found me. Claire?"

"Preston."

"Claire Preston, I'd like you to meet Eileen Parent."

They returned greetings and Claire got up to leave. She kissed her grandmother's cheek, finding it dry and warm. "I'll be in touch soon. Thanks, Grandma."

"For what, dear?"

"For being so nice."

They shared a smile before Claire slipped by the caretaker; the snapshot clutched in her hand. She opened the front door and hurried outside into the wicked wind. Impossibly, it seemed to be blowing even harder. An arid odor scorched her nostrils. Her stomach clenched tight, recognizing the frightening smell. No human alive didn't know what it represented. Fire.

She hurried up to Jake. "Do you smell that?"

He gave her a worried look. "Yeah. Wildfire. I freaking hate fire. I'd like to get up into a helicopter or small plane even time this happens. Find the source. It's been a couple of years since we had a bad one, that Loop fire up north in the Angeles National Forest. Hell of a disaster. It killed a number of Hotshots, all good men."

She laid a hand on his arm. "I have some news. I've got a photo of the man my grandma thinks might possibly be my father."

His expression cleared. "That's good. I have an eyewitness to the man she was in the pawn shop with. He may be able to help. Let's go."

The haze from the smoke busy filling the Los Angeles basin had already reduced visibility in the city. Claire kept her mind off it and instead studied the black-and-white photograph while Jake drove in silence, his expression distant. The tall, dark-haired man in the snapshot stood unsmiling and stiff while her diminutive mother appeared happy, smiling as the sun shone down on her blonde hair. The man's eyes were dark against his pale skin, while her mother's eyes appeared to be blue or green. If only the image were in color. She sighed, wishing she could speak to the young couple in the photo. Ask them a slew of questions that had built up over the past few months, and now added to observing the picture. *Why did you drop me at an orphanage? Why didn't you marry her? Are you my father?*

Finally, she looked over at Jake, wondering why she hadn't asked the question before. "Are you married? Children?"

He gave her a startled look. "Aw, no, not married now. No children."

"But you were. Divorced?"

"No."

"Separated?"

He cleared his throat. "She died a few years back."

"Oh, I'm sorry." She felt bad for pressing, making him say the hard words out loud. What was it about a crisis that made people step outside their comfort zone? She'd never push for personal information on a normal day.

"I'm over it. We had separated before she died. A cop's life is such I should never have married in the first place. And now that I'm a PI, it's impossible to have any kind of relationship. This business takes its toll. You might want to rethink your career choice."

"Hmmm."

He turned to give her a look, like he wanted to sleuth inside her brain. More and more she was beginning to think this was exactly the job she wanted. People had to know. The drive for the truth was too intense, too important to ignore.

CHAPTER 19
THE PAST IS A CRUEL TEACHER

JAKE'S MIND WAS FILLED BY THE IMAGE OF THE ANSWERING machine hidden in the bottom of his file cabinet. The Model 100 Robosonics that held the last words of his dead wife was brought out only after having consumed too much whiskey. Kept him relatively sober, most days.

"Do you have a boyfriend?" Tit for tat. Fair play.

She shook her head. "No. No luck with men."

"You'll have even less luck with the opposite sex if you become a PI."

"You think so?" She seemed bemused now. "Maybe I'll become a nun instead."

"Now that would be an incredible waste. *There is no trap so deadly as the one you set for yourself.*"

"Right about now, I could see myself drinking enough to wake up in a place like Singapore."

"Hopefully without the full beard," he quipped back. He liked trading the Raymond Chandler quotes with her far more than he should. *Careful, Jake.*

She barked a laugh in response as he parked the Mustang in front of Sunset Pawn and killed the motor. Down the street he could see the hippies he'd

147

bribed to move their act. Today they appeared to have a male in the group, standing to the side and watching them. Probably wanted to keep an eye on the money. Pimp?

"I don't get the panhandling, especially with a baby," Claire said, her mouth firming into a grim line. "All this smoke can't be good for delicate lungs."

"No. It's not good for anyone's." He got out and hurried around to open her door, but she was already on the sidewalk and striding toward the pawn shop entrance.

He managed to reach the door of the pawn shop before she did, holding it open for her. Old habits die hard.

"Thanks."

They were greeted by Bill, who had been standing and peering out the window, looking less annoyed than yesterday since the freeloaders moved off. Well, not free, since they'd taken a pair of Jacksons with them. That led to a vivid reminder of his assistant's objections to his liberal use of money. Sorry, Mae, call it the cost of doing business.

"Hey, Jake. Who's the pretty lady?" The man smoothed down his short hair, straightened his tie, and sucked in his gut.

"Nice to meet you. I'm Claire Preston." She stepped forward and shook his hand.

"Claire. What are you doing with this guy?" Bill softened his words with a smile.

"This is the case I told you about. Why we needed you to find that pawn slip. I was wondering if Gunny's around? Got a photo for him to identify."

Bill's eyes flicked to the photograph that Claire held in her hand. "Sure, in the back like always. May I offer you refreshments, Claire? A cold drink or coffee? The wind's making everyone darned thirsty today."

"I'm fine, but thanks for the offer."

"Horrible with the smoke. Know anything about it?" Jake asked, scrubbing a hand over his jaw and chin.

"Heard on the radio it's up north in the National Forest. We should be okay if you're not asthmatic."

The three of them walked to the back. Bill held open the curtain for them to step through.

"Gunny. Jake's back and wants you to have a gander at a photo."

Gunny turned from working on one of the many disassembled items on the bench. He grabbed a rag and wiped his hands. "You think to bring that mickey, boy? The wind's making me parched today."

He didn't make a federal case out of the moniker boy. "We hurried right over and didn't take the time to stop. Claire, Gunny."

"You're getting better taste," Gunny remarked, appraising Claire.

She ignored the compliment and held out the snapshot. The old man took it from her hand and studied it.

"Do you know him?" Claire asked, her face strained with the asking, and yet hopeful enough to damn near break his heart. He steeled himself, this young woman was suckering him in too tight, too soon. And the worry about her friend pounced again. He needed to make some calls. Find out if Agent Mann had discovered anything about Claire's case. But more urgent was calling Detective Bachman. See if he had heard anything more about Serena. A clock had begun to tick in his mind sometime this morning that he now acknowledged; time was counting down for finding Serena. If she had been abducted, the first forty-eight hours was

149

crucial to the investigation. If they wanted to find her alive.

The elderly man stabbed a bony finger at the pair in the picture, his snow-white hair feathering around his skull from the abrupt movement. "That's him. That damn Nazi bastard. And the pretty lady who shouldn't have been with him. The one always pawning her brooch." He looked up with an inquiring look. "Who are they to you?"

Claire turned so white she'd give a ghost a run for their money. Jake swallowed. Hard as it was to hear, she had to know the truth. No point in running from it.

"I think he might be my father. The young woman's my mother."

The old man's expression softened. "I'm sorry. I shouldn't have been so hard. Not your fault whose loins you come from."

"Can you tell me anything about my mother?"

"She was a nice girl. You know, you do look like her—pretty, though her hair was blonde, not that sweet cherry red. And she was always polite and came back and retrieved her goods whenever she could. Never quibbled about the cost of doing business." They seemed to have made a tactile agreement not to mention the man in the photo again.

"Thank you for that. Can I offer you anything for your help?"

"It's covered. Jake's promised to bring over a bottle of the best stuff. Haven't you?" The old man turned a sly eye in his direction.

"Of course, soon as I can."

"You might want to stick a couple of Jacksons in the bag."

Jake's nose twitched. "Okay, we should head out. I've got some calls to make."

"Hang on a sec, Jake. I need to tell you something in private. This will put a little sparkle in your piss."

He hung back while Claire and Bill left.

"The guy had a tattoo I'd forgotten about. Not one of those blood type tattoos that some SS have on their inner arms above the elbow. This was on the back of his wrist. I saw it when he reached to look at something and his sleeve slipped up. A small black swastika." Gunny shuddered with disdain, shaking his head. "I should have taken him down then."

"Thanks, Gunny."

He took his departure and rejoined Claire and Bill at the front door.

"It was a great pleasure to meet you, Miss Preston. If there's ever anything I can do for you, don't hesitate to ask." Bill's face beamed with sincere intent. Huh.

"Nice to meet you, Bill. Thanks for your help."

"Anytime. I'm here every day, rain or shine."

The exchange rankled more than it should.

Since they'd entered the shop, the girl and her baby had left the group of freeloaders at the end of the block and now hovered nearby. She'd spotted her mark again.

Jake pushed open the door and stood shielding Claire to speak with the woman who wore the same clothes, though the baby still looked clean and cared for.

"Hey, mister. Charlie has a message for you. He wants you to come visit us. Says he can help you gain enlightenment. We're out at the Spahn Movie ranch. North of town, past Chatsworth in the Simi Hills at 1200 Santa Susana Pass Road. You're welcome to visit anytime. Share a meal with us." She sounded breathless, like she had been waiting all morning to deliver it word for word.

"Thanks, but I got all the enlightenment I can handle." He reached into his pocket and drew out another bill, handing it off to the young girl. Her eyes lit up. He hoped it went for food, and not a drug trip. The valley was saturated with enough LSD and marijuana to send the entire population on an extended high until 1970.

"Thanks, but think about it. Charlie's the message. The new Messiah come back to earth to save the chosen. We're all groovy to that. Time's running out, mister. Think about saving yourself." She skipped away, holding the baby tight to her chest.

"Strange. Twice in one week to hear mention of the Spahn ranch."

"How so?"

"Doctor Vogel at the studio mentioned he lived near a ranch owned by a man with that name, and that he was pretty upset a commune of hippies had descended on it. Thought the guy should know better than take them in. Maybe he meant them?"

"Maybe. Not that common a name. Did he mention the address?"

"No, except that he had to drive into the city each day." She grimaced. "Used it in reference for my being tardy for the appointment. Who's Charlie?"

"Darned if I know, but shysters like that are a dime a dozen now. Stay clear of them, Claire. They'll sucker you in. Take all your possessions and money and offer a lesson in extreme humility in return. Feeds their swollen egos. They prey on the unsuspecting, the innocent looking for someone to show them the way."

"No problem." She shrugged. "I'm a born skeptic. But

maybe, if it makes them feel part of something bigger than themselves, it's not so bad."

He groaned. "See, I'm right to worry. You're already giving them the benefit of the doubt. Promise me, if ever someone approaches you, and it sounds too good to be true, you'll call me first?"

"You worry too much, but okay, I promise."

"Good. I gotta get back to the office and make some calls. Do you want me to drop you back at home?"

"Can I come with you? I was hoping to see more about how it all works, this private investigator business. Plus, I want to know what Gunny shared." She gave him a direct look, her eyes boring into his with intent.

"Okay, I'll tell you in the car."

Claire hurried over and jumped inside the Mustang. She shut the door against the invading smoke. He joined her and sat back, staring out the windshield at the group of committed hippies accosting passersby with razorlike precision.

"Gunny saw a tattoo on the man's wrist that helped prove his case. A symbol of Nazi Germany, the swastika."

She drew in a ragged breath and let it out in a solid whoosh of air. "So, it's true then. Oh my god, Jake, what if he's my father?"

"We don't know that for certain." He shrugged nonchalantly. "And like Gunny said, we have no control over who our ancestors are. Luck of the draw. But here's the thing, the more we dig, the more dirt gets disturbed. You want that for yourself? Some people can't handle the truth. It's okay if you're one of them, Claire. There could be rough waters ahead. And with Serena missing, it's only going to make things worse for you. You really up for this? You've discovered your grandmother. That's a positive thing right there. Could be the place to stop for you?"

He watched her absorb the cold facts. She stared off into the distance. What was she seeing? If anything at all? Psychology had always interested him. What motivates a human being to action was fascinating stuff. And if it helped him catch an evil man, all the better.

"I have to do this. I need to know. All of it. The good and the bad." She turned to look at him, her eyes shining with an intelligent gleam that spoke of a deep well of sureness, her features firmed by resolve.

"Okay then." He started the motor and drove the short distance to his office. His thoughts slipped back to the professor. In good conscience, he should call the man and return his money. With all that was going on with recent developments, he had no time to devote to another case.

Soon as he escorted Claire through the door, Mae looked up from her desk.

"Jake, Agent Mann called. Asked that you call him back right away. Said it was urgent. I left the number on your desk." She glanced at Claire with interest riding high in her eyes.

"Nice to see you, Claire. How are you?"

"All right. And you?"

"Good, thanks for asking."

Mae looked entirely too smug. The addition of a sly wink was uncalled for.

"*Tall aren't you, tall aren't you,*" Bishop yelled as Jake opened the door to his inner office.

Claire walked right up to the parrot. "*I didn't mean to be.*"

He hopped up and down, looking at her intently, like he was waiting for the next cue.

"What's your name?" she asked.

He kept eyeing her and she repeated the phrase a few more times.

"What's your name?" he finally asked, his beady eyes intently focused on watching Claire. He got it. Watching Claire could become a full-time occupation if he wasn't careful.

"Nice job, Jake." She offered Bishop a few sunflower seeds she'd chosen from an open bowl, laying them on her open palm. The parrot fastidiously took them into his beak, one by one, his green eyes glowing with utter satisfaction.

Her approval pleased him. He responded with a self-effacing shrug. "He needed some new lines. I thought Chandler would approve."

"I believe he would."

He picked up the phone and dialed Mann's number. He answered it on the second ring.

"What's up?"

"Jake, good you called. That file you were asking about?"

"Yes."

Mann lowered his voice to a whisper. "We need to talk."

"Where do you want to meet?"

"O'Hara's, but I can't until later tonight. Eleven, eleven thirty at the earliest."

"Fine. I'll wait."

He hung up and immediately redialed.

"LAPD. Detective Bachman."

"It's Jake, anything new on the Serena Sands case?"

"The van's been found. Abandoned. In the river a few miles away, partially submerged in the water. A couple of boys fishing spotted it. Forensics is going over it as we speak. Doubt they find anything. Looks like it was wiped clean by a perfectionist who loved the smell of bleach in the morning. We're dragging the riverbed. If it's there, it can't have gone far. Current's slow."

Jake groaned, praying they didn't find Serena's body in the water. "Well, let me know if they find anything."

"Will do. I also paid a visit to the asshole that was bothering her. William Costanza?"

"Discover anything?"

"Yeah, usual celebrity bullshit, thinks he's above the law. I corrected him on his misconception."

Problem was, for some A-list celebrities, the sense of being untouchable had been a correct notion. Hollywood fed the life's blood of tinsel town. And if he thought it was bad now, he was more than aware of the scandals of past decades. The LAPD had taken its lumps but had worked hard to clean up its act. Didn't mean there wasn't still work to be done. But he was one hundred percent certain that Detective Ted Bachman was legit. They'd grown up in the neighborhood together and had each other's back more times than he could count.

"And that's why the Black Dalia case is so hard to crack," he said, allowing the disgust to spill over in his voice.

"Phttt, no kidding. But we're looking into where Costanza was at the time of the disappearance. Talk later. The chief's giving me the eye."

He set the phone carefully in its cradle. He gave Claire a brief rundown of the facts, trying not to see the tears that appeared, making her blink in rapid succession. She earned his admiration when she managed to keep the waterworks at bay and asked, "What's our next move?"

"I'm going to want to interview anyone that Serena had contact with, especially in the last few days."

"I prepared a list earlier." She handed the slip of paper over, covered with precise printing.

"Good job. Remind me to give you a couple of manuals before we leave to help bring you up to speed on the business." The list had the addresses included along with names and phone numbers, even specific notations to intel Claire was party to. "I think a visit to speak with the only witness is in order, then over to see her agent before checking out her friends."

"I want to tag along. It might help as I know most of the people on the list."

"Sure. I'm fine with that." *More than fine.*

CHAPTER 20

A MOUNTAIN TOO HIGH

FIRST, THEY DROPPED OFF MARLOWE, NOT WANTING TO leave him in the vehicle. Then the fiery hot, difficult to breathe day was spent in the endless pursuit of any tidbit of information someone could remember with careful prompting. Claire was jittery from the endless cups of coffee and sugar donuts that fueled their sprint around town by the time night fell. The worse part, they were no closer to finding Serena. Though she had to admire the way Jake worked the case, methodical and exacting with each person on the list, by the end of the day, she wanted action. Finally she understood wanting to shake someone up to get them to spill the beans.

"What do we do next?" She chewed on a fingernail. Her nerves were shot.

"I'm taking you home."

"But we haven't found her! How can I give up and go home? She's out there somewhere. And she needs our help. If I keep looking surely—"

"You need to rest. Exhaustion's not going to help find your friend. A level head, that's what's necessary."

She didn't like hearing his words and worked to find a logical response. Before she could, he spoke again.

"Besides, I need to meet someone soon. Someone who can possibly help with your case."

"Right now, that's the least of my worries. You can pull back on my case until we find Serena." Her concerns seemed so insignificant with her friend's life at stake.

"Okay, but the ball was already rolling on this one. No point in not following through. Let's see how you feel in the morning, okay? We can move forward when you're ready. In the meantime, we'll focus on your friend." He pulled to a stop in front of her building, leaving the motor of the Mustang running.

She picked up the manuals he'd lent her and the photo of her mother, then reached for the door handle. "Thanks for all this."

"I didn't do that much. I want to see your friend safe, same as you. We will do everything in our power to find her, I promise you, Claire."

She got out and closed the vehicle door, then walked up to the front door of her building. The arid odor of smoke dried her nostrils and made her skin crawl. When she turned to look back, she found Jake still watching her. She waved and slipped inside, realizing he was just wanting to see her safely home. It was a comfort.

"Did you find Serena?" Herman pounced before she could collect her mail from the small letterbox in the foyer of the apartment complex. They'd spoken with him only hours ago, but she understood. The guy was obviously upset it had happened on his watch.

She shook her head, her throat tightening. "Not yet. We'll get an early start in the morning."

"But it's not good, finding the van in the water, is it?" His reiterating the dreadful fact wasn't a help.

"No, but it might not mean anything. We don't know if she was even in the van. No one saw her get in." She kept hoping it wasn't the case, though it seemed the only answer as the hours and minutes slipped by. Otherwise, her friend would have called her. She knew that without a doubt. She rubbed her scar, feeling more drained than she could remember.

"It's my fault! If I hadn't been distracted by Mrs. Ferguson, I would have seen it all. Maybe stopped the guy."

She didn't have the strength for this discussion. Reassuring the guy all over again seemed like a mountain too high.

"No, it's fine." She decided her mail could wait. "I'll let you know when we find anything out."

"Thank you, that means a lot to me. If you need me to do anything, please ask. I'm only a phone call or knock on the door from being there for you. I mean it, don't worry. I'm a light sleeper."

She nodded once and hurried away. A minute later she was safe inside her apartment with the door closed behind her, thankful for the quiet. She set the manuals on the table near the door, then stood staring at the photo of her mother while studiously ignoring the man by her side. *Where are you, Mom?*

Marlowe chuffed softly and ambled over to greet her, making her want to grab him and cry for as long as it took. But she made herself focus on getting his dinner, then hers. Not fair to upset him. But even though she kept a stiff upper lip, Marlow seemed to absorb her somber mood, just eating, and laying down nearby. She made herself eat a few bites of the hastily prepared sandwich she'd pulled together from some leftover luncheon meat, but it stuck in her throat.

Giving up on the food, she dumped it in the garbage. Even though the air was polluted by smoke and she dreaded going out again, Marlowe still needed his constitutional.

"Sorry, boy, I'm not much company tonight. Time for walkies?"

Marlowe got up and wagged his tail. She attached the lead to his collar and they headed outside. She stayed far away from the spot where Serena was most likely taken, not needing the reminder. The smoke was as annoying as earlier and she hurried the dog through the necessary protocols. He didn't fight it, just did his business, and wanted back inside.

After grabbing a glass of wine and a scribbler for notes, she sat on the sofa and opened the first instruction manual for the private investigation business. She needed something, anything to get her mind off of her friend, or she'd go crazy. No hopes of sleeping this night. She looked up at the pill bottles standing enticingly close at hand. Then shook her head. No. When her body was tired, she'd sleep, until then she's put up with it. But she was taking the rest of the week off from work, or however long it took to find Serena, no questions asked.

CHAPTER 21
CATCH 22

JAKE OPENED THE FRONT DOOR TO O'HARA'S BAR, THE favorite hangout of off-duty cops, wannabees, and sticky bar flies. He took a good look around the poorly lit space. Liam and Jimmy O'Hara, the brothers who ran the joint, had no need to make the décor more inviting. The dark dinginess of the place was the draw. No Whiskey a Go-Go celebrity hype at O'Hara's. No sign of Mann either, not that he'd expected there to be. He was running early. The bar was quiet tonight, a fact he was grateful for, not being exactly the most popular man among the men in blue.

"Hey, Jake, what can I do you for?" Liam asked, busy wiping down the bar with an old piece of cloth. He looked up to greet Jake, raising thick, ginger-colored eyebrows. Dressed in the prerequisite black tee and jeans, the clothing did nothing to add any menace to his cherub appearance. But then the brothers didn't have to worry with a bar full of cops always ready to work off the stress of the job by dealing personally with any infractions. He'd done some work for the brothers, tracked down a former customer who'd owed a whopping bar bill. Made him pay up, and not the brothers. Goodwill comes in handy in the trade.

"Usual, thanks."

Liam poured him a whiskey with a beer chaser and set them in front of him, and took the saw buck he offered.

"Keep the change."

Liam tucked the bill in his pocket.

"Quiet tonight," Jake observed, picking up the beer and taking a large gulp. Maybe it would help with the raw taste of smoke.

"Hmm." Liam was his usual chatty self. But then no one came to O'Hara's for the chitchat.

"How's that bird of yours?" The question took him by surprise.

"Good. Why?"

"Thinking of getting one for the bar."

"Really?" He could only imagine the lingo that would be picked up by a parrot in this joint where most patrons would be left saying nothing with all their four-letter words stripped away.

"Ah, better watch your back. Jigger just walked in with a couple of his cronies." Liam nodded, giving the bar one last swipe before throwing the rag in a bin. Jake could hear the thud of boots on the floor.

"Well, if it isn't one of LA Central Division's rejects." The annoying sound of Jigger's voice echoed loud and clear.

"Out to impress your friends, are you, Jigger?"

"Nothing about you impresses me, Sterling." The rank odor of alcohol permeated the air within ten feet of the cop who had never made detective. Too volatile by nature. And it was worse when he was drunk. And Jigger was drunk, though he hid it well. Lots of practice.

"Then we see eye-to-eye."

"I'm not putting up with any shit from the likes of you. A former cop who abandoned the job when the going got too rough. You don't deserve to drink with LAPD's finest."

"I'm not." Jake knew better, but this guy stuck in his craw. Whenever their paths crossed, it was always the same posturing bullshit. And tonight, after a day of chasing ghosts, he'd had enough.

Liam reached down and picked up the baseball bat he kept at the ready behind the bar, brandishing it about. "You want to drink here—you show some respect."

Jigger's expression turned deadly. "Take the side of a two-bit hustler, why don't you."

"Not taking sides. Just trying to keep my investment intact."

Jigger was almost painful to watch as he rolled the situation around in his mind. Nothing changes. Thinking would always trouble the man.

"Come on, Jigger, let's find a table far away from this stench." One of his cronies pulled on his sleeve.

Jigger allowed himself to be led away. Jake kept the trio in his line of vision until they had corralled a table in the darkest part of the bar.

"Not all LAPD cops hate your guts."

Jake snorted. "Maybe not. But enough do that I need to keep a clear head. I'll have a glass of water, if you stock any?"

Liam's turn to snort as he set the baseball bat under the bar again. It was a famous Louisville slugger, once used to knock sense into a pair of famous Chicago mobsters who shall remain unnamed. They had shown up in the bar one night. Picked an unadvisable fight with the O'Hara brothers over unwanted attentions to a certain barmaid who had consequently married one of them. Since then, no woman had worked the floor. Less eye candy, but a whole lot less testosterone to fuel fights. "It can be arranged, for a pittance."

The door opened again and Jake turned his head to see Mann advancing toward him.

"Hey, Jake." Connor Mann looked dead tired as he nodded at the bartender, making his stomach clench into a bundle of knots. Usually Mann was as hearty as his moniker. Dressed in his office attire, perquisite black suit, white starched shirt, and regulation black tie, now loosened, his sandy-blond hair neatly combed to the side, he was a lean, mean fighting machine, and had earned the respect of his fellow agents with his bulldog-like attention to solving cases. You want a lead or an answer, you called Special Agent Connor Mann.

"Mann, what can I do you for?" Liam asked.

"Draft and keep them coming."

"Let's find a table," Jake said.

They chose a table near the door, away from the bar flies.

"So, you look like you've been dropped in it," Mann said, taking in the bruised condition of his face, noticeable even in the dim lighting that passed for ambiance at O'Hara's.

"Yeah. But enough about me. What's going on, Connor?"

"You're not going to like this. But this file you're looking for missing from the children's home? Too hot to handle, buddy. I tracked down a guy who says it's as hush, hush as it gets."

"Can I talk to him?"

"Unlikely, but I'll ask. You don't want to be pushing it

too hard. Not with your license hanging out there in the wind."

"That bad, huh."

Mann shook his head. "You have no idea. I was put through the wringer with the inquiry."

"It's all beginning to add up."

"How so?" Mann asked.

"The guy who is most likely the suspect that's causing the mess—a former Nazi."

Mann whistled. "You're shitting me. Well, that does shed some light. Most likely he was up to no good after they hid his origins, and now they never want it brought to anyone's attention."

"Yup."

They both sat and stared at their empty beer glasses.

"I've heard tell of Project Paperclip. We recruited former Nazis with specialized skills in medicine and engineering after the war to keep the information out of Russian hands. He could have been part of that," Mann said, his expression troubled.

"Then he was up to no good in our country as well, and they are hiding everything to avoid exposure. Adds up."

"It does."

"And if that's the case, the guy's dangerous. So dangerous they don't want us to know about it."

"I wonder if they've kept tabs on him?"

Mann shrugged. "It would be good to know."

"I need to speak with your contact." A terrible sense of urgency filled Jake. "Tell the guy that they might be threatened with exposure if the guy's operating here. Use the leverage. Explain it will be kept confidential. I really need to help my client."

"All I can do is try. But don't count on it. We might both get our asses chewed off for this one."

"How's it going with your cold case?"

"Not good. The informant has vanished."

Jake shook his head. "Dark times in LA right now. Add in a fire, and it's beginning to feel a bit too much like Armageddon for my liking. Waiting for a plague of blood or locusts to descend next."

"More beer?" Liam asked, a pitcher at the ready.

Jake nodded absently, his mind struggling to put together the pieces of the puzzle. Some gut feeling told him that Serena's abduction had something to do with all this. It was far too timely.

CHAPTER 22

EVIL IS AS EVIL DOETH

RANK FEAR FILLED THE ROOM WITH ITS DISTINCTIVE WILD, musty, oh so sweet odor. He checked her vitals, drawing one finger down the tender skin of her pale cheek. So far, her heart had withstood the effects of the operation. But she was teetering on the edge far sooner than expected. Was she going to be another disappointment and not add the necessary data to his log? He needed outliers. Patients that proved his thesis. The well was filled with those who had not lived up to expectations. Succumbed before they added any vital intel.

He moved away from the hospital bed and stood in front of the camera that gave a full view of the front yard, his mind filling in the rest. It overlooked the scabby land that comprised the ranch. Land that seemed only capable of growing cacti and tumbleweeds, their prickly glory a sad testament to lack of water. Thoughts of his homeland filled his mind's eye. Vast fields of green in summer. Stooks of cut grain, piled in tidy precise rows into the vast curving distance in the fall. Golden against the bluest of skies. The rhythm of the planting, he missed it as much as he was capable of.

He turned now from the sight, his lip curling with distaste as he thought about the Spahn Movie ranch that butted up against his property. A group of disgusting, dirty hippies had recently moved onto the land. They threatened his entire operation while offering nothing in return. Not the proper sort of neighbor at all. Something would have to be done. Too bad he couldn't use them for his research, though they wouldn't be of much use anyway, that type would most likely succumb far too easy. Hmm. An idea struck like lightning, providing the perfect solution. It had already begun to the east, what was a few more acres?

CHAPTER 23
FOR WHOM THE BELL TOLLS

CLAIRE SPENT THE NIGHT TOSSING AND TURNING, IMAGES striking her tired mind like a series of electric shocks. Painful and repetitious, a looped roll of horror. Serena lying dead out in the desert. Serena lying dead in the river. Serena lying dead in the morgue.

When first light crept in the westward facing window of her bedroom, she wearily slipped out from under the strewn covers and swept her tangled hair back from her face. Marlowe looked up from the foot of the single bed, his brown eyes astute, as if asking if she were okay.

"I'm fine, fellow. Time for breakfast?"

He jumped to the floor and padded after her to the kitchen nook. As she dug out a can of Marlowe's favorite dog food, everything that had happened lately kept pressing on her brain. The missing file from the orphanage. Louisa keeping those few things for her from that guy looking to steal them. Finding her great-grandmother. The fact the guy in the photo with her mother who might be her father. A suspected Nazi. That thought made her swallow. Hard. Then the attack at the party and Deanna's assertions that Elle would ask her clients to do things they would never do in their right minds, not hyped on achieving fame. Her mind seized on the idea. Could Deanna know anything about it? Even if inadvertently? She knew Jake had talked to her, but maybe with a woman she'd open up more?

She set a bowl of food and one of fresh water down for Marlowe, started a pot of coffee, then hurried to the bathroom to prepare for the day. She had an avenue of inquiry to explore. For the first time she understood the drive that Jake must feel much of the time, working to expose the truth.

Twenty minutes later she picked up the phone. "Deanna. Can I swing by your office this morning? I need to speak with you. It's about Serena." Claire juggled a cup of coffee and a piece of toast as she made the call. Marlowe gave her a look. The one that said how pitifully he was being treated. She relented and fed him the last bit of the buttered toast with strawberry jam. The gleam in his chocolate brown eyes was thanks enough.

"Serena? Has anything happened? Do you know anything more?" The reporter's voice was troubled.

"No. But after our conversation at the party the other night, I think you might know something without realizing it."

"I already told the police and that private investigator, Jake Sterling, everything I know." Deanna's tone was brisk.

"Please, a few minutes of your time. It's important to me, Deanna, or I wouldn't call. I'm worried sick about Serena."

"We all are, hon. Okay. Be here within the hour. I've got an appointment at nine sharp."

"Thanks. I'll leave now."

Claire raced out the door, locking it behind her

before half jogging down the hallway in her tennis shoes. She'd dressed casually this morning in faded blue jeans and a white sleeveless blouse that buttoned down the front. She left the building grateful there wasn't a soul in sight and headed toward her car in the lot, getting safely inside in mere seconds. The air was somewhat better this morning and she hoped that meant the fire was under control. She locked the driver's door of the white Volkswagen bug she'd gotten to replace the Fairlane for good measure. With Serena possibly taken from the parking lot, she was not taking chances. In that moment she realized her life had changed drastically. Apparently, the one thing you could count on, life changed. Best get used to it.

She parked outside The Tattler, the rag that Deanna worked for and cut the motor. It felt good to be on the case. Working to find out what was going on. She hadn't felt this energized in a long time. Certainly not since her accident, and maybe, if she was being honest, long before then.

In the lobby, she pushed the elevator button to the seventh floor where Deanna's office was located. The whoosh of the doors opening and closing at each floor as people got off and on, the sounds of the forgettable music emulating through the speakers inside the confined space, kept her company for the ride. The goldfish swimming in the tank built into one of the elevator walls was over the top, but fascinating to watch. It kept her fellow passengers quiet watching as well. Not a bad thing. Too early in the morning for small talk.

On the seventh floor, she got out and hurried down the hall. Deanna's office was listed as 705 in the building's directory. She knocked. A voice called out to enter.

Upon opening the door, she was greeted by the

sight of Deanna sitting at her typewriter behind a small desk. The click-clacking of the keys striking the white paper she was working on completed the picture of a woman hard at work. Impressive so early in the morning.

"Hey, hon, come in. I'm nearly finished." The woman's fingers danced over the keys as she frowned at the old standard black typewriter. Claire sat down on one of the two wooden chairs available to visitors. Other than a corkboard, a plant that had seen better days, and a bottle of water, the room was empty.

"Okay. Done." Deanna sat back and yanked the page out of the device. She placed it beside the bemouth. "What can I do for you, Claire?"

"Thanks for seeing me. It's about Serena." She hesitated, unsure how to ask now that she was there.

"Of course. Go on." The woman was dressed in a black pencil skirt and a long-sleeved white shirt, the picture of efficiency with her flame-red hair pulled back into a low bun with a pencil tucked inside.

"When we were at the party, you mentioned that Elle often leads her clients into uncomfortable situations, in efforts to obtain parts?"

"Yeah, I've seen a bit too much over the years."

"Serena was attacked at the party."

Deanna scratched her nose. "I was advised of that. Terrible thing. You think it's connected to her disappearance?"

"Hard to believe it isn't, considering how soon after she disappeared? I was wondering if you can tell me anything from the party that might help?"

She shrugged. "I didn't see much that night. Only talked to a few people. I may not be the one with the answers that can help you."

"You know what Hollywood's capable of more than anyone I know."

"You got that right. Say, did Dr. Vogel ever contact Jake Sterling about his interest in hiring him?"

"Not that I know of? Why?"

"Just wondering."

"Did someone give him the information?"

"You had thanked Elle for suggesting Jake, and he was on it like white on rice."

"Thanks. That's interesting." She filed it away. Every little detail gleamed was important to a PI. That much she had learned about the profession already. "Did you mention this to anyone else?"

"No, I don't think so. Didn't seem relevant to Serena's case. Why? Do you think it's connected?"

"No idea."

"Well, you be careful."

"Thanks, I will."

"If that's all, I gotta get this down to Fred. The guy's been after me already this morning." Deanna grimaced and picked up the page she'd recently typed again.

"Sure." Claire got up and offered her hand to the woman. "Thanks for seeing me."

"Let me know what you find out about Serena, okay? Anything at all. I know she's your friend, but it's news too."

It was Claire's turn to make a face. "I know. And you do need to warn others if something amiss is going on."

"Exactly, though we don't run a public service here, I do what I can."

Claire let herself out and headed for her car. Time to speak to her partner.

A short while later she pulled up in front of Sterling Investigations. Hmm, maybe one day it would read

Preston & Sterling? The thought made her smile as she scrambled out of the bug. She locked the car door, then looked up to catch a glimpse of a man leaving Jake's office. He had a familiar look to him and when he caught her checking him out, he ducked his head and limped quickly away.

She frowned, then crossed the sidewalk and pushed open the front door. Mae wasn't in evidence yet, so she ventured further inside and knocked on the inner door.

"Come in."

"What's your name?" Bishop greeted her first. Jake was busy making a pot of coffee, his back to her.

"Morning, Bishop. Tell your boss that Claire's here to see him."

"Morning." Jake returned her smile. "Coffee?"

"Please." She fed Bishop a few sunflower seeds before taking the cup Jake offered her. She took a deep satisfying breath of the steam emulating from the rich brown liquid, enjoying the lovely fragrance of invigorating beans.

She sat down across from Jake and eyed him over the rim. "Who was that man that just limped out of here?"

"A client. Well, former client. Why?"

"He looked familiar. I can't place him. You said former?"

"I had to turn down the case. I can't fit it in what with Serena missing and heated developments in your case. I did get him started in the right direction though with some sage advice. I'll give him this, he took it well. Actually, surprised me *how* well. Maybe I'm losing my edge?" Jake took a sip of his coffee, his eyes thoughtful.

"My case?"

Jake cleared his throat. "Yeah, last night I talked to an agent at the FBI, Connor Mann. Learned something new. Seems your case is one hot potato. So much so that Mann's advising us to leave it alone."

"Will we?"

"Hell no!"

Claire almost snorted coffee through her nose. She set the half-empty cup down. "What do you think it means? Is this is tied to that guy in the photo with my mother?"

"Probably. Obviously, the bureau has something to hide. After the war, a lot of Nazis made it out of Germany as refugees. Lots of countries took them in, some inadvertently due to false identity cards and letters of reference, others wanting to access their knowledge in science and medicine. Shortly after the Second World War, the Cold War began, and it changed the political focus drastically. The allies wanted to keep the knowledge out of the hands of the Russians, so we got into bed with the snakes."

"You think the guy in the photo's a spy?"

Jake shrugged. "Could be."

"But what would that have to do with my mother?"

"I don't know. Maybe she discovered what was going on, left you in the orphanage for safe keeping, and hid out somewhere?"

"But then why didn't she come back to see her family? Surely she could have done that without his knowledge?"

"He knew where her family—your family lived. Maybe he threatened her about exposing them or harming them in some way?"

"God, I hope I'm not related to that creep."

"I know, some stones are best left unturned."

For the first time regrets for starting on the journey filled her. But then she thought of her great-grandmother and the pressure eased. It was worth it to have a little time with her.

"What now?" Claire asked.

"Want to take a little drive? I always wanted to see a movie ranch."

"The Spahn ranch? Sure. By the way I went and talked with Deanna St. James from The Tattler this morning. She didn't know much, though she's worried about Serena same as we are. She's quite tuned in to this city. Worries about what it does to people."

"Doesn't keep her from writing those speculative stories."

"My guess is she has to make a living like the rest of us. That reminds me. She mentioned that the doctor at the studio, Dr. Vogel, wanted to hire you. Have you heard from him?"

"No. And no time now to start a new case, so it's for the best." Jake came around from behind his desk. "Ready to go?"

"Sure. Bye-bye, Bishop," she said, giving the friendly parrot a wave.

"Bye-Bye, Bishop. *Vengeance is mine sayeth the Lord.*"

Claire laughed. "That's one clever parrot you got there, Jake."

"Yeah, he's a laugh a minute."

CHAPTER 24
TOO HOT TO HANDLE

THE ARID ODOR OF SMOKE THAT HAD DECREASED OVER LA in the past twenty-four hours began to increase again the closer Jake drove them north toward the ranch in the Simi Hills. He found himself focusing more and more on his worry about the young girl and the baby, concerned that the smoke and living conditions weren't up to code even as he filled his own lungs with the stuff from his favorite Export A cigarettes. He recognized the irony but ignored it. One of his foibles, more worried about others than himself. When he turned the Mustang onto the 118 and headed east to Chatsworth, the air became hazy ahead with particles of smoke and ash.

"Bloody smoke's a hazard," he said.

"You're worried about the baby."

It wasn't a question. He glanced at Claire, noting the concern riding high in her expression. She looked lovely today in her casual yet chic outfit, something he knew better than to mention. If indeed they were to become working partners, best to keep everything professional. But impossible to miss the treat for his eyes which seldom were gifted with such a view sitting so close. He particularly enjoyed the elegant lines of her long neck, and the way she had of holding her head in a certain way as if she expected the earth to speak to her. It was endearing and maddening at the same time.

"Yeah. It's getting thicker. It's the wind, it's blowing this way from the fire."

Twenty minutes later, they turned off the highway onto a narrow dirt laneway at the signpost for 1200 Santa Susana Pass Road. The first thing they saw when the few stunted trees vanished at a curve in the road was a few Volkswagen bugs, most appearing to have been heavily modified to look like dune buggies.

"The followers of this Charlie must be into mechanics. They've been busy rascals," he said, taking a look around as he drove up to the main house. The rest of the buildings were rustic, relics of another era. Cowboys versus rustlers and bankers. Human nature never changes. He could well understand the call of adventure to living at such a location.

"I guess it makes sense, dune buggies in the desert."

Suddenly a group of a dozen or more people spilled out from one of the rustic buildings, everyone long-haired and jean-clad. Some wearing love beads. Most of them broke away into smaller groups of two or three, headed to what looked like a stable. Jack was aware that procuring trail rides was the way the ranch stayed afloat. Two other people, a man and a woman, began to stride quickly toward the Mustang. He didn't see the woman and her baby anywhere. Maybe she was still in town begging for funds to keep this ragtag group from starving? He hadn't seen her on the Strip today, so he hoped to run into her on the property. Check on her welfare.

"Looks like we have company."

"You wait here. I'll talk to them," he said. Claire didn't

look happy about it, but she didn't complain, just giving him the leery eye.

He got out and pasted on a smile. "Hi, I'm Jake Sterling. I met one of your members the other day and she said to come out anytime, that we have a permanent invitation to visit y'all and break bread."

"That so. Who was it you spoke to?" The greasy-haired sun-burned man asked, tugging at the light-brown straggle that did nothing to enhance his weak chin. Dusty Roman sandals scuffed at the dry ground, raising little poofs of dust with feet that were an undeterminable color. Last time he checked; soap was only pennies a bar.

"She called herself Sunshine. And she had her baby with her. Cute little duffer. I gave her some money."

"Money? How much money?"

"The first time a pair of Jacksons."

"You got more of those?" the man asked, before coughing up and spitting a splash of phlegm on the ground.

"Possibly. Business pays good."

"What business is that?"

His female partner stood quietly at his side, her eyes darting around in a thin ferret face. Her lank brown hair was parted in the middle and hung down well past the middle of her back. It was obvious she had no bra on under the light-colored top she wore, especially when she stretched her back like a cat to draw attention to her assets.

"I'm in the business of helping people."

"I'll see if Charlie wants to talk with you. Who's the girl?" He nodded toward his car.

"An acquaintance."

"Very pretty girl. She looking to help us too?"

Jake twisted his lips in an effort to avoid spilling out something that would get them driven off the ranch before he could even begin to discover anything. The predatory look in the hippie's eyes told the tale. The female squinted over at Claire, looking disgruntled by her partner's astute observation.

"No, only me."

"You'd stand a better chance you brought her along with ya. Wait here."

The man turned and strode over to the wooden boardwalk before vanishing inside one of the larger buildings. The saloon doors that guarded the opening swung smartly in the wind created by Mr. Clean pushing it open with a show of force. The building looked properly authentic for a cowboy movie shoot. He could see Sheriff Matt Dillon and Miss Kitty of Gunsmoke fame having one of their awkward meets inside.

"You looking to join up with us?" the ragged girl asked, sticking a questionable finger into her mouth and squinting up at him.

"Looking to check if Sunshine and her baby are doing okay?"

"Sure, they are. Charlie loves babies. Everyone knows that!" The girl looked offended, like he's tried to tarnish the Madonna.

"Good to know. Are they any other babies out here?"

She shrugged. "Yeah, a couple. They're doing fine too. Charlie wants lots more babies, raised by all of us. He knows that parents are up to no good. We need to raise the babies together."

"Interesting philosophy. Charlie's quite the man."

"He sure is. Knows more than *anybody*. He's all about getting us to know ourselves. Stripping away our egos and being true to our basic nature. Sends us on trips to work it out. You ever been on a happy, happy trip, mister?"

He assumed she meant LSD. "No, other than driving my Mustang around. But you do provide an excellent character reference."

She sniffed and squinted her eyes up at him again. "You don't wear glasses?"

"No, why?"

"Charlie don't allow no glasses. Keeps us from being true to our nature. Charlie's so out there. He knows, man, he knows."

Explained a lot. The poor girl kept squinting because she couldn't see well. Sometimes nature sucked.

His attention was taken by the saloon doors swinging opening. Out strode a short, slightly disheveled looking man in fancy buckskins tied together with leather thongs. His short statue surprised him, but the panther-like walk did not. A few steps behind walked the other guy.

The shorter man strode right over, glanced with approval at Claire still sitting in his Mustang, then peered at Jake. Up close the man had such dark brown eyes they appeared almost black. His head appeared large for his body, like his growth had been stunted somehow. Lack of nutrition? His worry for Sunshine and her baby surfaced again. He'd put up with this shite to gain knowledge of the pair.

"Welcome to paradise, Jake Sterling," he said, holding out his hand. "Are you ready?"

"For what?" Jake shook the offered appendage. The shake was firm at least.

Charlie gestured wide with his hands, pointing at nothing and everything. "For understanding the beginning of it all being over. For accepting the new truth."

"Never had trouble with the truth. *The truth will set you free.*" Bishop would be proud.

"John 8:32."

"You read the Bible?"

"Only book Charlie allows," squinty-eyed gal chimed in, looking far more pleased by the revelation than a thinking individual would find rational.

"All you need. The good book tells all." He gestured with his hands held wide, an animated expression making squinty-eyed gal near swoon with appreciation.

"Charlie knows all," she said, in case he was hard of hearing.

"I can see that. Then perhaps you can tell me how Sunshine and her baby are doing?"

"First, I want to meet the girl you brought. We have no secrets around here. Everyone shares in all things," Charlie said.

"Fine. If I can talk with your girl?"

"Sunshine's out on a food run. Should be back soon," taller guy added, directing the intel chiefly at Charlie.

Charlie nodded. "Good. You are both invited to stay for dinner with us. Share our humble repast."

"You must make good money here or get a lot of donations?" Jake wasn't agreeing to a meal without knowing more about the operation. He wouldn't subject Claire to food that was of questionable quality.

"Charlie provides everything we need," the girl said with pride.

"Nice setup. Where do you purchase your foodstuffs?"

"No need to buy. The land provides. Ever looked inside a garbage bin? It's a crime the amount of food thrown away. Wasted. We live well without having to pay the company man," Charlie said, his expression smug.

Right. No way was he subjecting Claire to garbage bin food. But maybe an introduction wouldn't harm anyone. If he stalled for time, maybe Sunshine would get back soon and he could have a talk with her. Make sure she knew what she was doing hooking up with this group.

But before he could gesture to Claire to join them, a commotion broke out.

A loud explosion reverberated in the air. Smoke began to pour from one of the buildings. Screams and shouts followed.

Stunned for a second, no one moved.

Then Jake started running. He observed a few people stumbling from the wooden structure near the end of the lot and he rushed toward them. Everyone was coughing and shambling about in a daze. Probably concussed.

His heart pounding, he came upon the first person. The young woman was disorientated, pale, her eyes widened by shock. She was trembling badly, her hair in wild disarray.

He realized someone was right behind him and he turned to find the taller man looking worried and gazing about as if he needed instructions on what to do.

"Do you have any blankets?"

"Sadie, go and get some blankets," he instructed the young girl with that had fawned over Charlie. She took off running back to the main house.

Charlie hurried past him at that moment, going up to one of the men who stood stunned nearby. "What happened?"

"I don't know."

Fire was now visible. Hungry fingers licked out through the blown windows and at the roof of the building. A loud crack of thunder nearby made everyone jump. Claire joined him and held a blanket out. He recognized it as the car blanket he kept in the back seat. He took it and he tucked it around the young woman, pulling it over her shoulders.

"You're going to be okay. What's your name?"

"Lyn...ette. Wha...what's yours?"

"Jake. This is Claire."

The woman nodded. Her teeth were chattering with enough power to break them. The odor of ozone permeated the air, only adding to the thickness of the lingering smoke.

Suddenly, a darkness moved in. Cold air rushed to follow. He looked up to observe a rare fall storm bearing down on them at punishing speed. He panned his view further to the right and saw Charlie with his hands raised in supposition. *Phttt*, opportunist. Low rumbles reverberated all around them. He felt the hair rise up on his scalp. Looked over to see Claire's red hair rising as well, creating a wild halo around her beautiful face. A sheet of lightning erupted, a dazzling display of power, giving everyone an eerie appearance. A surrealness that a film director would be hard pressed to capture.

"Rain! Rain! Rain!" the wannabee god cried to the blackened sky. His followers stood and watched their leader with awe. Each face, when highlighted by the near continuous lightning, beatified by wonder. *Give me a break. Mother nature beat him by a country mile.*

Loud peals of thunder continued to crack the air at an alarming rate. Silhouettes leaped and writhed on all sides, everything looking strangely distorted. Then a chain of spectacular thunderbolts rent the sky in two.

Seemed Thor was beyond angry. Being caught out in it made no sense.

"We need to get everyone inside. Now!"

He turned to help those in need and felt the sting of burning pain on his upper arm.

What the hell!

Rain began to pound down on them. Entirely predictable. He was soaked through to the skin in mere seconds. A veil of water obscured the land, making him blink harder in efforts to see. He grabbed Claire by the hand and pulled her along toward the Mustang. Time to get out of Dodge. They'd have to visit Sunshine and her baby another day.

CHAPTER 25
COOL WHIP PLUS

CLAIRE SLAMMED THE CAR DOOR SHUT AGAINST THE deluge. Then winced. "Sorry. I know how much you love this car."

He shrugged. "More worried about you, kiddo. You're shivering." He turned the heater on full blast. She thrust the wet hair away from her face and swiped the water off her dripping nose. She'd given their only blanket away so he had nothing to wrap around her. Beyond the windscreen nothing could be seen. Water drops pelted the land.

"Kid?" She gave him a look. "I'm not that much younger than you."

"You're what, twenty-one?"

She nodded.

"I'm thirty-three. Thirty-four next January."

"The age Christ was when he died," she said. Then realized it was a strange statement. Must be due to that Charlie guy acting so weird. She didn't have to hear all his words, just watch his pantomimes. Like he knew it all. Yeah, *right*. No one does. Least of all a god wannabee.

"I think our Charlie would prefer to be the one compared to Jesus."

"No doubt." She rubbed her bare arms. Her goose bumps had goose bumps. "I hope it lets up soon. I would love to get away from here."

"At least the rain has put out the fire. I wonder what the heck happened there?"

"Someone using propane?" Claire suggested.

"Maybe. Or doing something illegal? Like making drugs or storing weapons."

A loud knock on the passenger side window made her about leap out of the seat. She rolled it down a few inches to see Charlie's face leering in at her.

"Rain is God's gift. You must be Claire."

"Yes. You must be Charlie."

His face split in a wide grin. "At your service, milady. Stopping by to tell you to come inside."

"Sorry, we can't. Got to get back to town. I need to feed my dog." Lame, but it was all she could come up with looking at spooky guy. With his hair plastered to his head, his eyes looked far too large for his face. They were mesmerizing in their striking intensity.

"That's too bad. The invite stays open. You come back and visit with us. Anytime, Claire. I would *love* to share the word with you. Spend time with you, because time's running out. Soon it will be too late. Everything will *cease to exist.*"

"Thanks. I'll keep that in mind. Do you know what caused the explosion and fire?"

He made an expressive face, contorting his features in an odd way. "No idea. But I know who caused the rain and saved the day!"

Right. Was this guy full enough of himself? "Good timing. Bye, Charlie."

She rolled up the window and watched the man do a strange kind of arms-raised-to-the-sky-dance from the vehicle. Certifiable.

"Interesting fellow," Jake deadpanned.

She laughed. Then sneezed. Shivering, she hugged her body with her arms. The heater helped, but wet clothing was wet clothing.

"Let's get you home."

She looked at him and froze. His shirt was wet with more than just rain. And he had what looked like a burn hole in the sleeve. "Good grief, you're bleeding!"

Jake tore the existing hole in his shirt sleeve wider, exposing a long, angry, horizontal crease across his upper bicep.

"I'm not too popular today. Good thing whoever it was is a lousy shot."

"That's nothing to joke about. They could have killed you!" Her worries spilled over and she heard her voice crack with emotion. She liked Jake, finding him one of the good guys who wanted to catch the bad guys in the act. He'd come all the way out to Spahn ranch today to check on the girl he'd only met twice for a few brief minutes. And then she only wanted to rip him off and take his money. Then she remembered the baby and admitted she would panhandle or most anything to see a child of hers looked after, if it came to that.

"I'm fine, Claire. It's only a flesh wound. I have a medical kit in the glove box."

She opened it as instructed and pulled out the small white box with the red cross branded on the lid. Inside she found two types of antiseptics, and a large variety of compresses and bandages.

"This happen often?" she asked. "You seem prepared."

"On occasion." He shrugged. "PI business can be

dangerous. But this is the first time I've been shot at since I left the force. It's usually just fisticuffs."

"*Just.* Good grief, Jake, that's crazy." She tore open a package containing a compress, added some peroxide to the pad, and pressed it to the bleeding wound. The bullet had dug a good sized furrow, taking a chunk of skin and flesh with it. She held it there to stem the flow of blood.

The rain had dampened his hair and clothing, and seeing him more vulnerable, yet still confident and joking, tugged at her heartstrings. She swallowed, averting her eyes. The odor of smoke emanated from both of them, their clothes reeking of it, the fragrance of soap or cologne long gone. But even with the stench of smoke, he was nice to be around.

When the area was clean and dry, she applied a large bandage, sticking it firmly to his upper arm, making sure the wound was entirely covered.

"Thanks. You make a fine nurse, kid. Helpful in this business. Though I imagine you might be having grave doubts about now. No pun intended." He smiled crookedly.

"No doubts at all. I want in, *Dad*. Big time. I'll take self-defense courses and learn how to shoot straight. You can teach me. Dads are great teachers."

He groaned. "Don't call me *dad* and I won't call you kid."

"Deal. How about Preston and Sterling? We can even put up a sign."

"Preston and Sterling. Shouldn't that be Sterling and Preston?"

"Preston and Sterling sounds better." She quirked her lips, more than pleased with her cheeky suggestion.

"The rain's letting up." He turned and looked at her with a serious expression. "I need to tell them about the threat, in case it means something. We can't ignore this. But I need your promise that you'll wait here. Do I have it?"

"Okay." She really didn't want to face that weird crew again anyway. The vibes given off by them gave her the creeps. Far too much adulation for her liking.

"And lock the doors."

"Yes, *Dad*."

He shot her a look and got out of the Mustang, then waited for her to do as he asked. She locked the doors and gave him the roll of the eyes signal.

She sat and watched the rain drip off drenched foliage. At least the fire appeared to be totally out. Only black burn streaks marred the side and roof of the building facing her. She was grateful it hadn't spread. Last thing they needed was another fire started, spreading deadly consequences into the area that was normally dry as a tinderbox this time of year.

Jake was back and banging on the driver's door, catching her off guard. She unlocked his door and he joined her in the front seat.

"I should drive. You've got a wounded wing."

"It's nothing. I'm fine."

"What did they say about your being shot?"

"Not much. Seemed unconcerned. Strange crew." He shook his head with what looked like frustration. "But at least they've been warned."

He started the Mustang's motor and made a quick U-turn to take them back down the lane to the highway. The grounds were deserted. Jake stopped before the turn just as a beat-up old brown van slowed down to turn onto the ranch road from the opposite direction.

He honked the horn and the van pulled alongside them. In the front seat sat the woman they called

Sunshine. Another young girl sat in the passenger seat holding the sleeping baby in her arms. A third girl sat perched between the seats. They looked a lot alike with center-parted hair styles, thin faces, and simple clothing choices. Not appearing happy exactly, but not sad either. More neutral and watchful. Whereas Claire knew if she were the one having to come back to this ranch, she's be looking more than pissed. Charlie was nothing but a hound dog. And some sniper in the hills was taking potshots at them.

Jake rolled down the window. Claire moved forward in her seat to see better around him. "Sunshine, good to see you," he said in a cheerful tone of voice.

"Hey, man, I know you. Jake-o. You come out to break bread with us? We got lots of Cool Whip this trip. A whole case. Yummy stuff. And even some salad and cheese bread. Good haul. Plenty to go around. And maybe Charlie will even bless us with a song or two on his guitar tonight. He's *really* good. One day he'll be famous, you know. He wrote a song, 'Cease to Exist.' It's going to be important. Everyone the whole world over will know Charlie, when it's released."

"Love to but we've got an appointment with the man in town. You understand. We did meet up with your Charlie though."

Sunshine's eyes lit up with a fervor that frightened Claire.

"Isn't he everything I said he was! He knows, man."

"Yes, he knows all right."

Claire admired how well Jake handled it, sounding nothing but interested.

"How are you doing? Is the baby okay?" he asked. His expression turned pensive.

Sunshine smiled widely. "Baby's fine. Sweet, happy, baby."

Her answer made Claire wonder if the baby was named Baby?

"That's good to hear. You know, I do want you to call me if you need something. You know that, right?"

Claire grabbed one of Jake's business cards from the dash, found a pencil in the glove box, then scribbled her name and number on the back.

"Give her this. It has my phone number on the back."

The girl took the card from his outstretched hands and tucked it in her blouse. "Sure, Jake-o. Thanks. But we got to get moving. Everyone's always hungry. I mean, before we feed them." She obviously didn't want them thinking poorly of them.

Sunshine waved a hand at them as she drove away, lurching down the potholed road made worse from the recent driving rain.

"What do you think, Jake-o?" she asked.

He frowned at her use of the nickname. "I think it's a complicated mess that needs ironing out."

"Yeah, sorry I was so flippant. Won't happen again, boss."

He smiled. "Boss has a ring to it."

"So does Preston and Sterling."

He smiled wider. "That it does, Claire-o."

"Okay, okay, Jake and Claire it is. You look pretty good for a guy who's been shot."

"How about we check in at the office? See if there are any new developments?"

How could she be joking about with Jake with her friend missing? It was wrong. Reality hit her straight between the eyes. "Right." She began to chew on a finger-nail, once more imagining the worst.

"It's okay to keep the world at bay with off-the-cuff comments, Claire. Sometimes that's the only thing keeping you sane. Mash units do it all the time, police departments, emergency departments—because it works. Don't lose that precious sense of humor. It maybe all you have between you and the darkness."

The perspective helped. "Yeah, I could see that."

They settled into a companionable silence for the drive back to LA. Claire kept wondering what caused people to want to join with someone who wanted to tell them how to live their lives, turning all their control over to someone like Charlie? But mostly she worried about finding Serena. Who had taken her? And for what sick purpose?

CHAPTER 26
A GUN SHOT FROM THE GRASSY KNOLL

IT WAS TIME. HE SHIFTED FROM THE PRONE POSITION AND stretched out farther on his stomach, moving his body slightly forward.

He'd held the stance for the past half hour with the rifle braced on bipod legs, situated on top of a deadgrass knoll not far from the movie set. The people screaming and streaming out of the old saloon as the explosion went off right on schedule made him almost smile. Perfect. He spat out his now tasteless gum onto the ground dried to powder by the harsh Southern California sunshine, the air percolating with ozone fumes. A storm was brewing, off to the west he could see darkened skies. It was moving fast, making him feel the urge to hurry his actions.

He squinted through the scope. His vantage point, reconnoitered weeks ago, gave an unobstructed view yet offered ample protection against discovery. His finger froze in place on the trigger as he waited. Scumbags like this ragtag group needed a wake-up call. The Family indeed. More like deficient sub-humans joining together to create chaos. Not that such a group would ever be able to pull off much, they didn't have the brains for it. They had enough trouble just keeping themselves fed. He'd seen the girls begging for handouts. Disgusting behavior.

The outside world silenced. Firing a rifle over such a long distance was a confluence of many things: chemistry, mechanical engineering, optics, geophysics, and meteorology—all taught to him by an excellent marksman in his former army. A man he'd admired for his complete and utter dedication to the Third Reich's vision. Thanks to Heiner, he knew the exact distance he needed to aim above the target to allow for the curvature of the Earth and the pull of gravity to put the bullet exactly where he wanted it to go. He now aimed the muzzle above the target to assist nature in curving the bullet downward to find its loathsome target. Charles Milles Manson.

Then a new development stopped him.

A man he recognized appeared in his scope sights. That nosy private investigator, Jake Sterling.

His mind divided. Which one?

Then he realized it was obvious. Now only ancient biology stood in the way. He slowed his heart rate, breathed in and out, waiting between heartbeats. The roaring in his ears ceased as his brain calmed. The vibrations of his physical body lessened.

His forefinger squeezed gently on the trigger. He breathed out. One heartbeat. Another heartbeat. A third heartbeat. He fired just as a thunderclap rent the sky, spoiling his aim as his body jerked slightly backward.

The bullet was now off target and spinning outward at fifteen hundred feet a second, its hand-polished copper jacket flying straight and true to the exact wrong spot. The heavy sound of the shot cracked and echoed in

the air a half second later. He accepted the instant reper-
cussion in his shoulder from the stock of the rifle. The
odor of sulfur instantly filled his airways, the gun hot
from the recoil burning his hands.

An intense anger consumed him. He'd only winged
his target, but before he could reload, the flood hit. A
harsh rain that instantly make it almost impossible to see
even a few feet in front of him.

He quickly set to work putting the rifle back in its
secure carrier. No doubt he'd get another opportunity.
*The opportunity of defeating the enemy is provided by the
enemy himself.*

197

CHAPTER 27
TEMPERATURES RISING

JAKE PICKED UP THE OFFICE PHONE AND MADE THE CALL, aware that Claire was hovering at his shoulder, antsy for news of Serena. They'd made a little side trip to her apartment for clean clothes while he'd changed into spare clothes he kept in the trunk of his car. Another lesson in the business of always being prepared. He had a lot of information to share on the subject, and for the first time since his wife had died, he found he wanted very much for that to happen. To mentor someone until they became a full partner may be the price of a ticket to letting go of the past.

"LAPD. Detective Bachman."

"Afternoon, Ted. Jake here. Any news on the Serena Sands case?"

A huge sigh answered the question without the words that followed. "We got nothing. All leads have been going nowhere. Worst case scenario I've seen in years."

"Is there anything I can do to help? Do you need more manpower?"

"It's not only a question of manpower though Lord

knows we always need more of that, it's a question of dead ends. No one saw anything or they're not talking. The van was stolen, but no one saw anything. It was abandoned, and no one saw anything. Only person to see something was that guy at the apartment and he didn't see his face. We do have round the clock surveillance on Constanza."

"Okay. And there's something else." He explained events at the ranch.

"We might want to do a welfare check on the children. Thanks for the heads up, Jake. I'll be in touch."

He set the phone down. "Sorry, nothing yet."

"Is that normal? Things taking so long?"

"Every case varies. No guarantees."

"I can't sit around waiting for something to happen! I'm going crazy with worry."

"I know. It sucks."

The phone rang. He picked it up. "Sterling and Preston." He earned a slight smile for his troubles.

"Jake? Who's Preston?" Agent Mann asked.

"My soon-to-be partner. You'll like her. You got something for me, Connor?"

"She?"

"I'm all about equal opportunity."

"Right." Slight hesitation before he continued. "That guy we talked about? He says he'll meet with you. Tonight. Same place, same time."

"You going to be there?"

"Wouldn't miss it for the world."

He hung up and filled Claire in. She listened, before bestowing on him a look filled with meaning. "You should have your arm checked out by a doctor."

"Why bother. Nothing to stitch up and it will only lead to a lot of questions. I have extra medical supplies in the office and a guy down the street if it comes to it."

"Okay, you know best." The twitch of her lips suggested her true feelings on the subject were most likely being repressed. "What's next?"

"Headed downtown to talk with my guy in real estate to discuss land maps and titles. The shot came from the west or southwest, far as I can figure. I want to see who else lives close by. Maybe your Dr. Vogel was sending a message to the hippies next door and hit me by accident in that freak storm, or maybe it was another disgruntled neighbor? I want to see the layout and the different properties involved. And grab a bite to eat on the way."

"Let's go then."

Bishop woke up, fluffed, and settled his wings, then noticed he had a visitor.

"*Hell-o Gorgeous. Hell-o Gorgeous,*" he announced with glee, trying to get Claire's attention.

"I should start calling him Bishop Two-times." The smile that spread across Claire's beautiful face was thanks enough.

"Hello, Bishop. You're looking fine today. You're gorgeous yourself, you big awesome bird you." He watched her head over to feed the preening scoundrel a few sunflower seeds, which was Bishop's hoped for intention.

"Have a nice day, Bishop," Claire added with a small wave goodbye before exiting the office.

Mae looked up from her desk, a pencil tucked behind her ear, her expression distracted. She was busy working on the mountain of paperwork that consumed most of her day.

"Mae, we're headed downtown to see George Lamb.

I'll be awhile. I'll check back with you in a couple of hours in case anyone calls."

"Will do. I need to head over to the bank sometime this afternoon, but it shouldn't take too long. I have to pick up some more ready cash." She gave him *the look*.

"Thanks. I'll try to make it last longer."

Mae chuckled. "Right."

Steamy heat rose from the blistering pavement in waves as he opened the front door for Claire, hitting them like a blast furnace. He took a deep breath. But at least the smoke had let up, meaning the fire must be coming under better control.

He opened the car door for Claire, earning another significant look, then walked around the front of the Mustang and slide into the driver's seat.

"Blame my mother if you must. She was a stickler for etiquette rules."

"It's fine. Do you see your parent's much?"

He shrugged and started up the vehicle. The instant purr of the well-maintained motor offered satisfaction every time. "Couple of times a year. But I get lots of phone calls."

"I should call my grandmother later. Go and see her soon."

"Good idea. I'll drive you if you like."

"Thanks. But you're busy."

"Always got time for you." He headed the Mustang into traffic, dismayed to find it already near rush hour capacity. He checked his wristwatch.

"Can you wait to eat until after we check in with George at Lamb's Real Estate? This traffic's going to hold us up."

"Sure."

"Jake, how do we know this is going to help us find Serena?"

"We don't. But I've learned that you can't know what's most important. All you can do is follow up all the leads. Do you believe in coincidence, Claire?"

"Not really. I'm more of the things-happen-for a-reason school of thought."

"Right. Cause and effect. Being shot at is important on some level. The police have Limp Willie under surveillance, so if he's involved, they'll know. Even though he thinks he's above the law like lots of these puffed-up Hollywood types, he'll find out that's a myth when it comes to LAPD's finest."

"Limp Willie?" Claire erupted into peels of laughter. "I love it!"

Jake grinned at her. "It was a bit more than our Mr. William Costanza could handle. Now, I could have called George Lamb instead of driving across town for this meet. But it's good for you to connect with the network needed for this job. Remember, a personal visit always beats a phone call if it can be arranged. Especially if you don't see them very often. That way, you can remind them they owe you. Far easier to do that in person."

"What do you have on poor George?"

"Old George needed a cheapie divorce a few years back to marry his pregnant mistress. Third divorce. I was able to sleuth out his wife was also having an elicit affair. Allowed him to keep his business intact."

"I would think divorces are the bread and butter of agencies."

"Yeah, they are. Especially in this town. Seems every movie shoot, someone falls for the magic and gets involved with someone they shouldn't. Just like partners in a business should always keep it professional." He slid in the intel while watching out for a park spot, having driven around the block twice in efforts to secure one.

"Yes, professional works for me."

He wasn't certain if he was happy, she agreed so quickly, or wished he'd kept his damn mouth shut.

"People need to start sharing rides again like they did after the war in those car clubs my dad used to talk about," he grumbled. "Two and a half million of us and everyone wants their own ride."

"Your dad served in the war?"

"Yeah, never talked about it much though. Most servicemen came back stateside and got into the business of living again. Got this country going so that we can be free to choose. One person in a car. Or not."

"Yeah, this city's half mad in their need to be free-wheeling. I'm guilty too. Maybe we should always try to take the same vehicle, Jake, on a stakeout or otherwise? Like today?"

The thought of long hours cooped up with Claire was appealing, if not practical.

"Maybe."

They disembarked and hurried inside the tall building of which the bottom floor was dedicated in its entirety to the real estate business, ignoring the stifling heat of the late day.

"Hey, Jake, long time no see buddy!" George Lamb strode right over to greet them, his booming personality out front and center. His high Elvis hair and long side-burns were in perfect order as was his choice of clothing: wide-label houndstooth's sports jacket and wide-legged pants. The white faux leather shoes might have been a bit over the top but at least they matched his belt. "And who is this beautiful lady? You been holding out on me?"

"George Lamb, I'd like you to meet Claire Preston. We're working a case together."

George took her hand and kissed the back of it in an exaggerated gesture, lingering over the moment. "It's lovely to meet you, *Miss* Claire Preston, I presume, seeing no wedding ring?"

"Nice to meet you. No, I'm not married." Claire handled George's pushy inquisitive nature with aplomb.

"Engaged? Boyfriend? Significant other?"

Trust George to push it too far. Perhaps he should have driven here alone today? He eyed George with a bit more annoyance. Was the guy pushing for a fourth divorce?

Claire shook her head with a snort of laughter. "No, none of the above."

"*I can feel my temperature rising!*" George sang being a little too fond of the very slight similarity between him and Presley, before adding, "Come to the back. I've got a nice selection of drinks if you'd care to partake?"

Claire leaned in and whispered. "I can only hope he's not as much as a hound dog as the singer is rumored to be."

Jake struggled to keep a straight face as George led them into his office.

"A club soda would be great," she said to George, standing at the mini bar.

Smart girl.

"What will you have, Jake?"

"Same."

George raised his eyebrows, but poured the drinks requested. Then poured himself three fingers of top shelf scotch.

He handed them each a heavy-bottomed glass and gestured for them to have a seat. The office looked the same as always. Spacious and uncluttered. A photo of George's sailboat decorated the wall behind his desk. Probably to remind him why he needed to work and squeeze out every penny.

Jake sat back in the fine leather chair and took a good swig of the soda before setting it down on a coaster atop the desk. Claire did the same. He watched her give the office a good perusal.

"Nice boat, George. Do you sail much?" she asked.

"Every weekend I can. Do you like boats, Claire?" He leaned forward on his desk like her answer was the most important thing he'd hear all day long, never taking his eyes off her for a second. One of George's strong suits was his interest in others. Sold a lot of real estate. Caused a lot of divorces. An unfortunate side-effect.

"As it happens, yes. Not that I've ever had much opportunity to go sailing."

"We must rectify that. This weekend. Say you'll come out on the water with me? You too Jake, if you want?" The second part of the invite wasn't nearly as sincere as the first part.

"We're here because Claire's friend is missing," Jake said before Claire got a chance to answer.

"I am truly sorry to hear it. Can I help in anyway?"

"As a matter of fact, you can. I was shot at today. Just a graze. Out on the Spahn Movie ranch, where they used to shoot westerns. And we need to know who owns the property around it."

"Glad to see you're in one piece, buddy. Yeah, I can look into it for you. That ranch covers about fifty-five acres if I'm not mistaken. Nice piece of real estate. If you like horses and scorpions."

"Heck of a thunder and lightning show there yesterday," Claire added.

"That so? Hope it didn't set more fires." George took a long swallow of his scotch and set the glass aside.

"I don't think so, a monsoon hit right after," Jake added.

The phone rang on the desk. "Excuse me a moment." He picked up the receiver. "Lamb real estate for all your family needs. George speaking."

"Uh-uh. It's for you, Jake."

George handed the phone over with a frown. "Something about a fire at your office?"

"What?" Jake grabbed the receiver. "What's going on?" he barked into the phone.

"Jake, it's Mae. Bad news I'm afraid. When I came back from the bank the office was already on fire. I called the fire department, but it looks really bad, smoke pouring out of the windows."

"Are you okay? Is Bishop, okay?"

The line went quiet. The longest few seconds of his life. Then Mae spoke again.

"I'm fine, but Bishop's missing. I could use a little help here." Her normally calm and patient tone crackled with panic.

Jake closed his eyes. "I'm on my way." How the hell had that happened? Two fires in two days were no coincidence. Something huge was going on and it drove him mad not to know what it was. He tamped down his anger that he could not allow. Anger is a luxury. Clouds the mind. He focused instead on trying to figure out who he had pissed off this badly.

"What's going on, Jake?" Claire asked, her expression concerned.

"Mae came back from the bank to find the office on fire. Bishop's missing. We need to get back. *Now*." He stood up, adrenaline coursing through him.

"I'll let you know what I find out," George said. "*Go*. We'll talk soon."

"Thanks. Let's go, Claire."

They ran out of the building and jumped into the Mustang, slamming the doors. He thrust the key into the ignition and took off in a squeal of tires. Burning rubber assaulted his nose and for once, he didn't care. If he didn't get to the bottom of this mystery soon, he didn't know what would happen next. His stomach roiled. He had a bad feeling that things were aligning against them.

CHAPTER 28
THE LEDGER

HE WROTE DOWN THE FINAL ENTRY FOR THE SUBJECT, tucked the ribbon over the page to mark his place, and closed the blue-ruled, black-bound ledger with a thud. Disappointment consumed him. What had begun so promising had petered out in ten hours less time than the last experiment. Female #1349-12 had not advanced his understanding of the effects of pain or even managed to replicate other findings. He sighed. Nothing left to do but to add her remains to the others.

He unlocked the door to exit the hidden underground cistern he used as his laboratory to retrieve a thick canvas body bag and his portable wheeler to tie the body to. Once it was dark, he'd transport the subject up to the main floor, then outside. Lifting the heavy fifty-pound cement cover off the two-hundred-foot deep well, he'd pull up the thick steel insert that kept the bodies below the water line, undo the restraining ropes and dump her in. With the steel grating keeping the water level of the well free of any suspicious floating items, the bodies under the heavy grate would never be seen. Now or a hundred years from now. His only concern was how full was the well getting. Was it time to have another one dug?

At the bottom of the staircase, he switched on the lights, illuminating the steps. *You can never be too careful not to take a fall.* No one visited this part of his ranch for weeks on end. One misstep and it could all be over for him. The thought sent his mind back to relive his one recent slip of the tongue. Telling his next chosen subject about the hippies on Spahn ranch. He shrugged. It was a very small mistake. Highly unlikely it had registered in any way.

A slight moan drew his attention. He stood still and listened. What was that?

He walked the few steps back into the chilled air of the heavy cement cistern to peer at the body. Had he made a mistake? Was she still alive? How was that possible? He had been unable to detect any signs of life. Perhaps he had been too hasty. He hurried to check, picking up the stethoscope from the tray, then laying the end against her bare chest. He listened with hushed expectations for a few seconds, then detected a very faint heartbeat. His pulse quickened. Yes. She was still alive.

CHAPTER 29
SMOKE AND MIRRORS

THEY MADE IT ACROSS TOWN IN RECORD TIME. AFTER checking in with Mae, Claire watched Jake speak with the firemen working to douse the flames in hopes of the fire not spreading to the surrounding businesses.

The rank odor of smoke and chemicals made breathing difficult in the heat of late day.

Where was Bishop? She prayed with all her heart that the clever bird was fine and spreading the gospel somewhere nearby.

"I'm going to check out the alley," she said to Mae. She couldn't stand around and wait. Her body was too jumpy with anxiety, like she could run a four-minute mile in under three.

Mae nodded, her expression still shell-shocked. "He might hide in one of the bins out back."

"You okay if I go look?"

"Go. I'll be fine."

Claire hurried away, going down the block until she found a narrow step way to the back alley. Her heart in her throat, she began calling out to the parrot. "Bishop, where's my pretty bird?"

She checked between doorways, behind garbage bins, and pulling out empty cardboard boxes that someone had piled against the wall of one business.

"Bishop, *the truth shall set you free.* Hey, Bishop, you can come out now. It's Claire. Come on big guy, where are you hiding? No more games. Come out and show yourself."

She checked carefully down one side of the alley, then crossed over and began on the other side. Where was he? *Please, dear God, don't let him have been trapped inside.*

When she came to the back door of Jake's former offices, she noticed the door was propped open a few inches. The sight gave her renewed hope and she doubled the intensity of the search.

She even opened a few back doors that were unlocked and called out to anyone inside, to ask if anyone had seen him? No one had, and as time escaped, the lump in her throat grew larger until it threatened to cut off her air supply.

"Bishop, come on big guy, you must be here some place." She heard the desperation in her voice. Damn it. He had to be alive.

Maybe he flew up and landed on top one of the buildings?

She was about to climb a fire ladder that led to the roof of a building of one of the businesses when she heard, "*Hello, Gorgeous.*" Her heart nearly stopped as the words registered.

"Bishop! Where are you?"

She scanned the alley. Where was he hiding?

"*Hello, Gorgeous. Vengeance is mine.*"

"You bet it is, big boy. Keep talking to me." Was he over there in that basement window well? She hurried over and dug out a length of cardboard obscuring it.

A pair of beady bright eyes peered up at her. *Thank you, God.*

"Bishop! You're safe!" She got on her hands and knees. Then reached down and tried to lift him up from the confined space. The window was barred, and the large bird was pressed up against them. The drop had to be two feet deep.

He pecked at her. "Sorry, did I hurt you?"

"Hello, Gorgeous."

"Hello, yourself. Can I lift you out, or do I need to go and get Jake?"

She gave it another try, and this time he cooperated, letting her lift him up and out. She held him in her arms and gave him a look over.

"You're looking gorgeous yourself. No harm done. Well, other than your perch has gone up in smoke, plus everything around it."

She tucked the large bird against her body and walked him down the alley, then back up the narrow chasm between two businesses to the front sidewalk.

She caught sight of Jake just as he caught sight of her and Bishop. He broke out into a run and joined them in mere seconds.

"Hey, Bishop. Claire's found you. You okay?"

"Hello, Gorgeous."

Claire laughed with relief. "That's how I found him, saying that phrase."

"Thanks for finding him."

"Believe me, the pleasure's all mine."

Jake petted the parrot's head and checked him over. "He looks okay."

"He was hiding in a window well. Says vengeance is his now."

"Yeah, I'd like some of that myself. Let's put him in the car, keep him safe."

Claire handed Bishop off to Jake and watched him carefully situate him in the front passenger seat of the Mustang.

"Looks like the fire's under control?"

"Yeah. I'll need to take Bishop home. I've got that meeting later."

Claire took a deep breath, staring at the shelled-out remains of Jake's former business. How to persuade him?

"I *need* to be there, Jake. Please, this is my life we're talking about here. I can't just sit by and let things fall apart around me. So much has happened—all out of my control. Serena's still missing. God knows where! You've been beaten up and shot at. Now your offices have gone up in smoke. What on earth is going on?"

"I understand your frustration. But it's not safe. What if someone sees you that's connected to this thing? Takes a pot shot at you next?" Jake rubbed at his neck. A gesture she well knew. He was as frustrated as she was.

"I'll wear a disguise. A dark wig and glasses. No one will know who I am."

She saw him hesitate. Pressed her advantage. "Two people listening to the intel will bring more to the table. Not to mention a woman's perspective can be an asset to any discussion. Didn't Marlowe say as much?"

"I doubt that. Philip Marlowe wasn't big on most females." He blew out a deep breath. "But okay. You can listen in. But please keep as discrete as possible. And the use of some dowdy clothes would help tone things down as well."

"It's a deal."

"I just hope I don't live to regret this." He shook his head slowly, his expression dark and troubled.

"You won't. And no matter what happens, or what I learn, I won't either. *Nothing but the truth,* that is what matters to me. It stands for something. Something I can get behind."

"Okay, I'll drop you off and pick you up at eleven. You try and get some sleep in the meantime. I gotta get Bishop home."

Claire looked over at the bird now perched on the dash of the Mustang. He appeared rather subdued; his feathers droopy, his wings folded in tightly. But thank the good Lord he had escaped physically unscathed.

Fifteen minutes later she let herself into the apartment. Marlowe ambled over to greet her, but no Serena. She absently patted his head. She kept seeing her friend everywhere. Her eyes filled with tears. She could still smell her perfume in the air, see her personal things spread out over the space.

She went into Serena's bedroom and picked up her favorite stuffed bunny from the bed, smoothing its ears. One ear had been half torn off in childhood and yet her friend refused to give it up. What was she going to do if her friend never came home again?

Tears flooded her eyes and she gave into the instinct to let it all out. She didn't notice Marlowe climbing up beside her until he nudged at her, his nose wet. She swiped the tears away and looked into his whiskey brown eyes filled with such touching worry.

"It's okay, buddy. I just needed a moment. Ready for walkies?"

He chuffed and got down to the floor before padding down the hallway to the door. She joined him, fastened his leash, and let him lead them outside into the twilight.

A quick constitutional and they headed home to eat. The entire day had flown by and she hadn't filled her belly since toast at breakfast. Keep this up and she'd be pulling in her belt a notch.

She fed them both, then went to Serena's closet to dig out what she would need for the meeting. Finding the short gamine wig that her friend had bought to play around with, she added it to the pile already containing a bulky drab gray sweatshirt and loose petal pusher pants. No makeup, flat shoes and she was all set.

She lay down on the bed after setting the alarm clock for ten. But it was no use. She tossed and turned, unable to get comfortable. The meeting with the agent from the bureau who might know something about her past was front and center in her mind. What would he have to say about her father? Was he the monster that Gunny thought he was?

She gave up trying to get some sleep. She got up and showered. Then dressed and pinned up her hair, tucking it carefully under the wig. The dark wig was odd against her skin coloring when she looked into the mirror, making her look far too pale. But it did make her look unrecognizable. Satisfied, she went into the living room. Marlowe raised his head from the rug as she went by but didn't react. She obviously still smelled like herself. Too bad this wasn't a day meeting, she'd wear sunglasses. But anyone wearing shades after dark was suspicious and would draw more attention. Unless you were blind. But that would require a white cane. Not a bad idea for a future disguise though.

She made herself a cup of tea instead of having the drink she wanted. She needed to stay sharp tonight, keep her wits about her.

A loud knock at the door make her nearly drop her

teacup. As it was it sloshed over onto her lap. Cursing, she got up and picked up the tea towel hung over the stove's oven handle and blotted at the stain.

Answering the second knock, she came face to face with Herman.

He looked startled at her appearance, and she remembered the wig. "Sorry to bother you, Claire. But I was just checking if you heard anything more about Serena?"

She bit her lip. "No, nothing."

"Okay, well, I needed to check." He pointed at his own head. "Is that a wig or did you do something to your hair?" The way he said it was obvious he disapproved.

"Wig." She didn't elaborate.

"If you hear anything, anything at all."

"I'll call you if I do. Now, I have to go." She needed to change, being covered in brown tea stains was going a bit too far. Dowdy was one thing, dirty quite another.

"Okay, well, take care. Oh, the office at the studio called and wants a meeting with me tomorrow. Can you make it? It's at two o'clock."

She tried not to groan out loud.

"I'll try. I can't promise though."

He looked crushed.

"Okay, I'll see if I can move some things around."

"Thanks! I truly appreciate it."

She closed the door and hurried to the bedroom to find another outfit.

A long maxi dress was a possible contender. The fabric was limp and beige and would cover her head to toe. She changed and pursed her lips, checking herself out in the full-length mirror. It would have to do. Most of hers and Serena's clothes were fashionable items and up to the moment, with rare exceptions.

She glanced at the clock. Five minutes to eleven. Time to meet Jake.

She waited in the lobby where she could keep an eye on the street, waiting for Jake to pull up. The sun had set on a hot day and the streetlights had turned on, adding to the pot lights on the pavement in front of the block.

A horn honked as Jake pulled up. Taking a deep breath, she exited the building and got into the vehicle, letting him hold open the door for her.

"That's a good disguise. I almost didn't recognize you. Though you smell just the same."

"What do I smell like?" His thoughts on how she smelled intrigued her.

"Ah, kind of sweet, like the fresh scent of a pink or white carnation."

"That works." She slid onto the leather seat and buckled up. He came around and got in behind the wheel.

"I managed to find a place to rent. A couple of blocks down from my current address. It belongs to Gunny. I can move in tomorrow morning. In this business, it's who you know that counts."

"That's good news. I can help you with the move— lend a hand setting things up. I didn't know Gunny was into real estate?"

"Thanks, I can use all the help I can get. Gunny's been around a long time. He's into a lot of things."

He didn't elaborate and she sat and chewed on a fingernail, thinking of the meeting to come.

"You'll be fine. Just let it unfold as it wants to."

"Okay." She dropped her hands into her lap.

A few minutes later they pulled into the lot behind O'Hara's bar and grill. Jake killed the motor and disembarked.

"Nothing fancy about this place, but if you don't mind the stink of testosterone, it's relatively safe."

"Don't worry, I can handle it. Probably no more stink than the usual Monday morning pitch meeting with the studio department head. They can get rather intense. I won't miss that part of the job when I quit."

"Every business has its drawbacks," Jake said conversationally, then held the door open for her and she proceeded him inside. Soon as her eyes focused to the dimness, she noted the half-empty bar held mostly cops, and what she would call regulars. Patrons that hugged their barstools like Armageddon was nigh. Most didn't even bother to look up as they entered, holding onto their beer glasses or shots of whiskey.

"It's a long way from Whiskey a Go-Go," Claire whispered.

"About as far as you can get. I like that. The brothers who run it are honest and keep the peace. Best you can ask for."

"What's their names?"

"Liam and Jimmy. Looks like Liam's working tonight." Jake escorted her right up to the bar.

"Hey, Liam."

Liam gave them a friendly grin. He was a medium height, stocky, ginger-haired man, his coloring screamed I'm Irish. She liked him immediately.

Jake made quick introductions.

"Nice to meet you, Claire."

"Likewise. Nice bar you got here."

"It's okay. Pays the bills."

"How's things going?" Jake asked.

"Can't complain. Jimmy's off to Boston to visit the family, taking the hit. Lost the coin toss. Beats tangling with my relatives. Funeral for Great-Uncle Morris. Irish wakes are best to avoid if you can. I got myself a parrot, like you suggested."

"Good. What are you going to call him?"

"Thor. How's Bishop doing?"

Jake explained the events of the day.

"My-oh-my, a fire. You must be thirsty. What can I get for you? On the house. Least I can do considering the day you've had."

"A beer. Tap's fine."

"You, young lady?"

"It's Claire. Same."

Liam poured two large glasses of foamy, amber-colored beer and set them down in front of them.

"Here you go."

They both took a sip. "It's good, thanks," she said.

Liam shrugged, but she could see he was pleased.

"We're waiting for Mann," Jake said.

"Haven't seen him yet tonight."

The front door opened, drawing few glances from the patrons.

Jake leaned over and whispered in her ear. "Connor Mann just walked in."

Claire looked toward the entrance. A large man in a black suit, white shirt, black tie, and short sandy-colored hair that did nothing to hide he was an FBI agent strode across the floor. Her heart skipped a beat. What was she going to find out tonight?

CHAPTER 30
A SECRET REVEALED

JAKE GLANCED AT CLAIRE, NOTING HER STRAINED expression. Was she up to this? It had been a hell of a day so far. He had to give her kudos just for hanging in there.

"Special Agent Connor Mann, I'd like you to meet, Claire Preston. She's the young woman I told you about."

Claire took the agent's hand. "Nice to meet you."

"Likewise. Can I get a shot of whiskey with a beer chaser, Liam?"

"Sure thing."

"Is your guy going to meet us here?" Jake asked.

"He's not coming."

Jake felt the stirrings of hot anger prickle in his belly. "Why not?"

"Let's have a seat and I'll explain."

"O—kay."

Jake led them to a small table in the back of the bar, far from the shuffleboard table. Customers might play on it and listen in at some point in the evening otherwise. The three of them sat down. He waited for Connor to speak.

"I know you're both disappointed not to hear this

from the guy who was there. But he refused to come. Though he did share the intel with me. I'm fairly certain I have the answers you want."

"Okay. Fire away. What did you learn?"

Claire grimaced at the word *fire* but kept her cool. He made a mental note to choose less colorful words.

Connor took a deep breath, his fingers working to peel the label off the beer bottle he'd insisted on having instead of draft. He'd already swallowed the shot of whiskey in one go. "I'm afraid the intel is explosive. You need to prepare yourself."

"Just say it. I can handle it." Claire clutched her hands together so tightly around her glass of beer it was in danger of shattering.

"The man in the photograph? He's been protected for years by our government. My informant says he was a liability to the bureau. The cover up goes deep, Jake. The man left a baby on the steps of an orphanage twenty-one years ago. He called his handler looking for help. Explained he had no choice but to do what he did as the woman had found him out—discovered an identify card and an incriminating photograph. There was no prosecution. It would have brought too much to light— brought the agency under too much scrutiny. His handler cleaned things up, even going so far as taking Claire's file from the orphanage. I'm sorry, it's been lost over the years. If my guy hadn't told me what he did, we'd not even know this much. Proof of his existence has long been eliminated. He said he was most likely still alive somewhere living under the radar. Normally, the bureau is informed if a death occurs."

"My father killed my mother?" Claire's pale face looked ghostly and strained in the poor lighting. Jake wanted to reach out and reassure her but didn't dare. It looked like she was an inch away from freaking out.

Mann pressed his lips together. "I'm sorry to have to tell you, but yes, that's the unfortunate facts of the case. My guy said he had little doubt she was pregnant by him."

"Are there any recent photographs of the man?" Jake asked. "That would be helpful. If he's still alive, give us a place to start to look."

He shook his head. "Not that I'm aware of. The agent might know what he looks like? You want me to ask?"

"Definitely. Any little detail would be of help."

"There was one other thing. He had a burn mark on his wrist. My guy said it was not an uncommon way to hide identifying marks after the war. Burn or cut them out."

Jake's pulse skittered. "A burn mark. The man in the photo had a tattoo on his wrist of a Nazi swastika. A friend of mine saw it once when he came into the pawn shop with Claire's mother. A burn mark must have been used to cover it up after that last visit." The idea gave him pause. Just recently he'd seen a burn mark on someone else's wrist. *Yes.* The professor had one.

"What are you thinking, Jake?" Mann asked, instantly picking up on his interest. Claire remained silent, even paler if it was possible. He felt her pain. The facts were brutal. Her father had murdered her mother before abandoning her.

"I've seen a burn mark on someone's wrist lately. He'd be the right age, but hard to think he's the one. A professor here at UCLA. The guy I told you about, Claire, that I didn't have time to look into his situation properly? He was being threatened by someone. Came to me for help. Took it well when I had to turn him down because I was too busy after Serena Sands disappeared to work the case."

"I saw him that day when he was leaving your office. He looked a bit familiar to me." She shook her head, her expression grim. "But I don't know where from. I remember he had a limp."

"I'll be looking into Professor Edward Smith ASAP." Jake went on to tell the events of the day to his friend.

"Do you think the potshot and fire had anything to do with Serena's case?" Mann asked. "Maybe you're getting too close to figuring things out?"

"I wish. The facts of this case are beyond the pale. Nothing fits yet. But I intend to dig until they do if it's the last thing I do."

Claire sat up straighter. "I need to find the guy that murdered my mother. See justice done. Can you help with that?"

Mann shook his head, his distaste obvious. "Beyond what I've shared with you which is confidential to begin with, no, there's not much I can do. I'm sorry. Even if you do find him, it's unlikely he'll ever be prosecuted for a murder the department didn't want exposed to begin with. I'm afraid he has escaped justice."

"I'm not going to let him get away with it," she hissed. "Someone's got to do something to make it right." A flash of deep anger in her eyes made her face regain some color with bright spots of pink staining both cheeks.

"If you do find the guy, if he turns out to be this professor, which is unlikely, don't confront him. Lots of people get burns on their hands and wrists from cooking. Best advice I got is leave this alone. Be satisfied with finding your grandmother. The truth is a hard mistress."

"Thanks for coming and telling us, Connor. I know it can't have been easy for you."

He shrugged. "Wish it was better news. Maybe someday the department will want to see this shameful period of our history exposed and dealt with, but I doubt it. Sweeping it under the rug has worked until now."

"If you can't do anything, that I can. *No way* is he getting away with this if he's still alive. I will hunt him down and do what you guys should have done long ago."

The vitriol in her tone surprised Jake. He knew her need for the truth went as deep as his own. What he hadn't realized was her need for justice paralleled it as well.

"Be careful, please. If the guy killed once to avoid exposure, he might be prepared to do it again."

"*Phttt.* The time for careful is long gone, Agent Mann. It's time for action. I won't rest until I see this through."

Connor shook his head. "I wish I hadn't shared it now. It's only stirred up the past. Put you in a dark place. But I'm sorry, I need to be going. It was good to meet you, Claire. I'm wish I could have had better news for you." He got up and nodded, his expression grave.

"Me too." Claire remained seated.

Mann leaned forward and whispered close to his ear. "Look after her. She's in a bad way."

"I will." Jake got to his feet and shook his friend's hand. "Thanks for coming."

"I'll let you know if a photograph exists. Can't promise you anything more than that."

"You've been a big help."

Mann's lips pressed into a straight line. "Not much of one I'm afraid. Talk soon, buddy." He strode across the bar and right out the front door.

Jake sat back down and signaled for a second round of beers and a couple shots of whiskey from Liam. He brought them right over.

"Drink it," he ordered her. "You need to calm down."

She glared at him but took the whiskey, downing it in one gulp. She grimaced and took a sip of beer.

"Better?"

"I'm fine."

"First rule of being a PI. Stay calm. The mind does not function properly when it's riled up."

"How do you do it? Stay calm when you learn shit like that?"

"Truth is a double-edged sword. You said you could handle it, remember?"

"There's truth and *there's truth*, it seems. This one's beyond sick." She paused, looking pensive and calmer. "Do you really think the professor could be the guy we're looking for?"

He noticed she didn't use any parent terminology. He couldn't blame her. "No idea. But I'm going to find out."

"Good. I need to know." She gulped down the rest of her beer. "I need to get home. I want to help you in the morning, then I have an appointment at the studio in the afternoon."

"Keeping your options open?"

"Trying to help out a friend with the ins and outs of having a viable script. This story we're living through right now—" Her face took on a disgusted look. "No one would believe it. Our own government being involved in the cover up."

"Let's go." He paid the tab and escorted her from the bar. In the car she tugged off the wig, letting her long locks flow around her shoulders. The gesture aroused his interest, but he immediately quashed it.

"I checked the security camera over the back door earlier tonight, but it was of no use. It had melted from the heat of the fire."

She sighed. "We sure haven't been getting any breaks."

"No, but we are slowly unraveling it. Give it time, Claire. We will find out all there is to know."

"Yeah, I guess." She surprised him by leaning over and kissing his cheek.

"What's that for?" he asked before thinking better of it.

"For helping me. For making me believe finding out all the truth is possible. Even though I know it may take years or not happen at all."

"Let's get you home. Tomorrow's going to be a busy day."

"You know, this might sound crazy, but do you think it's possible the two cases are connected? That somehow the guy who's taken Serena is connected to mine? If this Nazi guy is as bad as they say, maybe he's responsible? If he's still around the area, that is. Maybe he's still even active. You know, murdered others?"

"It's possible, though unlikely. Too many murders would bring him under scrutiny, no matter that he's been protected in the past. Which reminds me, I need to check in with George Lamb. See if he's discovered anything about our Dr. Vogel possibly owning property nearby? If he's the guy's responsible for taking pot shots on a ranch with women and children in attendance, he has to be stopped."

"It's after midnight," Claire said, checking her watch. "Think he's still up?"

"George is a night hawk. It's one of the reasons why he's had so many wives. There's a pay phone around the corner, I'll call from there."

He started the Mustang and drove down the alley, hanging a right at the intersection. He got out again and headed over to the lighted booth, leaving the vehicle running. Claire sat and tried to remain calm and rise above the recent explosive intel, but it was harder work than just getting angry and hitting something in her frustration. Maybe it was time to join a boxing gym?

She didn't notice Jake had left the phone booth until the car door opened again and he got back inside, settling himself behind the wheel.

She pounced. "What did you learn?"

"Turns out our good doctor does own land that butts up against the Spahn ranch. An even larger spread of more than a hundred acres. If that bastard has been taking potshots at those hippies, he's going to answer for it. I'll be checking on him along with the professor." He banged the steering wheel. It startled her. He was the one always telling her not to let her emotions overcome her. "Damn the fire for slowing things down."

"No kidding." But this was something she could handle for them. Confront him tomorrow at the studio, she was going to be there anyway for the meeting. He wouldn't be expecting her questions and she's most likely learn something of value. The thought energized her. Finally, something she could do.

"Sorry about the outburst. Okay, time to get you home. I'm not always the best role model."

"You do fine. We're all human, Jake."

At her apartment, she made her goodbyes quick and jumped out.

"See you in the morning," Jake called after her. Then he waited at the curb for her to walk down the sidewalk and enter the front door of the block. She couldn't help but smile at his old-fashioned chivalry. He was one of a kind. More a question of what kind? Like most people he was filled with contradictions telling her to stay calm even though he felt the same anger, and didn't always know what he was going to do until the time arose to act, even though his moral compass seemed to be more intact than most.

Her mind took a darker turn. Would he help make sure that the monster who sired her was brought down? Hell, was she capable of it? That's if they ever found him. Would she do what needed to be done? Or would it make her as bad as him? No way. She shook her head. Finding a way to bring him down was an entirely different thing from what he had done. It wouldn't make her be like that vile person at all, right? But it bothered her. The moral dilemma.

In high school, she once argued with her teacher that state sanctioned murder was wrong, that it made you just like them. She had slowly grown away from that ideal to the point she now wondered if she had taken it too far? Did she carry the genes of a murderer which had influenced her more than she knew? Well, if she did, she would use it to make herself stronger. Capable of handing out vigilante justice.

She had reached her suite and she opened the door, more than certain, that if they ever found the man who killed her mother, and the law wouldn't do it, she'd somehow make sure he went down for the count. Even if she had to do it herself. She'd pay the price herself after the fact. Her mother deserved that much at least.

She swallowed hard as Marlowe jumped up to greet her. She just hoped she wasn't fooling herself.

CHAPTER 31
AN IMPOSTOR

"I THINK PUTTING THE DESK BY THE WINDOW WOULD BE A nice change," Claire suggested. "Sunlight's good for a person. You've been cooped up in a back office for years."

"Not a bad idea," Jake agreed. Between the three of them they had cleaned, tidied and were now filling the twenty by thirty space with slightly used office furniture from the pawn shop. His one regret was the loss of his father's desk. Maybe some refurbishing might restore it? Until then it would spend time in his garage.

The front door opened and in popped Bill with a wheeled dolly. "I got the third desk you asked for. Where do you want it?"

"A third desk?" Mae asked, looking up with keen interest from arranging her typewriter and office supplies. They'd have to make do with partitions between their work areas until the back office was painted and ready for occupancy. At least the place had a decent bathroom along with a few extra feet of square footage. Not a bad spot to have landed. Get a new sign for out front and they'd be all set.

"Yeah, thought the newest member of our team needed her own workspace."

He more than enjoyed watching Claire's eyes pop open with surprise. Gorgeous as she was, and she was gorgeous, he admired her brains the most. Getting her into the fold would be his best move in a long time.

"For me?" She rushed to check out the offering, running her hands over the slightly scarred surface.

"It needs a bit of smoothing down around the edges. But it's sound," Bill said.

"It's perfect. Thank you, Bill." She kissed the pawn-shop owner's cheek. He blushed, then demonstrated an oh-shucks look that rivaled Barney Fife's. Jake narrowed his eyes.

"What about my thanks?" he asked.

"You got your kiss last night, so we're about even, I'm thinking."

Mae's eyebrows rose toward her hairline while Bill frowned at the intel.

"I thought that was for working on your case? Not for welcoming you to the fold. Well, that is, after you pass your exams, give notice at the studio, and move Marlowe in. I'm fairly certain him and Bishop will make friends." Flirting with Claire was already the highlight of his day.

"You don't know Marlowe. He's liable to discover he's a bird dog. And not in a good way. He's got retriever blood."

"Well, then we'll just have to get Bishop a gilded cage."

"No way. It was because he was free that he escaped the fire."

The thought brought him up short. The others felt the same judging by their expressions. "Yeah, guess that's not going to happen. Marlowe's back in doggie day care for now."

"I can watch them. Check if they get along all right. Lots of different species do. I was watching this special on TV the other night and a goat adopted a pet kitten; let the kitten ride around on its back. So, it's entirely possible they'll get along fine," Mae said. "Spray them both with vanilla, that's the key. If they smell the same, they'll be good to go."

Mae had more off-beat info than anyone he knew. And it came in handy more times than he could say.

"O—kay, we'll take that under advisement. I gotta run. Head over to the studio for a couple of meetings," Claire said.

"Stay away from the good doctor, and I mean it. If he's the one taking potshots, he's not to be trusted. I'm heading over to the campus shortly to check out the professor. We'll meet up later."

"Fine."

A busy couple of hours later and driving through heavy traffic to the university, Jake searched in vain for a parking spot. Finally settling on leaving his emergency blinkers firing off with a short prayer sent off to the campus police for mercy, he headed inside the administrative building to check on the location of his quarry.

Entering the lobby, he was certain he could detect the sharp odor of ivory tower bullshit that permeated the hallowed walls, doubting it had changed much in the years since he graduated on the Dean's Honor roll. Like anyone cared about his excellent scholastic record in his current business or when he had been a cop. All people cared about were results. He got it. Book learning and good intentions did not guarantee a proper solution.

He approached the front desk. When he asked the

female clerk where he could find the professor's office, she gave him the skeptical once over.

"I'm sorry, but Professor Smith is away on—sabbatical," she said, pausing a split-second before her explanation which suggested she could be lying while answering with a briskness to her tone that suggested he was annoying just in the asking.

He ignored her edgy prissiness. "When did this happen? I just talked to him."

"A few days ago."

What was he missing here? The professor hadn't mentioned he was taking time off. Guilt struck. He really had been too busy to take on the man's case but it still bothered him.

"Did he say why?"

"Excuse me, but I don't think it's any of your business." The prissiness ratcheted up tenfold.

"It is if he's in danger. He came to me because he was being threatened. Surely you can understand that I want to be certain the man's okay?"

"Threatened? Professor Smith? Are you quite certain we're talking about the same person? He's one of our most beloved professors here on campus."

"We are if he's your history professor that's been getting threatening notes." He remembered belatedly that the man would prefer others not know about his situation, but a sense of unease filled him. If he was in mortal danger, it overrode everything else.

"Would it be possible to speak with anyone who knows him well? A colleague or graduate student?"

"This is a big campus and I don't see how I'm expected to know who knows who? If you'll excuse me, I have work to do."

"Are you wanting to know about Professor Smith?" a

voice interjected. Jake spun around to find a young male student standing there with a sheath of stabled paper in one hand and a coffee cup in the other.

"How do you know him?"

"I'm one of his graduate students. I've known him for a few years. It's not like him to leave us all in the lurch like this. And, sorry, but I overheard you say he's being threatened?"

"From an unknown source. Would you have time to sit and speak with me?"

The administration clerk gave the young grad student a piercing look. He blushed and shook his head.

"Sorry, I'm running late. Maybe another time?"

"I'll walk you wherever it is you're going. Look, I only need a few minutes. If you're worried about the professor, you have a right to be. He hired me to look into his case. Try to find the perpetrator." He was stretching the being currently employed by the guy.

The twenty-something looked nervous, his Adam's apple moving so quickly it ping ponged up and down. "Ah, sure, man. I'm headed to meet up with some friends. I just need to drop off this paper first with Helen."

"Okay."

He moved a few feet away and watched as Jake handed the pages over to the clerk.

"This is for Professor Collins. Thanks for taking care of seeing she gets it."

"I'll see that it makes it into the correct hands. Have a good day, David."

Who was she kidding? She meant that like the rival team wants the home team to win the season ender.

Jake let David set the pace down the long hall and into a small cafeteria empty of patrons.

"Coffee?" he asked, his politeness instincts obviously overriding the clerk's silent admonishments.

"Sure."

They retrieved standard white mugs from a pyramid pile placed at the beginning of the assembly line and took turns holding them under the sprout of a tall coffee urn, pulling back on the spigot to fill their cups. The student added liberal doses of cream and sugar while Jake left his black. At the till, he reached into his pocket and paid for the two coffees and the apple pie that his companion chose from the slim selection of desserts.

"Thanks," David said, nabbing a fork and napkins, then leading the way over to a small round cafeteria table where they could watch passersby through the glass windows that ran along one side.

"No problem." Jake sat down and took a sip of the bitter liquid. At least it was hot.

"I remember what it was like to be a student and low on funds."

"You went to school here?" David asked, digging into his pie with gusto. It appeared standard fare, flabby crust with tinned apple filling. Looked like nothing had changed since he graduated. Bullshit, condescension, and lousy pie in spades. Hmm, maybe he was getting a tad jaded? Nah, just a realist.

"Yeah, over a decade ago. Took criminology. Helped in my career as a policeman."

David's eyes bugged out, though he kept up the steady attack on the pie. "You a cop?"

"No, not anymore. I have my own private investigator business."

"Really? With a degree in criminology, you could have risen quickly through the ranks. Even been police captain one day." Then he must have realized how that sounded and added. "That must be an interesting job?"

"You have no idea." Jake shook his head, thinking of the blur of cases these past years. "As nice as it is to chitchat with you, I want to talk about Professor Smith, and I know you're in a hurry. Any idea why he's bailed on his grad students?" His stomach roiled again, warning him that things were in flux, and not in a good way.

"The official reason was a family matter, but—" The student pressed his lips together and shook his head ominously before continuing. "There's talk it was more. That something's being hushed up. The professor was last seen in the company of a tall man who seemed to be intimidating him. They got into a nondescript white van. Professor Smith always took the bus, so maybe the guy was just offering him a ride home? But one of my friends, a fellow grad student, said he looked uncomfortable."

"A white van. And a tall man? Any idea of what the man looked like?"

"The taller guy? No. But Professor Smith's so short, they'd be easy to spot."

"Short? How short? Did he have a limp?" Jake's heart rate jacked up. Things were not adding up.

David shook his head. "Five foot four or five at most. And no limp. He was quite a vigorous man, short, but full of energy. He's known for his energetic lectures."

"Did the tall man have a limp?" Jake asked.

"No one said he did. Is that important?"

"Did anyone go to the police with this information?'

"Not that I know of. It's hardly incriminating. And no one has reported him missing. He called in to take a sabbatical and everything seemed all right. You think some harm's come to him? Because of the threats?"

Jake shrugged. "I need to look into things. I'd like to speak to the student or students that last saw him with that tall guy. Can it be arranged?"

"I could ask." David finished his pie and drank the last of his coffee to wash it down. "Give me a number and I'll have Sean call you. He's my friend that last saw Professor Smith. But I need to get going now. Meeting someone." He didn't elaborate but got up from the table and carried his dirty dishes to the collection tray.

Jake followed him and pulled out a pad of paper and pen from his shirt pocket. "Write down your phone number. In case I need to get in touch."

David hesitated, then took the items from him and scribbled something down.

"I can't in good conscious give you Sean's, without his permission, you understand?"

Jake handed him a business card. "Have Sean call me. I have a secretary he can leave the information with if I'm not there."

He needed confirmation of Professor Smith's identity. A photo would suffice. He strode outside and headed toward the main Faulty Center building, intent on dealing with it now. If the man asking for help in his office was an impostor, the water just got murky enough to float a boat load full of crap.

Pushing open the door of the stately building built after the war, he took note of all the mugshots of the different professors that line the hallway. Damn. Sure enough Professor Smith's professional portrait looked nothing like the man he'd met. This guy looked like a happy cherub while the man in his office was darker and leaner, far more intense. Why would someone pretend to be him? Did this have something to do with the fire at his place? Was the man only there to scope out his joint?

Playing a game with him? Had he offended the guy in the past? Sinister thoughts pressed in. He was missing something of vital importance and his gut roiled with it. Something that could get someone killed.

A harder thought hit him. Claire had said the guy looked kind of familiar. Did he know her? Maybe it had something to do with her case? If only he had a photograph of the fake professor. He needed to speak with that unknown operative. Now. If the Nazi guy was still alive, and it was very likely the case, then he might have been alerted that someone was looking for him. Got him running scared.

And what if the real professor was in trouble? He had enough to talk with the cops about the fake identity scam. Jake rubbed the back of his neck where a headache threatened. It's always darkest in the hour before sunrise. No truer words could be spoken about this case. If it got any darker, dawn would be put off permanently.

CLAIRE SLIPPED INTO HER CHAIR BESIDE A PERSPIRING Herman. Circles of sweat had leaked through his shirt. The conference room was deserted except for the pair of them, but she'd anticipated that. One of Cuthbert's favorite ploys was to make his opponent nervous. She laid a comforting hand on Herman's forearm.

"Don't worry. They like your story. And if you're okay with the changes they suggest, the meeting will go along fine. You do know that first-time screenwriters don't make much renumeration?"

"I didn't sweat blood and tears for no money. That doesn't seem fair." Herman's knees were bouncing up and down under the table, making his chair squeak in protest.

"Not *no* money. But less than an established screenwriter. If this one does well at the box office, then you can call the shots. More people see your movie, the better standing you will be in. That's why you need to be certain you want changes to your script? If your vision is changed too much and the movie bombs, then you'll blame yourself for letting it happen. Afraid it's a double-edged sword, my friend. Complain too much and it won't get made, don't complain, and you have to live with the results."

The circles grew on Herman's shirt as he chewed over her words.

"It sucks. Here I thought the hard part was coming up with the script."

"Well, if it helps, you're already won. You're in a position that only a very small percentage of the screenwriter community ever gets to experience. You had your script read and approved. That, Herman, *is* a monumental milestone. Amazing for a first-time author. You should be proud. I just want you to know the facts going forward, that's all."

"Well getting it read and approved is mostly thanks to you."

"No, it's your flair for writing. I could never get a lame script approved in a million years."

The door opened and in popped Tess Evans, her next-door cubicle mate.

"I wanted to tell you Dr. Vogel called. He's expecting you when you're done here."

Claire made a face. "I don't think I have time."

"Your choice. I'm just the messenger. Catch you later."

"Who was that?" Herman had perked up considerably from his first glimpse of her gorgeous friend.

"A colleague. Tess Evans. She reads scripts as well."

"Maybe I could meet her sometime? You know if you ever go for drinks or something?"

She was spared from letting him down easy by the door opening again for the flotilla of Cuthbert and Wendy, plus entourage.

Herman's eyes bugged out alarmingly as he watched the five-person power crew sit down in solidarity across the table from the two of them. A silly ploy. Never worked before in her case, not going to work now. *That I can promise you, Herman.*

"Okay, let's talk about this little picture of yours," Cuthbert Murdock said. He sat back in his chair, his fedora set at what he thought of as a rakish angle, and he straightened his bolo tie. He checked his appearance in the fancy mirror scribed with the company logo conveniently positioned on the wall across from him, then smiled and winked at his reflection. *Vanity goes before a fall, you soulless mutt.*

"Let's get at this. I can't wait to see the audience reaction when it hits the big screen. Herman, you should be so proud. You've written an outstanding screenplay," Claire said.

Cuthbert frowned in her direction. And so it went. By the time they'd hammered out all the details, it was just a matter of hours until she had a pink slip added to her file. *So be it.* Spending the time fighting tooth and nail had helped her tremendously. Kept her from sliding down the slippery slope of worry and dread of what the next few days might reveal about her missing friend.

The company filed out and Claire got to her feet. She shook Herman's sweaty hand, trying not to grimace.

"Well done."

"Thanks, you were a big help, Claire. I can't thank you enough. I hope your boss isn't too mad at you?"

Ah, so he had picked up on it. Guy was a good study of human nature which is why he was also a good screenwriter.

"No problem. Now, go home and have a drink to celebrate."

"Care to join me? I have a bottle of bubbly with your name on it. Just say the word—"

"No, sorry, I can't. Apparently, I have to see a Dr. Vogel." At least she had a legitimate excuse. Damn, now she had to make a showing, or she'd have been lying to Herman on her last day at work and that wasn't how she wanted to go out. A high note was more her style.

"Okay then. Another time. And I mean that, I want to thank you properly for all you've done for me."

She walked him out to the front foyer. Then headed in to speak with Tess.

"So, how did it go?"

"You got a date with the guy any time you want it."

"Yeah. He seemed rather sweet and nice. Not the usual scoundrel I date." Tess shook her head. "My track record sucks."

"How's your niece and nephew doing?"

A wide smile broke out on her face. "Great. Mom's taking them to the zoo today. They got a day off due to some teacher seminar thing. They were so excited this morning." She paused. "How did your meeting go?"

Claire sighed. "Great for Herman. Not so good for me. I'd bet the odds would be twenty to one in favor of the studio laying me off today. I stuck up for a screenwriter and you know how much they *love* that."

"Good for you. At least you'll be able to look yourself in the mirror."

"Yeah, maybe."

"What's the matter?"

"Just some stuff I discovered this week." She briefly outlined the tumultuous events that Tess had not been party to.

"My god, Claire. Your friend is missing, your PI gets shot at, the business he runs burns to the ground, you discover your great-grandmother still living and who your mother was, and then you find out this Nazi guy who the government has been covering up for may be your father? You write all that into a screenplay and no one would be believe it."

"Yup. And now Dr. Vogel wants me to spill my guts." She shook her head. "No way. I'll deal with this in my own way."

"I gotta agree with you. I'm not big on telling strangers my life story either. So, are you going to talk to him at all? Feed him some line of BS?"

"I guess." She sighed. "I got better things to do with my time. And especially since I'm probably out of a job anyway. Why wait for them to fire me? I'll leave with my chin held high and try not to trip on the way out the door."

"Ah, I'm going to miss you." Tears filled Tess's eyes.

Claire hugged her. "Don't worry. I'll be checking in with you lots. I did promise to babysit, remember?"

"That you did. I know you're a woman of your word so I'm holding you to it."

Claire gathered her few personal items from her cubicle and put them in a small cardboard box, including her favorite photo of Marlowe. She glanced with bitter-sweet fondness at the miniature pink-haired troll doll her mother had given her when she was five and placed it on top of the pile. Then left the office for the last time. Best to go now before they had the satisfaction of being the ones to make the decision. She'd at least take that away from fussy old Cuthbert.

Once in the parking lot, she looked back at the imposing low-riding building that she'd hunkered down in for the past eighteen months, experiencing mixed feelings about leaving a job she'd gotten a lot out of including a good friend, insane tales of an ego-driven boss to share for years to come, and a wealth of knowledge in how stories are created or not created as the case maybe. She took a deep breath. *Oh, what the hell, it was time.* She swiped away a couple of tears and heard her name being called.

"Claire Preston."

She spun around, then startled to discover Dr. Vogel standing too close for comfort. In her anguish at leaving her job, she'd missed his sneaking up on her.

She backed up a step and frowned, looking around. The parking lot was deserted. "I didn't hear you come up."

He smiled coyly; his eyes hidden behind dark shades. "I've been told I have the grace of a cougar, the silent swoop of an owl, and the keen eye of an eagle."

Huh. She might not be the only one that needed to talk to someone.

"In full disclosure, you should know I've just quit my job. Would the studio still want to cover the cost of my talking with you?" No way was she calling it therapy. This guy was no more capable of helping her make sense of her life than he was of doing open heart surgery right here in the studio parking lot.

He dismissed her objections with a grand wave of his hand. "Have no fear. I'd talk with you whether or not I get paid by the studio." He took a step closer. "Besides, today is my last day here too. Thinking of going back to private practice."

His revelations startled her. The coincidence was too odd to be believed.

"Really? Well, I do have a couple of questions I'd like

to ask," she said. She desperately wanted to talk to him, gain intel. But his closeness was making her more and more uncomfortable. And something else bothered her. Hadn't she seen this man somewhere before? Her mind hurt with the need to know, an answer that eluded her, but a little out of reach. The accident still affected some things, like short term memory loss the doctors promised should clear up in time. She rubbed at her forehead, a headache threatening to make remembering even harder.

"Questions for me? It's you I'm concerned for." He leaned in. She could feel his hot breath on her skin. She shuddered. Somehow the eerie stillness of the day was making it much worse.

"If this isn't a good time, I can come back another day." Then she remembered he wasn't going to be there. Her senses screamed something wasn't right, but her thoughts felt so jumbled. Then it hit her. The man on the sidewalk. The man looking to hire Jake.

She reached for the door handle to place the cardboard box inside her vehicle, cold chills raced up and down her spine. Why would Dr. Vogel pretend to be a professor? It made no sense. But whatever the reason, she wasn't comfortable in his presence any longer.

"I have to be going. I just remembered a pressing appointment." She set the box on the back seat, rushing her actions. The troll doll spilled off the top and landed on the floor. She was about to retrieve it when the doctor spoke again.

"I was afraid of that." Something pressed hard into her side, bruising her ribs. She faltered in her actions.

"What are you doing?" Fear rose up in her throat and she swallowed hard against the bitter bile. She remembered Jake's words about the importance of staying calm in any situation and it settled her enough to keep her legs from folding under her, sending her tumbling to the ground.

"I need you to do what I say. The gun is loaded, Miss Preston, with one in the chamber."

CHAPTER 33

NO ROCK UNTURNED

JAKE STRODE INTO THE HALLOWED WALLS OF THE FBI, ignoring the lineup of mug shots that decorated the long hallway so similar to those at UCLA. He needed answers. And he wasn't leaving until he had then.

He took the stairs two at a time. At Mann's office, he knocked once before opening the door.

Connor looked up in surprise from his desk, his expression serious. "Hey, Jake, wasn't expecting you."

"New developments need sorting." He quickly filled him in.

"And now I need to talk to that operative. I need a more recent photograph of the guy. What he looks like today. If he's who I think he might be, someone could get killed or have already been killed. I have LAPD checking on the location of the professor and I'm praying he's alive. Does your operator want more deaths on his conscious?"

"Christ, Jake, this is bad. I'll call him again."

Jake waited. His gut roiled with worry. He had the distinct sensation that something was happening that would blow his world apart. Or the world of someone he knew.

"Okay, he's coming here."

Jake counted off the minutes while he waited. Focused on rethinking every detail, praying he hadn't missed something of vital importance.

A quiet knock on the door and in came a middle-aged man that Jake had never met before. He was carrying a vanilla file folder. His non-descript, mealy-mouthed appearance gave the appearance of a man with a lot to hide. A man who knew more than he wanted to know. One of the problems with life is never being able to unsee things once they're seen. And it looked like this guy had lived that experience for far too long.

"Jake Sterling, Agent Paul Norrie."

The man nodded. "I know what you're here for. Okay, I'm ready to help you." He shook his head. "I always worried that psycho would rear his ugly head again."

"I need to rule him out. The whole thing has gotten so complicated. If he's not somehow the one involved, than at least I'll have a better sense of things. Thanks for coming and doing this."

"Well, from what Connor's told me, I'd best step up now. Take the flak if need be. I've lived with this a long time. Too long. Okay, I have a photo taken about a decade ago. The subject came looking for a handout."

Norrie opened the file and drew out an eight by ten black-and-white headshot. "This your guy?"

Jake took it and studied it closely. "Shit, this is the guy who pretended to be the professor, looking for my help. The limp was as fake as his hair."

"So, he is still operating." Norrie turned a whiter

shade of pale. "I had hoped he'd just slipped under the radar and had the sense to live low."

"We need to put out an APB on him," Jake said. "He may have already harmed Professor Smith over at UCLA and possibly set fire to my offices. And who knows what the hell else? The man's a chameleon. A charlatan." But why? Was he someone with a grudge against the world? Against him? Evil existed, no doubt about it. Sometimes the why is hard to sleuth out, try as he might. All he could do was uncover the facts in some cases, hope to prevent future tragedies.

"I'll take care of it," Mann said.

Fear hit him in the gut, freezing the very breath in his lungs. A horrifying thought had burst from the dark recesses of his mind. "I need to check on Claire Preston. He may know we've been working together. She may be at risk."

"Good point. Where is she now?"

Jake looked at the clock. 5:31. "At New Pictures Studio. She said she had a couple of meetings. She should be done soon. I also need to check on Dr. Vogel who works there. He has a ranch next door to the Spahn ranch—you know the one—movies are filmed there. He took a dislike to the hippies living there and I think he might have taken a potshot at me the other day."

"Thank you for coming forward, Agent Norrie." They shook hands.

"I'll check in with you later," Jake said. He exited the office and made the short drive over to Claire's workplace.

He headed to the front doors of New Pictures, stopping at the reception desk to ask to speak with Claire. The young attractive female receptionist gave him a measured look, her eyes filled with meaning.

"She quit today. Took her things and left."

"Today? Something happen?"

The girl leaned in as if to conspire with him. "She had a meeting with the head, Cuthbert Murdock and a new screenwriter friend of hers, Herman something-or-other, and I think it didn't go the way Mr. Murdock envisioned it."

"What about Dr. Vogel? Is he available?"

"I'll check. Please wait one moment." She picked up the phone and dialed a number, requesting the doctor. She hung up.

"His nurse says he's gone for the day."

"Could I speak with his nurse?"

"Sure. Just take that path through the jungle right over there," she said, pointing at the back lot filled with Quonset huts and relics of past films visible through the huge bank of windows. "Leads straight to the medical offices."

"Thanks."

He pushed open the door and hurried to get his feet on the proper path. On the way, he spared an admiring glance at Excalibur rising out of the rock. He had a sudden thought that Claire had been through here too, most likely more than a few times. He'd bet dimes to dollars that she had appreciated the monument.

He shoved open the medical clinic's door and advanced on the desk. The puny nurse behind the desk was a surprise. Male.

"I was wanting to speak to you about Dr. Vogel." He flashed his credentials.

The guy narrowed his eyes. "Dr. Vogel is gone for the day. You'll have to make an appointment." The prissy sound of his tone made the skin crawl on the back of Jake's neck.

"Look, Mr. Nurse, *Dr.* Vogel is wanted in connection with a suspected intent to murder or cause bodily harm warrant." Slight exaggeration, but worth it when the male nurse's eyes shot wide open. "And a lack of cooperation on your part could be seen as your being an accomplice to said crimes."

"He didn't say where he was going. But maybe he went home?"

"You have an address?"

"He has a ranch. Past that Spahn ranch where they make movies. I'll make a quick map for you."

Nice to see proper cooperation. Too bad it so often had to be created with threats.

The guy grabbed a pencil and paper and began to scribble furiously. He rubbed out a few things with the eraser on the back of the HB pencil, made corrections until he nodded with satisfaction. "Here you go. It's a bit complicated to get there. The access road is well hidden, rather overgrown with foliage. I've only been once. To take him some papers that needed his signature. He's not fond of visitors."

"Why do you say that?" Jake asked as he took the slip of paper.

"He didn't offer me refreshments or invite me inside or anything at all." The nurse pursed his lips like he was tasting something vile. "And that was after my taking the initiative to go all the way over there to save him the drive. Pay for my own gas even."

"Not very thankful of him. Have you worked for him long?" Jake tucked the paper into his shirt pocket.

"Only a few weeks. Dr. Vogel just got the job too. I rather thought with us both starting at the same time we could have a friendship outside of work. But he's a bit of a lone wolf apparently."

"Yeah. Some people are. Too bad for them."

"Am I in any trouble, detective?"

Jake shook his head. "You're cooperated. I'll put in a good word for you."

"Thanks." The nurse flashed a relieved smile.

"Can I use your phone? I need to make a quick call."

"Of course."

Jake called Claire's home number. No answer. Damn it. His bad feeling only grew stronger.

He placed a second call to Bachman at the LAPD. All the time a buzzing white noise grew louder in his brain. He was missing one vital connection and it ate at his marrow. And until he knew what it was, nobody was safe.

CHAPTER 34
ATONEMENT

CLAIRE SLID OVER THE CENTER CONSOLE TO THE DRIVER'S side as instructed. Dr. Vogel entered the vehicle right behind her, gun pressed to her side. He stayed in the passenger seat keeping the gun low, pointed at her belly.

"Drive."

"Where?" She fumbled trying to get the ignition key into its proper slot, her hands were shaking so violently they seemed incapable of the simple action. She took a couple of deep breaths, trying to steady herself. *The changes of survival for a victim go down significantly if taken from the abduction point to a second location.* The instruction from the manual made sense if the perp didn't have a gun pointed straight at her.

"Down the Strip. You've been to the Spahn ranch. Head there."

"How did you know that?"

"I saw you with that PI guy, Sterling. Drive."

"You shot at Jake? That was you? Is that what this is all about? He's going to be fine. Just grazed him. I doubt he presses any charges."

"Not worried about him. He's busy chasing ghosts. By

the time he's figured it out, I'll be long gone with a new identity."

"Why are you doing this?" Keep him talking. Build rapport.

"Why does anyone do anything?" He shrugged. "I need a steady supply of subjects. How else can I finish my important work?"

"You take me at gunpoint for therapy? Doesn't that defeat the purpose?" He was a doctor. Why take such chances? Her only hope was someone had seen them drive off together. Then she remembered he had ducked down low until they were a good distance away. Possibly no one knew anything. But Jake. He'd never give up. He'd scour the ends of the earth for her, of that she was absolutely certain.

"You think this is about therapy?" A surprised grunt accompanied his words.

"Then what is it about?" She had to know though the thought of his answer was beginning to terrify her.

"Just drive." He gestured with the gun for emphasis.

She swallowed her fear, realizing they were fast approaching the turnoff to head north. Another even more horrible thought occurred to her. "Did you have anything to do with my friend Serena's abduction?"

His lack of an answer made her glance at him. A certain smugness said it all.

"You have her? At your ranch? Why?"

"I need subjects. I told you. Lots of subjects."

"For what purpose?" She couldn't avoid wanting to look at him. She kept turning away from the view in front of her to observe his reactions.

A bump in the road pulled the wheel to the right, almost into oncoming traffic.

"Pay attention. You'll get us both killed," he growled.

"Is she all right? Did you hurt her?"

"She's where she belongs. Safe in the well. Gave me lots of good data in the end."

"Data on what?" The words *in the well* and *the end* lay stark between them. Her mind shied away from knowing what it meant. That her friend was gone.

"You'll know soon enough."

"How long have you been doing this? How are you getting away with it?"

"I have immunity. A deal for past services."

"How is that possible? No one gets to do anything they want to other people. It makes no sense at all."

"I've gotten away with it for over twenty years."

The words pierced her heart, making it bleed. "When did you start? With who?"

"It was a long time ago. No point in dragging it up."

She made herself ask the hard question. "How many?"

He shrugged. "Over the years, dozens."

"Are they in the well too?"

"You ask too many questions." The tone of his voice sharpened. Threatened violence.

She drove a few miles in silence, trying to wrap her mind around things. Nothing made sense. She couldn't think about her friend, what state she would find her in.

Driving by the Spahn ranch, he gestured for her to keep going. "Bloody hippies. Turn right at the next junction."

As their final destination came closer and closer, horrid thoughts pressed in from all sides. That he intended her great harm was no longer in doubt. He couldn't let her go any more than he could let Serena go. They'd both seen his face. Then she remembered about the man she'd seen outside Jake's office.

"Did you impersonate Professor Smith? Is he okay?"

"Phttt. *The opportunity of defeating the enemy is provided by the enemy himself.*"

"What's that mean?"

"A great man wrote those words. He understood war."

"War? Our country's not at war."

"We're always at war." He paused before continuing. "You know, you look like her."

"Who?"

He poked the gun tighter against her ribs. She refused to cry out.

"Your mother."

"My mother." Her throat tightened. "What about her?"

"She started this whole thing. Wanted to expose me to the press. Wanted me to atone for only doing my sworn duty to the homeland."

"Who are you?"

"I think you know."

Her father. He really was an evil villain that hid behind a thin façade of normalcy. She needed to know all the truth, no matter how brutal the revelations would be. This might be the only opportunity she'd ever have. But could she live with knowing? But the living was so in doubt now, what did it matter?

"What do you do to your subjects? What do you need them for?" She hated the inhumanity of the word 'subject' with every fiber of her being.

"Have you ever considered how much pain the human body can handle before succumbing to death? It's a fascinating study of human character and physiology. Back in Germany, subjects were readily available. In America I've had to make do. Find my own."

"In Germany? You mean the death camps?" The vastness of the horror shocked her to the very depths of her soul.

"What else could provide a steady stream of volunteers?"

The man was a devil. Unfit to be called human. She swallowed against the bile that threatened to spill out of her guts. She gripped the steering wheel with such force she was dimly aware her hands throbbed with the pain. The memory of the terrible stench of smoke that had filled the City of Los Angeles for days on end seared her mind with the thought of the ovens of Nazi Germany.

A sense of having to do something, anything, rose up from the dark recesses of her mind. Her head throbbed with it. This was the man who had torn her from her mother. Left her on the cold stone steps two decades ago. Who had gone on to destroy people in his inhuman experiments. It was better to go down fighting. Destroy this evil. *Now.* If she died at his hands, and she had no doubt that that was what he intended, then he would only choose another. And another. A monster who would strike over and over again until he was stopped. She kept her eyes peeled on the road, looking for the first opportunity.

Dry sagebrush clung to a huge rock a hundred yards ahead. Thirty feet off the road to the right. She pushed her foot down harder on the gas pedal. The bug lurched ahead even as she begged for forgiveness.

"What are you doing? Slow the fuck down!"

The gun pressed harder into her side, bringing acute pain with it. No matter. It was time. She was the spawn of an evil man. A man who had harmed innocents. A man who had taken the life of her mother. He must be stopped. And she had to do it. No matter the cost to her. If she had to give her life to save future victims, so be it.

She'd always thought she could do the right thing when called upon, now was her chance to step up. It may not be the revenged filled spree as pay back for hurting someone she loved, instead, it was ending the pain for others. And for herself. It was okay to admit it.

She quit thinking then and twisted the wheel to the right, the vehicle rushing ahead over the uneven terrain, the bottom hitting potholes and rocks. Bouncing toward its final destination. Death.

He was screaming something she couldn't understand. She ignored it.

She pressed the accelerator harder. The Volkswagen obeyed her every command, preparing for its death punch. *I'm sorry Marlowe. Jake will look after you. Jake!* His face rose up in her mind. *Please forgive me.*

An explosion. The screech of bursting metal. A brightness. White light. Then no more.

CHAPTER 35
END OF THE LINE

A TERRIBLE SENSE OF URGENCY ATE AT JAKE, LOOMING larger with every passing second. He headed straight for Spahn ranch. The directions from the nurse lay on the front passenger seat. He ignored them. He didn't need them until he reached the movie set location.

He stopped the Mustang on the side of the road, left it to idle while he picked up the map. Traced a forefinger over the route. Not far now. He resumed driving, his stomach in knots. If something happened to Claire on his watch, he'd never forgive himself. There had been no one since his wife died. No one had ever made him feel as alive as Claire had so easily managed. The shared love of the truth was something he intended to savor for years to come. *So, please, dear God, let her be okay.*

He traveled in silence, only the purr of the motor humming and a stone caught inside a hubcap making an annoying rattling sound for company.

He became aware of a thin stream of black smoke on the horizon. A fire? Damn it. Not again. Last thing this dry tinder box of a county needed was another fire. It looked contained. Maybe it was just starting? He had an extinguisher in the back if he could get there in time. He pressed down on the accelerator. The car surged again, reacting instantly to his command.

He drove closer, bumping and slamming over the potholes. Then realized it was a car on fire. Keeping one eye on the vehicle and one eye on the road until he was parallel to the vehicle, he slammed the Mustang into park. He jumped out and used his keys to retrieve the bright red fire extinguisher from the trunk. Then raced toward the vehicle that had gone off the road and slammed into a large bounder in its path.

A split-second later he recognized the car. Claire's white Volkswagen was a twisted-up mass of metal. The trunk that housed the engine was on fire.

Oh my god.

His throat tightened by fear, he jerked the extinguisher into position. A couple of long scary moments later and the fire succumbed to the onslaught of thick white retardant that boiled over onto the sparse grass.

He raced around to the driver's door. Claire lay unmoving behind the wheel, blood pouring out of a deep scalp wound. He tried to jerk the door open, but it was stuck fast from the impact.

Running back to the Mustang, he retrieved a crowbar. He tried again to force the door open. Braced the crowbar against the edge of the door and pulled with all his might. Gritting his teeth, he kept up the pressure until it began to move. Inch by inch. He increased the distance between the door and the vehicle's body until it was large enough to ease her out. He glanced once at the passenger, barely recognizing the man as that side of the vehicle had taken the brunt of the impact. The guy was out cold. He looked vaguely familiar, even covered in blood.

Then he kept his attention focused entirely on Claire. He swept her bloodied hair back from her face. Her eyes were closed and she was so pale.

"Claire. It's Jake."

No answer. He carefully checked for a pulse, laying two fingers on the side of her neck. A faint heartbeat. He took a deep breath. Hope flared in his chest.

He picked her up and bore her back to his vehicle, laying her gently on the back seat and covering her with a blanket. It would be far quicker to drive her to the hospital than wait for an ambulance at this distance.

He went back to the Volkswagen to see if the man was alive. That's when he saw the gun, laying on the floor. When he checked him for a pulse, he found none. What had gone on? No matter, it was over now. He'd let the police deal with the body.

He raced back to his car and got behind the wheel. Began driving, aware of the fragile state of his passenger. Each bump made his jaw hurt as he ground his teeth together. Time was running out. Each second the clock ticked pushed her closer to dying from her injuries. Who knew what was torn up inside that delicate body?

He hit a particularly hard rut and a slight moan from the back seat made him swing his head around.

"Claire, are you okay?"

Silence. But he could see the slight fluttering of her eyelids. He forced himself to drive safely, watch the road. No point in rescuing her and having another accident.

"Where...where am I?"

The almost indistinguishable words came out faint as a sigh.

"It's Jake, sweetheart. I'm driving you to the hospital. You've been in an accident."

"Dr. Vogel. My...father."

His mouth felt parched, his throat ached. Was that the guy that had abducted her? Taken her at gun point? All the pieces of the puzzle fell into place. The guy had played everyone. Himself included.

"Don't try to talk. Rest. We'll be there soon."

How had the accident happened? Traffic was so light on this stretch. Hard to believe they could have hit the biggest rock formation on this stretch of road. There must have been a struggle. Maybe over the gun?

Please, please let Claire recover. I'll ask nothing else for the rest of my days. Just this once, hear me.

Claire had lapsed into silence once more. He focused on getting them to medical help as quickly as possible, praying it wasn't too late.

A siren's loud wail erupted close behind them. He swore out loud.

He had to stop whether he wanted to or not.

He waited impatiently, the Mustang raring to go at the press of his itchy foot, and he considered driving away while the officer took his time disembarking his cruiser and strolling up to his window.

"License and registration, please. You are aware that you were doing thirty miles above the posted speed limit?"

"I have a badly injured woman in the back seat. Car accident. The vehicle was on fire, and I'm just racing her to the hospital. Can you assist?"

The officer startled, then recovered himself. "Where? I need to call it in. Any other persons in the vehicle?"

"A man with a gun. He held this woman at gunpoint. Claire Preston. Abducted her. A Dr. Vogel from New Pictures Studio. He's dead."

A moan from the back seat. "Serena...ranch...well."

Jake's attention was riveted on Claire. "Are you

saying that Dr. Vogel was responsible for Serena's abduction?" It made sense. He quickly gave the man his details on the ranch's location, handing over the map.

"I'll call this in and escort you ASAP. There may be a chance to save the woman. Wait here."

Two minutes later they were back on the road, sirens blaring as the officer cleared the space ahead of them. The frantic ride to the Los Angeles medical center, the closest one to their location, seemed to take hours. Sweat dripped in his eyes that he continually swiped away.

They were met at the emergency entrance. In seconds Claire was transported inside the building, the metal wheels of the gurney dinging noisily against the cement. He hovered nearby while she disappeared down a short hallway and into a room, a handful of medical staff accompanying her.

Waiting while the doctors examined her took even longer. He paced the floor, drinking cup after cup of bad coffee and scarcely noticing.

Finally, a doctor exited the room and approached him.

"You next of kin?"

"I work with her." He flashed his credentials. "Her only next of kin is a very old great-grandmother who can't be here. I'll contact her, report anything you have to say."

"Well, she's in a bad way. We've stopped the bleeding for now. She's suffered internal wounds along with a severe concussion. And she has a shattered tibia in her right leg. The next twenty-four hours are critical, as you can well imagine." He shrugged. "If she makes it through that, she stands a chance."

Jake nodded, swallowing against the hard lump in his throat. "She will. She's a fighter."

The doctor departed. Jake went in search of a phone. A bank of pay phones near the entrance drew his attention. Checking his pocket for coins, he placed a dime in the slot and dialed the number for his office. After filling in Mae, he called Bachman.

"Did they find Serena Sands?" he asked before the officer could speak.

"No word yet. They're in the process of tearing the place apart looking for her."

Then he realized exactly the three words Claire had used on the way to the hospital. *Serena, ranch, well.* What they meant. How truly evil the man had been. "Look in the well. I think you'll find her there with the others."

EPILOGUE

THREE MONTHS LATER

THE SOLEMN RIDE through the streets of Los Angeles was driven in complete silence. Claire glanced over at Jake a couple of times. She still bore the scars of the accident, inside and out. Healing would take its own good time. She struggled daily with the ending to the case. But *what ifs* could kill a person. And she had to keep going, sleuthing out the truth for others if she was going to keep her sanity. Make some kind of difference in this world. Atone.

Evergreen Cemetery's stone arches and wrought iron decoration stood silent sentinels as her partner drove the Mustang slowly through the open gates. Though it had been many months since she'd visited, it still looked just the same. A quiet place to lay the dead to rest. Forever. The beautiful clouds floating against the perfect blue skies seemed at odds with reality of the place, but helped give her heart. Jake parked the Mustang and they stepped out. She clutched a bouquet of white roses, her favorite, in her hand, a cane to steady herself in the other.

Jake let the way to the proper section, then left her alone.

She leaned down and touched the first headstone, running her fingers over the lettering, tears running down her cheeks: *In Ever Loving Memory of Serena Sands. 1947-1968. 'Til we meet again.*

Her murderer was gone, sent straight to hell. If there was any justice in the afterlife. She lay half of the roses on the grave. Said a silent prayer. She swiped the tears that lingered away.

She turned her attention to the next one: *In Ever Loving Memory of a loving daughter and mother. Fiona Mary Ruth Clarin 1924-1947. 'Til we meet again.* She laid the last of the lightly scented flowers down. Bowed her head to give a prayer, her hand pressed to the gravestone. *If only I could have known you.*

Jake waited for her a respectful distance away. He'd also visited a gravestone while she visited her dead. That of his wife. The pink roses he'd brought now gone.

It had been a long road to this place. And a longer road lay ahead. A road of endless searching for redemption, at least in her case. She would not let the blood of her father taint her future.

The accident had also closed something off inside, some link to the past that no longer pressed on her. Maybe it was for the best.

Back in the Mustang, they both seemed to let out a collectively held breath.

"Okay. Do you want to eat first or check in with Mae?"

She pulled out a pack of cigarettes from her purse and offered him one. "Food sounds good." Though she had scant appetite, eating was a way to appear normal until she achieved it for real.

He took one of the cigarettes and rolled down the driver's window. Then pulled a lighter out of his pocket and lit hers first. "Don't know how you can stand this kind? Weak as dishwater," he said.

"You know I'm trying to quit." She let a series of perfect smoke rings go. At least she hadn't lost her touch. Her leg should heal fine. A slight chance the limp was permanent, but with physical therapy, the prognosis was good.

"Hope that doesn't include good whiskey?"

"You call that stuff you serve good?"

He chuckled. "You don't know what you're missing."

They puffed in silence for a few minutes. A few minutes of calm in a promising to be very busy day. She watched a black crow fly over the cemetery. "That reminds me. Have you checked on that young woman connected to that Charlie guy and the group of hippies looking to be a family?"

"Yeah." He blew out a puff of smoke, his face turned to the window. "I drove them home. Sunshine and her baby. All the way back to Salt Lake City. I think I'll be checking in with that group from time to time. Charlie's a bit off."

"Do you think! But that's great news about Sunshine. I'm happy about that." She shifted in her seat, grimacing at the slight pain in her right leg. She stubbed out her cigarette. Though she didn't consider herself a vain person, she was glad her face had come out unscathed this time, the deep wound hidden under her hair.

"So, what do you think of my taking that PI exam soon? I've been studying. If I'm going to make this my permanent vocation, I should have my own ticket. Not be riding on yours."

"Any time you want. I'll even help you study. As Chandler wrote, *Mostly I just kill time and it dies hard.*"

She swatted at him. "Your time with me is *not* killing time, buddy. We make a productive team."

"Sure, if you say so." She took note of the slight upward curve to his lips.

"I do. Now, drive me to O'Hara's. You've made me thirsty with all this talk of whiskey. We need to drink to them." She nodded her head toward their gravestone.

"That we do. Got a new case just this morning. I waited to mention it until we were done here."

She nodded; her interest piqued. "What kind?"

"A case in Laurel Canyon. Music guy's been getting threats about a copyright issue. One of the California Boys. Wants us to look into it."

"Really?" Her heart rate speeded up. "They make great music."

"Then this should be right up your alley."

"You bet." She sobered. "Do you think they forgive us, Jake?"

He didn't ask who she meant, knowing she referred not only to Serena and her mother, but the professor and the dozens of other bodies found down the well. "I believe they do. But more importantly, you need to forgive yourself. None of it was your fault."

"Maybe. But it still doesn't stop me from feeling it."

Jake turned over the Mustang's engine in preparation for leaving the cemetery. "No, but use it to motivate yourself. Use it to help others."

"Aye, Aye Captain."

He gave her a pleased look of surprise. "Smart ass, aren't you."

"I didn't mean to be," she quipped.

ACKNOWLEDGMENTS

I want to thank everyone at Rough Edges Press for their wonderful support since I received the awesome news that they were interested in publishing my work. In particular, a special thank you to my amazing managing editor Rachel Del Grosso. For the cover that took my breath away as soon as it appeared in my inbox, kudos to the artist.

Thank you to my friend, Rebecca Baker, for all your support and encouragement over the past decade.

And to you, dear reader, thanks for taking the time to read and perhaps review and share my work with others. Absolutely nothing beats word of mouth in this industry! And if it gave you even a moment of entertainment or pleasure while captivating you to another world, it was worth all the time to create it.

IF YOU LIKE THIS, YOU MAY ALSO ENJOY: NO GOOD DEED

BY JANUARY BAIN

A gripping tale where good deeds intertwine with hidden crimes and a quest for truth...

Katie Kelly finally has the career and house of her dreams, but it's a life built on a shaky foundation. Everything she holds dear could be stripped away in a split-second if the truth were to become known and her secrets exposed. Her best friend, Sadie, is also involved in hiding the past. The pair have managed to move on since that day of reckoning that occurred when they were just teenagers, by helping others to escape bad situations.

When a young woman runs to Katie and begs for her help, Katie is compelled to come to her aid and hides her in a safe room, locked away from her abusive boyfriend.

But then the past rises up and threatens to derail her best efforts to help the young girl, exposing her and her best friend to the vulgarities of fate as the girl is discovered to have an unexpected agenda, harboring secrets of her own. Katie is left with few choices. With her entire life crashing down around her ears, she must act to save not only herself, but her dear friend as well.

Can Katie stop the past from destroying all hopes for a future?

AVAILABLE MAY 2024

ABOUT THE AUTHOR

January Bain is an award-winning author who firmly believes that stories unite us, that good stories help us to discover the commonality of the human experience by supporting values, empathy and understanding. She writes with her heart, mind, and soul, hoping that her novels will touch your life, giving you moments of freedom as you fly with her to other worlds.

Bain has had the pleasure of select novels being turned into games, and her work is also available in different languages.

January and her husband live in rural Canada on peaceful acreage where a variety of wildlife comes to visit regularly and expect to be fed and paid attention to.

www.ingramcontent.com/pod-product-compliance
Lightning Source LLC
Chambersburg PA
CBHW010729250626
47155CB00011B/3610

9 781685 497101